THE DECAGON HOUSE MURDERS

YUKITO AYATSUJI

TRANSLATED FROM THE
JAPANESE BY HO-LING WONG

PUSHKIN VERTIGO

Pushkin Press
71–75 Shelton Street
London WC2H 9JQ

Jukkakukan no Satsujin Shinsou Kaiteiban
© 2007 Yukito Ayatsuji. All Rights Reserved.

First published in Japan in 1987, by Kodansha Ltd., Tokyo
Publication rights for this English edition arranged through Kodansha Ltd.
English translation © Locked Room International, 2015

First published in English by Locked Room International in 2015
First published by Pushkin Press in 2020

5 7 9 8 6

ISBN 13: 978-1-78227-634-0

Designed and typeset by Tetragon, London
Printed in the United States

www.pushkinpress.com

Dedicated to all of my esteemed predecessors

CONTENTS

All names in the text of this work are given in Japanese order, family name preceding given name.

PROLOGUE

The sea at night. A time of peace.

The muffled sound of the waves welled up from the endless shadows, only to disappear again.

He sat down on the cold concrete of the breakwater and faced the deep darkness, his body veiled by the white vapour of his breath.

He had been suffering for months. He had been brooding for weeks. He had been thinking about just one thing for days. And now his mind was focusing on one single, clearly defined goal.

Everything had been planned.

Preparations were almost complete.

All he needed to do now was to wait for *them* to walk into the trap.

He knew his plan was far from perfect, but he'd never intended to plan everything in perfect detail in the first place.

No matter how hard he tries, no matter what he might think, Man will always be mere man, and never a god.

And how could anyone who was not a god predict the future, shaped as it was by human psychology, human behaviour and pure chance?

Even if the world were viewed as a chessboard, and every person on it a chess piece, there would still be a limit as to how far future moves could be predicted. The most meticulous plan, plotted to the last detail, could still go wrong sometime, somewhere, somehow. Reality is full of too many coincidences and decisions taken on a whim for even the craftiest scheme to succeed exactly as planned.

The best plan was not one that limited your own moves, but a flexible one that could adapt to circumstances: that was the conclusion he had come to.

He could not allow himself to be constrained.

It was not the plot that was vital, but the framework. A framework in which it was always possible to make the best choice, depending on the circumstances at the time.

Whether he could pull it off depended on his own intellect, quick thinking and, most of all, luck.

I know Man will never become a god.

But, in a way, he was undoubtedly about to take on that role.

Judgement. Yes, judgement.

In the name of revenge, he was going to pronounce judgement on them—on all of them.

Judgement outside the court of law.

He was not a god and so could never be forgiven for what he was about to do—he was completely conscious of that fact. The act would be called a "crime" by his fellow men and, if found out, he himself would be judged according to the law.

Nevertheless, the conventional approach would never have satisfied his emotions. Emotions? No, nothing as shallow as that. Absolutely not. This was not just some powerful feeling within him. It was the cry of his soul, his last tie to life, his reason for living.

The sea at night. A time of peace.

No flickering of the stars, no light of the ships offshore could disturb the darkness into which he gazed. He contemplated his plan once again.

Preparations were almost finished. Soon they, his sinful prey, would walk into his trap. A trap consisting of ten equal sides and interior angles.

They would arrive there suspecting nothing. Without any hesitation or fear they would walk into the decagonal trap, where they would be sentenced.

What would await them there was, of course, death. It was the obvious punishment for all of them.

And no simple death. Blowing them all up in one go would have been infinitely easier and more certain, but he would not choose that route.

He had to kill them in order, one by one. Precisely like that story written by the famous British writer—slowly, one after the other. He would show them. The suffering, the sadness, the pain and terror of death.

Perhaps he had become mentally unstable. He himself would have been the first to admit to that.

I know—no matter how I try to justify it, what I am planning to do is not sane.

He slowly shook his head at the pitch-black, roiling sea.

His hand, thrust into his coat pocket, touched something hard. He grabbed the object and took it out, holding it in front of his eyes.

It was a small, transparent bottle of green glass.

It was sealed off securely with a stopper, and bottled inside was all he had managed to gather from inside his heart: what people like to call "conscience". A few folded sheets of paper, sealed. On it he had printed in small letters the plan he was about to execute. It had no addressee. It was a letter of confession.

I know Man will never become a god.

And precisely because he understood that, he did not want to leave the final judgement to a human to make. It didn't matter where the bottle ended up. He just wanted to pose the question to the sea—the source of all life—whether, ultimately, he was right or not.

The wind blew harder.

A sharp coldness shot down his spine and his whole body shivered.

He threw the bottle into the darkness.

ONE

The First Day on the Island

1

"I'm afraid this will turn into the same old stale discussion," said Ellery.

He was a handsome young man, tall and lean.

"In my opinion, mystery fiction is, at its core, a kind of intellectual puzzle. An exciting game of reasoning in the form of a novel. A game between the reader and the great detective, or the reader and the author. Nothing more or less than that.

"So enough gritty social realism please. A female office worker is murdered in a one-bedroom apartment and, after wearing out the soles of his shoes through a painstaking investigation, the police detective finally arrests the victim's boss, who turns out to be her illicit lover. No more of that! No more of the corruption and secret dealings of the political world, no more tragedies brought forth by the stress of modern society and suchlike. What mystery novels need are—some might call me old-fashioned—a great detective, a mansion, a shady cast of residents, bloody murders, impossible crimes and never-before-seen tricks played by the murderer. Call it my castle in the sky, but I'm happy as long as I can enjoy such a world. But always in an intellectual manner."

They were on a fishing boat reeking of oil, surrounded by the peaceful waves of the sea. The engine was making worrying sounds, as if it were trying too hard.

"Well, personally, I think that stinks."

Carr, leaning against the boat rail, scowled, and stuck out his long, freshly shaven chin.

"Honestly, you and your 'in an intellectual manner', Ellery. Fair enough if you consider mystery fiction a game, but I can't stand you emphasizing that 'intellectual' every single time."

"That's surprising coming from you."

"It's just elitism. Not every reader is as oh-so-smart as you."

"That's so true," said Ellery with a poker face, "and it's very regrettable. I realize it all too well simply by walking around the campus. Not even all the members of our club are what you might call intelligent. There are one or two of them who might even be intellectually challenged."

"Are you trying to pick a fight?"

"I wouldn't dare."

Ellery shrugged, and went on.

"Nobody said you were one of them. What I mean by 'intelligent' is having a certain attitude towards the game. It's not just about being smart or stupid. On that measure, there's no one on the face of the earth who doesn't possess at least a modicum of intelligence. Similarly, there's no one on the face of the earth who doesn't enjoy games. What I'm talking about is an ability to play while maintaining an intellectual approach."

Carr snorted and turned his head away. A faintly mocking smile appeared on Ellery's face as he turned towards the boy with the youthful features and round glasses standing next to him.

"And furthermore, Leroux, detective fiction evolved based on its own set of rules, and if we consider it to be its own unique universe, in the form of an intellectual game, then we must admit that in these modern times, the foundations of that universe have been severely weakened."

Leroux looked doubtful. Ellery continued:

"It's a great problem for modern crime writers. Diligent police officers performing their jobs slowly but surely; solid, efficiently run organizations; the latest techniques in forensic investigation: the police can no longer be regarded as incompetent. They are almost *too* competent. Realistically, there's no place any more for the exploits of the great detectives of yore, with their little grey cells as their only weapon. Mr Holmes would be a laughing stock if he turned up in one of our modern cities."

"I think that might be an exaggeration. A modern Holmes, fit for our modern times, will surely appear."

"You're right, of course. He'll make his entrance as a master of the latest techniques in forensic pathology and science. And he'll explain it all to poor dear Watson, using complex specialist jargon and formulas that no reader will ever even begin to comprehend. Elementary, my dear Watson, were you not even aware of that?"

With his hands inside the pockets of his beige raincoat, Ellery shrugged again.

"I'm just taking the argument to the extreme, you understand. But it illustrates my point perfectly. I don't feel at all like applauding the victory of the unromantic police techniques over the magnificent logic of the great detectives of the Golden Age. Still, any author who wishes to write a detective story these days is bound to come up against this problem.

"And the simplest way round it—or rather let's say the most effective—is the 'chalet in the snowstorm' method of establishing a sealed environment."

"I see." Leroux nodded and tried to look serious. "So what you mean is that of all the methods used in classic detective fiction, the 'chalet in the snowstorm' is the one best suited for modern times."

It was late March, almost spring, but the wind blowing across the sea was still cold.

On the S— Peninsula on the east coast of the Ōita Prefecture in Kyūshū lay J— Cape. The boat had left the rustic S— Town harbour nearby, and was moving out to sea, leaving behind only its wake and the sight of the cape disappearing below the horizon. Its destination was a small island about five kilometres off the cape.

It was a clear day, but because of the dust storms so typical of spring in the region, the sky was more white than blue. The sunlight shining down turned the rippling waves to silver. The island lay ahead of them, wrapped in a misty veil of dust carried on the wind from the mainland.

"I don't see any other boats here."

The large man, who had been smoking silently while leaning on the boat rail opposite Ellery and the others, suddenly spoke. He had long, unkempt hair and a rough beard covered the lower half of his face. It was Poe.

"The tide on the other side of the island's too dangerous, so everyone avoids it," replied the elderly but energetic fisherman. "The fishing spots round here are more to the south, ya see, so ya won' see any boats goin' in the direction of the island, even those that've just left the 'arbour. By the way, y'all are really strange college students, aren't ya?"

"Do we really seem that strange?"

"Well, for one thing, y'all have strange names. I just heard ya use odd names like Lulu and Elroy and such."

"Yes, well, they're sort of nicknames."

"Do kids at universities all've these kinds of nicknames nowadays?"

"No, it's not like that."

"So ya really are an odd bunch, eh?"

The two young women, in front of the fisherman and Poe, were sitting on a long wooden box set in the centre of the boat, which served as a makeshift bench. Including the fisherman's son, who was steering the rudder in the back, the boat held eight people.

The six passengers besides the fisherman and his son were all students of K— University of O— City in the Ōita Prefecture and also members of the university's Mystery Club. "Ellery", "Carr" and "Leroux" were—as "Poe" had said—something like nicknames.

Needless to say, the names were derived from the American, British and French mystery writers they all respected so much: Ellery Queen, John Dickson Carr, Gaston Leroux and Edgar Allan Poe. The two women were called "Agatha" and "Orczy", the full original names being, of course, Agatha Christie, the Queen of Crime, and Baroness Orczy, known for *The Old Man in the Corner*.

"Look o'er there. Ya can see the building on Tsunojima now," the fisherman yelled out loudly. The six youngsters all turned to look at the island that was coming closer and closer.

Sheer cliffs rose from the sea, covered at the top by a dark fringe of vegetation. The island had three capes, or "horns", which had earned it the name of Tsunojima, or "Horn Island".

Because there were cliffs on all sides of the island, the boat could only make land via a small inlet, which was why the island was only occasionally visited by curious amateur fishermen. About twenty years ago, someone had moved there and constructed a strange building called the Blue Mansion, but now it was completely uninhabited.

"What's that on top of the cliff?" asked Agatha, getting up from the bench. She squinted her eyes in delight as she held one hand on her long, wavy hair dancing in the wind.

"That's the annex building that survived the fire. Heard the main mansion burned down to the ground completely," the fisherman shouted over the noise of the motor.

"So that's the 'Decagon House', eh, grandpa?" Ellery asked the fisherman. "Have you ever been on the island?"

"I've gone into the inlet a few times, to avoid the wind, but I've never set foot on the island itself. Haven't even come anywhere close to it since the incident. Y'all better be careful, too."

"Careful about what?" asked Agatha, turning round.

The fisherman lowered his voice.

"They say *it* appears on the island."

Agatha and Ellery gave each other a quick look, both puzzled by the answer.

"A ghost. Ya know, the ghost of the man who got murdered. Nakamura something."

The fisherman's dark, wrinkled face creased into a frown, then he grinned devilishly.

"I heard ya can see a white figure on the cliff o'er there if ya pass by here on a rainy day. 'Tis the ghost of that Nakamura guy, trying to lure ya there by wavin' his hands at ya. There're other stories too, like people havin' seen a light at the abandoned annex, or will-o'-the-wisps floatin' near the burnt-down mansion, or even one 'bout a boat with fishermen being sunk by the ghost."

"It's no good, grandpa." Ellery chuckled. "No use trying to scare us with those stories. We'll just get even more excited."

The only person among the six students who seemed to have been scared, even a little, was Orczy, who was still sitting on the wooden box. Agatha didn't seem at all perturbed—quite the contrary. "That's so awesome," she muttered to herself in delight. She turned towards the back of the boat.

"Hey, are those stories really true?" she excitedly asked the fisherman's son—still a boy—who was holding the rudder.

"All lies." He shot a glance at Agatha's face, then, looking quickly away as if dazzled, said gruffly: "I heard the rumours, but I've never seen a ghost myself."

"Not even once?" said Agatha, disappointed. But then she smiled mischievously. "Still, it wouldn't be all that strange if there were a ghost," she said. "Not after what happened there."

It was 11 o'clock in the morning of Wednesday, 26th March 1986.

2

The inlet was located on the west coast of the island.

It was flanked on both sides by steep cliffs. To the right, facing the inlet, was a dangerous-looking bare rock surface and this cliff wall, almost twenty metres high, continued towards the southern coast of the island. On the east side of the island, where the currents were very strong, the cliff wall even reached fifty metres in height. Directly in front of them was a steep incline, almost another cliff wall, with narrow stone steps crawling up it in a zigzag pattern. Dark green shrubs clung to the face here and there. (See Figure 1.)

The boat slowly entered the inlet.

The waves inside were not as fierce as those out at sea. The colour of the water was also different: an intense, dark green.

To their left inside the inlet there was a wooden pier; further back, a decrepit, shabby boathouse came into view.

"So I really don't have to check up on ya even once?" the fisherman asked the six as they set foot on the dangerously creaking pier. "Don' think phones work here."

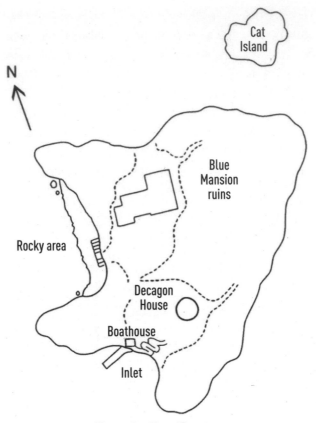

Figure 1   Map of Tsunojima

"It's all right, grandpa," Ellery answered. "We even have a doctor-in-training here," he added, placing his hand on the shoulder of Poe, who was smoking a cigarette while seated on a big knapsack.

The bearded Poe was a fourth-year student in the medical faculty.

"Yes, Ellery's right," Agatha pitched in. "It's not often we have a chance to visit an uninhabited island, and it would ruin the mood if someone kept coming to check up on us."

"You have a brave lil' miss there too, I see."

The fisherman exposed his strong white teeth as he laughed and undid the rope that was tied to a post of the pier.

"I'll come pick ya up Tuesday next week at ten in the morning, then. Be careful."

"Thanks, we'll be careful. Especially of ghosts."

At the top of the steep stone steps, the view suddenly widened. An overgrown grass lawn appeared to be the front garden of a small building with white walls and a blue roof, which stood there invitingly as if it had been waiting for the students.

The blue double doors right in front of them were probably the front entrance. A few steps led up to the doorway.

"So this is the Decagon House."

Ellery was the first to speak, but, having climbed the long stone staircase, he was out of breath. He dropped his camel-beige travelling bag on the ground and stood gazing up at the sky.

"Agatha, your thoughts?"

"Surprisingly lovely place," said Agatha, putting her handkerchief to her light-skinned forehead, which was gleaming with perspiration.

Leroux came up next, also out of breath. His arms were full of luggage, including Agatha's.

"Well… I was expecting… how to put it?… something more sinister."

"Can't always have what you want," replied Ellery. "Let's go inside. Van should have arrived here before us, but I don't see him."

No sooner had Ellery spoken than the blue window shutters immediately to the left of the front entrance opened, and a man looked out.

"Hey, everyone."

And so Van Dine made his appearance, the seventh member of the group of students who were to sleep and eat on this island, and in this building, for one week. His name was, of course, taken from S.S. Van Dine, the literary father of the great detective Philo Vance.

"Wait a sec, I'll come out," Van said in his strange, husky voice, and closed the shutters. A few moments later he came scurrying out of the front entrance.

"Sorry I didn't meet you at the pier. I seem to be coming down with something. I've got a bit of a fever so I was resting for a while. I was listening for your boat coming, though."

Van had arrived earlier on the island to prepare everything.

"Coming down with something? Nothing serious, I hope," Leroux asked with a worried look, pushing up his glasses, which had slipped down his sweaty nose.

"No, nothing serious… At least I hope not. Just a cold, I think."

A shudder went through Van's slim body, as he laughed uneasily.

Led by Van, the group entered the Decagon House.

Going through the blue double doors, they entered a large entrance hall—although they soon realized that it was smaller than it first appeared, its irregular shape creating an optical illusion on first sight. Looking closely, they realized the wall facing them was shorter than the one behind. The entrance hall was shaped like a trapezoid, becoming smaller as they went forward, with another set of double doors on the far wall leading further into the building.

Everyone except Van was puzzled by the strange layout of the room, which played with their sense of perspective, but once they had passed through the second set of doors and arrived in the main hall of the building, they began to understand. They were standing in a decagonal room, surrounded by ten walls, all of the same width.

To grasp the structure of the so-called Decagon House, it is probably best to look at a simple floor plan. (See Figure 2.)

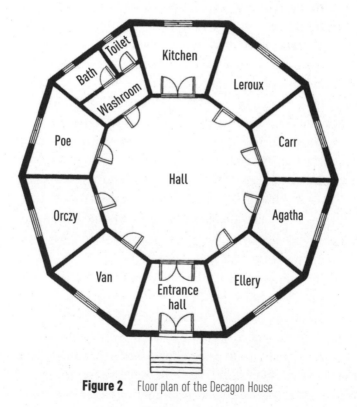

Figure 2   Floor plan of the Decagon House

The distinctive feature of the Decagon House is, as the name implies, that the outer walls form an equilateral decagon. Inside this outer decagon, ten separate blocks are set next to each other, surrounding the inner decagon that makes up the main hall. In other words, an equilateral inner decagon (the main hall) is surrounded by ten equal-sized trapezoidal rooms. The entrance hall they had just passed through was one such room.

"Well? Bizarre, right?"

Van, who had been leading the way, turned to the others.

"Those double doors over there, opposite the entrance, lead to the kitchen. To the left of that are the toilet and bathroom. The remaining seven rooms are the guest rooms."

"A decagonal building and a decagonal hall."

As he looked around the interior, Ellery walked towards a big table in the centre of the room. He tapped on it with his fingers.

"This is decagonal too. What a surprise. Could the murdered Nakamura Seiji have been suffering from monomania?"

"Perhaps," Leroux replied. "The burnt-down main mansion was called the Blue Mansion, and they say everything in there was painted blue: the floors, the ceilings and all the furniture."

The name of the individual who had moved to the island and built the Blue Mansion about twenty years ago was Nakamura Seiji. And the Decagon House, which was the annex of the main building was, of course, built by him too.

"All the same," said Agatha to no one in particular, "I wonder whether I'll be able to tell all these rooms apart."

The entrance and the portal to the kitchen opposite both had double doors, and both were decorated with figured glass set in a frame of plain wood. When the doors were closed there was no way to tell them apart. The four walls to each side of each set of double doors had doors leading to the other rooms. These plain wooden doors were also difficult to tell apart. There were no furnishings in the main hall that could serve as a guide, so Agatha's worries were quite natural. "You're right there. I myself got confused about the rooms several times this morning."

Van cast a wry smile. His eyelids looked puffy, perhaps because of the fever he had mentioned.

"How about making some nameplates and hanging them on the doors? Orczy, did you bring your sketchbook?"

Orczy looked up anxiously as her name was called.

She was a small woman. Mindful of her rather plump figure, she was always wearing dark clothes, but that only made her look out of fashion. She was the complete opposite of the brilliant Agatha and was always looking away with timid eyes. But she was very skilful at her hobby: traditional painting.

"Yes. I have it with me. Shall I take it out now?"

"No, later is OK. Take a look at your rooms for now. They're all the same, so you don't have to fight over them. I'm already using this room though." Van pointed to one of the doors. "I was given the keys, so I've left them in the keyholes."

"OK, gotcha," Ellery answered brightly.

"Great, you get settled in then we'll go and explore the island."

3

The rooms were quickly divvied up.

Counting from the front entrance, Van, Orczy and Poe occupied the rooms on the left and Ellery, Agatha, Carr and Leroux those on the right.

After the six had disappeared into their rooms with their luggage, Van leant back against the door of his own room, took out a Seven Stars cigarette from his ivory down jacket, put it in his mouth and stared keenly into the dimly lit decagonal hall.

The walls were made of white plaster. The floor was covered with oversized blue tiles and, unlike most Japanese homes, you could walk inside with your shoes on. The ceiling rose diagonally upwards from the ten walls and in the centre was a decagonal skylight, from which light kissed the exposed rafters before falling on the white decagonal table. Ten chairs with blue cloth covering their whitewood framework surrounded the table. Those were the only decorations in the room, save for the round lamp hanging from the rafters like a pendulum.

There was no electricity. Natural light from the skylight was the only source of illumination, which is why, even during the day, a mysterious atmosphere permeated the hall.

After a while Poe, dressed in faded jeans and a light-blue shirt, stepped languidly out of his room.

"Oh, you're fast. Wait, I'll make some coffee now."

Holding his half-smoked cigarette between his fingers, Van walked to the kitchen. He was currently a third-year student in the science faculty, which meant he was one year younger than Poe, who was a fourth-year medical student.

"Thanks. Must have been a hassle bringing the big stuff like the blankets."

"Not at all. I had some people help me."

Agatha also appeared from her door, busy tying her long hair back with a scarf.

"These are pretty good rooms, Van. I'd expected something much worse… Coffee? I'll make it."

Cheerfully Agatha walked into the kitchen, where she saw a glass jar with a black label on the counter.

"Instant coffee?"

She picked the jar up with a look of displeasure and shook it.

"Don't be picky," replied Van. "You're not at a resort hotel, you're on an uninhabited island."

Agatha pouted her rose-coloured lips.

"And the food?"

"In the fridge. But it isn't working, as the electricity and phone lines all went down in the fire. Hope that's OK."

"Oh, well, it'll probably keep. There's water, I hope?"

"Yes, I've already connected the water line. I also hooked up the propane-gas tank I brought, so you can also use the gas heater and the boiler. I don't recommend it, but you could even use the bath."

"Good job. Hmm, there are still some pans and tableware left, I see. Or did you bring those with you too?"

"No, they were here already. Three kitchen knives, too. There's a lot of mould on this cutting board, though."

Timidly, Orczy joined them.

"Orczy, you come and help too," Agatha said briskly. "Luckily there's a lot here, but we'll need to clean everything first."

Agatha shrugged and took off her black leather jacket. She turned to Van and Poe, who were stood behind Orczy, peeking into the kitchen.

"If you aren't going to help us, then please leave. Go and explore the island or something. You won't get any coffee before we're finished."

Putting her hands to her hips, she glared at the two of them. Van grinned sheepishly and retreated, together with Poe.

"And don't forget the nameplates," Agatha called after them. "I won't have you coming into our rooms when we're undressing!"

By now, Ellery and Leroux had also emerged from their rooms into the hall.

"Thrown out by the Queen, I see," said Ellery with a laugh.

"Indeed," replied Van.

"So now I suggest we follow Her Majesty's orders and take a look at the island!"

"That's probably the best... Wait, where's Carr? Still in his room?"

"He's gone out. On his own," said Leroux, and he glanced towards the entrance.

"Already?" asked Poe.

"He likes to play hard to get," Ellery said archly.

A row of high pine trees grew to the north of the Decagon House. There was a break in the line and the branches of the black pines on either side had connected to form an arch, which the four passed through to reach the ruins of the Blue Mansion.

All that remained on the site were the foundations, together with a few dirty stone blocks. The desolate front garden had been covered by a thick layer of black ash, and the sight of the surrounding trees, scorched in the fire and rotting where they stood, was striking.

"Completely burnt down. Must have been a tremendous fire," said Ellery, letting out a sigh as he surveyed the dismal scene.

"There's really nothing left," added Van.

"So, Van, is this your first visit too?" Ellery asked.

Van nodded.

"My uncle told me a lot about the island, but today is the first time I've been here. I had to carry all the luggage this morning and then what with my fever I didn't think it'd be wise to explore the island on my own."

"That was sensible. But there's really nothing but ashes and bricks here."

"I guess a corpse would have made you happy, Ellery?" Leroux grinned.

"Lay off. That's something more up your street, isn't it?"

A little path opened into a pine grove to the west. It led straight to the cliffs. On the other side of the wide azure sea they could just make out the black shadow that was J— Cape.

"Great weather today. The sea's almost tranquil, you could say."

Ellery faced the water and stretched. Wrapping his hands in the hem of his yellow sweatshirt, Leroux also turned his small body towards the sea.

"You're right, Ellery," agreed Leroux. "It's almost unbeliev-able that only six months ago, at this very place, such a horrific incident occurred…"

"Horrific… That's the word. A mysterious quadruple murder, right here in Nakamura Seiji's home, the Blue Mansion."

"I'm quite used to quintuple, even decuple murders in books, but this one was real and happened relatively close by, too. Somehow the fact that Nakamura is such an ordinary family name made the whole incident seem even stranger. I was really shocked when I saw it on the news," said Leroux with a shudder.

"I seem to recall it happened in the early morning of the 20th of September? A fire broke out and the building burned down completely. Four bodies were discovered in the ruins: that of Nakamura Seiji, his wife Kazue and the bodies of the servant couple who lived there."

Ellery went on, his voice calm and detached.

"A significant quantity of a sleeping drug was found in all four bodies, but the police also discovered that they had not all died of the same cause. The two servants had been tied up with rope in their own rooms and their heads had been smashed in with an axe. The head of the household, Seiji, had been doused with kerosene and burnt to death. His wife Kazue, who was found in the same room, was found to have been strangled to death with a rope-like object. What's more, her left hand had been cut off at the wrist using a sharp instrument. The hand was not recovered from the ruins of the fire. I think those were the main points of the case, Leroux?"

"I think there was also a gardener who disappeared."

"Ah, you're right. The police couldn't find the gardener, who was supposed to have arrived on the island some days earlier to work there. He seemed to have disappeared completely."

"Yes."

"There are two views on that. One is that the gardener was the murderer and that's why he disappeared. The other view is that someone else was the murderer, and there's another explanation for his disappearance. For example, the gardener might have been fleeing from the murderer and accidentally fallen off the cliffs and been swept away by the current."

"The police seemed to have gone with the 'gardener equals murderer' theory. I don't know what results further investigations uncovered, though. What do you think about the case, Ellery?"

"Well." Ellery brushed away a lock of hair that had been displaced by the wind blowing from the sea. "Regrettably, we have too little data. All we know is the information we were given in the few days the media were all over the case."

"Not like you to be so unsure of yourself."

"Well, so should anyone be. It's easy to come up with a fairly reasonable hypothesis, but there's too little data to prove any one theory and declare QED. In this particular case, the police investigation was also rather poorly handled. But then again, this is all that was left of the crime scene. And there were no other survivors on the island. It's quite natural that the police would consider the missing gardener the criminal."

"True."

"So the truth is hidden beneath these ashes."

Ellery turned and walked back to the remaining stone blocks and picked up a piece of wood. Crouching, he looked at what lay beneath it.

"What's the matter?" asked Leroux, puzzled.

"Wouldn't it be interesting if I'd just found the wife's hand here?" Ellery said with a straight face. "Or maybe we'll find the skeleton of the gardener beneath the floor of the Decagon House."

"You're crazy," cut in Poe, who had been listening to their conversation in silence. He stroked his beard, looking worried. "You have a rather peculiar sense of humour, don't you, Ellery?"

"I agree," chimed in Leroux. "It's as you all said on the boat: if something happened on this island tomorrow, it would be just like the 'chalet in the snowstorm' Ellery loves so much. How happy he'd be if there were a series of murders like in *And Then There Were None*."

"And he'd be the first to get himself killed."

Poe spoke very little, but sometimes came out with some harsh words.

Leroux and Van looked at each other and laughed.

"A series of murders on a remote island. That sounds just the thing," Ellery said with good grace. "Precisely what's in order. And then I'll take on the role of the detective. So? Anybody want to challenge me, Ellery Queen?"

4

"When it comes down to something like this, we women are always the worst off, aren't we? They think we're their servants," Agatha grumbled as she quickly took care of the dishes. Orczy stood beside her, staring at the white, supple fingers swiftly doing their work, until she realized she wasn't doing any work of her own.

"Let's have the boys do some work in the kitchen, too. They shouldn't think they're off the hook just because the two of us are here. Don't you agree?"

"Eh, y-yes."

"It'd be hilarious to see Ellery wearing an apron and holding a ladle with that nonchalant expression of his. He might actually look cute in it."

Agatha laughed gaily. Orczy cast a glimpse at her beautiful profile and sighed.

A bright face with a shapely nose. Eyes that had been accentuated by a light touch of violet eyeshadow. Well-kept long, wavy hair.

Agatha was always cheerful and full of confidence. She seemed to enjoy the looks she received from the men who flocked around her glamorous beauty.

Compared to her, I'm just...

A small, round nose. Childish red cheeks covered in freckles. She did have big, wide eyes, but they weren't in balance with the rest of her face, which gave her a permanently anxious expression. Even if she could use make-up the way Agatha did, she knew it wouldn't suit her. She hated her own timidity, her constant worrying and the fact that, despite all that, she was also very unaware of what was going on around her.

It had always been like this. Agatha and she, as the only females in the group, inevitably seemed to end up together, and it got to Orczy.

I shouldn't have come, she had even begun to think.

She had never wanted to come to this island in the first place. It felt… disrespectful. But she had also been too timid to decline her friends' invitation.

"Orczy, what a wonderful ring," Agatha said, looking at the middle finger of Orczy's left hand. "Have you always had it?"

"No."

"Was it a present from someone special?"

"No, nothing like that."

Orczy had considered carefully before making up her mind to come to the island. The trip wasn't an intrusion: she was paying her respects. *I will go to the island to pay my respects to the dead.* And that's why she had to come.

"Orczy, you're always like that, aren't you?"

"What?"

"Always keeping your thoughts to yourself. We've known each other for two years now, and I still feel as if I don't know anything at all about you. It's fine, of course, but still, it's so strange."

"Strange?"

"Yes. I sometimes feel like that when I read the stories you write for the club magazine. You're always so lively and bright in your own stories."

"Because that's a made-up world." Orczy turned away from Agatha's gaze and smiled awkwardly. "I'm not so good with reality. I'm not really very keen on my real self."

"What are you saying?" Agatha laughed and ran her fingers through Orczy's neat short hair. "You need to have more

35

self-confidence. You know, you're cute. You just don't know it yourself. Stop looking at your feet all the time and stand proud."

"Thanks, Agatha. You're very kind."

"Let's clean this mess up fast and have lunch, OK?"

Ellery, Leroux and Van were still at what remained of the Blue Mansion. Poe had gone over to the grove on the other side of the ruins on his own.

"Listen, Ellery, and you too, Van," Leroux began. "We're going to be here for seven days, so I'd really like to ask you something…" Behind his comical silver-rimmed round glasses, which he himself didn't find comical at all, Leroux's eyes were gleaming. "I'm not asking for a hundred pages, but at least give me fifty."

"Tell me you're joking, Leroux?"

"I'm always serious, Ellery."

"But this is completely out of the blue. We didn't come here to write, don't you agree, Van?"

"I'm with Ellery."

"But I already explained it to you earlier. I want to publish the new issue of *Dead Island* a bit sooner than usual, around mid-April. We can use it to attract some new members, and it would also be a special issue to commemorate the tenth anniversary of our Mystery Club. I'll be the new editor-in-chief soon, so I want to give it my all. I can't come out with a flimsy club magazine for the first issue in my new job."

Leroux, a second-year literature student, would take on the role of editor-in-chief of the club magazine *Dead Island* from April onwards.

"But, Leroux…"

Ellery took out a new pack of Salem cigarettes from the pocket of his wine-red shirt and removed the seal. Ellery was in the third year of his law degree. He was also the current editor-in-chief of *Dead Island*.

"...Carr is the one you need to butter up. I won't comment on the quality of his work, but he is the most productive writer in the Mystery Club. Sorry. Van, have you got a light?"

"It's not often you two fall out so badly," said Van.

"Not my fault. Carr started it."

"Now you mention it, Carr does seem to be in a bad mood," Van agreed. Ellery chuckled and blew smoke out of his mouth.

"He has reason to be."

"Oh, why's that?"

"A while back, our poor Carr made advances to Agatha and was immediately rebuffed."

"He went for Dame Agatha? Wow, he had guts."

"And... I think it might have been out of spite, but he then tried his luck with Orczy, but even she wasn't interested."

Van frowned.

"Orczy too?" he muttered.

"And so our great writer is not amused," Ellery concluded.

"Well, of course he wouldn't be amused," agreed Leroux. "Together under one roof with the two girls who rejected him."

"Exactly. So, my dear Leroux, if you want something from Carr, you'll need to be a smooth talker."

At that moment they saw Agatha coming from the direction of the Decagon House. She stopped under the arch of black pine trees and waved at the three men.

"Lunch is ready—where are Poe and Carr? Weren't you together?"

The little path led into the pine grove behind the Decagon House.

He had started along it to take a look at the cliffs on the eastern coast, but the path had become narrower and narrower as he proceeded. It was also full of twists and turns, so he hadn't even gone fifty metres before he lost his sense of direction.

It was dark and gloomy under the pines. The long *sasa* bamboo shoots that grew between the trees clung to his clothes with every step, and the ground was uneven. He had almost tripped several times.

He had considered turning back, but he didn't feel like doing that either. It was a small island. There was no way he could get lost.

The collar of the black turtleneck sweater he wore beneath his jacket was getting soaked in perspiration, but he struggled on. Just as it was becoming unbearable, the path finally led him out of the grove.

He was at the top of the cliffs. The bright reflection from the water dazzled his eyes. A big man was standing on the clifftop already, looking out to sea—it was Poe.

"Hmm? Oh, it's you, Carr."

Poe had turned around at the sound of footsteps, but when he saw it was Carr, he turned back again to the sea.

"This is the north coast. I think that's Cat Island over there," he said, pointing to some rocks sticking up out of the waves. Considering its size, it could barely be called an island. Only a few bushes grew on its barren surface. As the name suggested, it resembled a dark animal crouching in the sea.

"What's the matter, Carr? Why the long face?"

"I'm beginning to regret coming here," said Carr with a scowl. "Just because something happened here last year doesn't mean there's anything interesting here now. I came hoping it might stimulate my imagination, but now just the thought that I'll be looking at those same faces every day for a whole week… You should have a long face, too."

Like Ellery, Carr was a third-year law student. But because Carr had failed the university entrance exams his first year, he was actually as old as Poe, who was one year above him.

Carr was of average height and build. But he looked smaller than he was because he stooped and had a short neck.

"And what are you doing all alone in a place like this?" he asked.

"Nothing in particular."

Poe squinted, his small eyes peering out from beneath thick eyebrows. He took out a cigarette from the birchwood cigarette case which hung from his waist, and put it in his mouth. He held the case out to Carr.

"How many boxes did you bring? Offering cigarettes to others like this, while you're a heavy smoker yourself."

Poe shrugged.

"Enough. I just like to smoke. Even though I study medicine."

"And always Lark cigarettes. Not a brand for the intelligentsia."

Despite this remark, Carr still took him up on the offer.

"But at least they're better than young Master Ellery's menthols."

"Carr, you shouldn't let Ellery get to you all the time. Your bickering affects us all, you know. Even if you try to fight him, he'll just laugh about it and make fun of you for it."

Carr used his own lighter on the cigarette and turned away.

"Look who's talking."

Poe didn't seem to mind. He enjoyed his smoke in silence.

After a while Carr threw his half-smoked Lark into the sea. He sat down on a nearby rock and took out a whisky flask. He jerked the cap off and took a swig.

"Boozing during the day?"

"None of your business."

"I can't say I approve."

Poe's tone became stern.

"You really should drink less, you know. Not just during the daytime, but…"

"Hah. Are you still thinking about *that*?"

"Yes, so you see—"

"No, I don't see. How long has it been? We can't keep on thinking about what happened."

Ignoring Poe's silent, reproachful look, Carr took another swig.

"It's not just Ellery who's got me upset. Whose idea was it to bring women here, to an uninhabited island?"

"It might be uninhabited, but we're not here on a survival trip."

"Huh. Even so, I don't like being cooped up with someone as arrogant as Agatha. And then there's Orczy. The seven of us have somehow became what you might call 'a close group' these last two years, so I can't say this in front of everyone, but that girl's all gloom, no redeeming features, and painfully self-conscious to boot."

"Now you're being unfair."

"Oh, of course. I'd forgotten you and Orczy have been friends since you were little."

Sourly, Poe threw his cigarette to the ground and rubbed it out with his foot. Then, as though he'd just remembered something, he looked at his wristwatch.

"It's already half-past one. If we don't hurry back, we won't get any lunch."

"Before we eat, I've an announcement to make."

Wearing delicate, golden, plain-glass spectacles, Ellery spoke to the party.

"Our next editor-in-chief has something to say to us all."

Lunch was already laid out on the decagonal table. Bacon and eggs, a simple salad, baguettes and coffee.

"Err, sorry to delay your meal," Leroux said, rising from his chair. "I'd simply like to introduce myself as the new editor-in-chief—" He broke off and coughed to clear his throat before continuing.

"We talked about coming to the Decagon House at the club's New Year's party. Of course, nobody imagined it would actually come true at that time. But then Van told us his uncle had come into possession of the island and he generously invited us to visit."

"It wasn't as though I invited you personally," objected Van. "I just said I could ask my uncle, if you really wanted to go."

"Don't be modest. Anyway, as you all know, Van's uncle is an estate agent in S— Town. He's also a talented entrepreneur and has big plans to transform Tsunojima into a holiday resort for the young. Right, Van?"

"I don't think his plans are all that big."

"Well, anyway, we're here today also as a sort of test group. Van came here this morning to make the preparations for our stay, so we'll have to thank him first. We all really appreciate it."

Leroux made a deep bow to Van.

"And now for my main announcement—"

"The bacon and eggs are getting cold," interrupted Agatha.

"I'm almost finished—ah, what does it matter, the food will get cold. Please have your lunch as I speak.

"The talents of everyone gathered here have been acknowledged by our club seniors—who have already graduated—and the seven of us have inherited their names. This is a gathering of the core writing group of our Mystery Club."

It had been a tradition of the K— University Mystery Club since its foundation that club members called each other by nicknames. Ten years ago, the founding members had decided to give everyone names taken from famous writers from Britain, France and the United States, an idea born from the innate childishness of fans of crime fiction. Of course, with new members joining every year, fewer and fewer names were available. The solution to that problem was "inheritance", a system whereby graduating members would pass on their name to a junior member of their choice.

In time, successors of names came to be chosen based on their contributions to the club magazine. Therefore, the seven present, who bore the names of the most famous mystery writers, were considered the core of the club and often gathered for various occasions.

"…We core members will stay here on this island for one week, starting now, with nothing to distract us. I suggest we all make good use of this time."

Leroux looked around the table.

"I've brought writing paper with me, and I would like to ask each of you to write one story for the upcoming club magazine in April."

"Ah!" Agatha yelled out. "So that's why you had so much luggage with you. You were plotting to spring this on us!"

"Yes, this is indeed my plot. Please do write something, Agatha, and you too, Orczy."

Leroux gave a shallow bow then stroked his round cheeks, chuckling. He looked like a lucky *fukusuke* doll, but with spectacles. Bitter smiles appeared on the faces of the rest of the group.

"You might only get 'murder on a remote island' stories, Leroux. What will you do then?" Poe asked.

"Then I'll say it's this issue's theme," said Leroux defiantly, sticking out his chest. "Better yet, let's go with that theme right from the start. That would be even better. The magazine's title, *Dead Island*, was taken from the first Japanese translation of Dame Agatha's masterpiece anyway."

"I fear we underestimated our new editor-in-chief," Ellery whispered to his neighbour, Van.

5

The first day ended without incident.

The group had no commitments other than to work on the stories Leroux had asked for. They were mostly solitary types, so as evening approached they had all gone their separate ways.

"Ellery, what are you doing with those playing cards all by yourself?" said Agatha, coming out of her room. The bright-yellow scarf that held back her long hair contrasted with her monochrome combination of a white blouse and black leather trousers.

"Oh, just a little something I've been dabbling with lately."

"Dabbling with what? Let me guess—fortune telling?"

"You must be joking. I'm not interested in that rubbish."

He shuffled the cards on the decagonal table and went on:

"Magic tricks, of course."

"Card magic?"

For a second Agatha looked confused, but then she nodded knowingly.

"I see. That's just the sort of thing you would be into."

"Why? What do you mean?"

"I mean you like tricking people!"

"You make it sound like a bad thing."

"Is that so?" Agatha laughed. "So show me something, then. I haven't seen much magic before."

"You surprise me. It's quite rare for someone who's interested in mystery fiction not to be interested in magic tricks as well."

"It's not that I'm not interested. I just haven't had that many opportunities to see any. So show me."

"OK. Come here and sit down."

The sun was setting, leaving the hall of the Decagon House in twilight. Agatha sat on the chair across the table from Ellery. He gathered his cards, arranged them on the tabletop and took out another deck from his coat pocket.

"Here I have two decks with different backs: one red and one blue. You and I will each use one deck. Which will you use?"

"Blue," Agatha answered instantly.

"All right. You take these cards."

Ellery passed the blue deck of cards across the table.

"First make sure there's nothing funny about them and then shuffle them anyway you like. I'll shuffle the red cards."

"OK. They look like ordinary cards to me. From the United States?"

"Bicycle Rider Back playing cards. There's an illustration of an angel riding a bicycle on their backs, do you see it? They're the most popular type of card over there."

Ellery placed his carefully shuffled deck of cards on the table.

"Now we'll exchange decks. You'll give me the blue, and I'll give you the red. OK. Now take a card out of the deck and memorize it. I'll take a card from your deck as well and memorize that."

"Any card I want?"

"Yes. Finished? Now place the card back on top of the deck. And now cut the deck once, just like me. Now the bottom half of the deck has been swapped with the upper half. Yep, yep, like that. Now repeat two or three times."

"Am I doing it right?"

"You're doing perfectly. And now we exchange our decks once more."

The blue deck returned to Agatha's hands. Ellery stared straight into her eyes and asked: "All right? So, to summarize what we just did: we each took one card from a shuffled deck, memorized the card, returned it and shuffled the deck again."

"Yes."

"Now, Agatha, please take out the card you've memorized from your deck, and place it on the table face down. I'll take out my card from this deck."

Two cards, one red, one blue, appeared on top of the table. Ellery took a deep breath and then asked Agatha to turn both cards over.

"Ah!"

Agatha shrieked in surprise. The cards were of the same suit and number.

"The Four of Hearts! But how did you know?"

Ellery laughed contentedly.

"Neat trick, don't you agree?"

After the sun had set, the antique oil lamp which stood in the middle of the decagonal table was lit. Van had brought it along, knowing there was no electricity in the house. He had also brought a number of thick candles for each of the guest rooms.

It was past seven when they finished their dinner.

"Ellery, why won't you explain the magic trick you did just now?" said Agatha, with a hand on his shoulder. She had just brought coffee for everyone.

"It's no use keeping on at me. It's taboo to reveal magic tricks. That's where magic differs from mystery fiction. No matter how mysterious the trick, you'll just be disappointed when you hear how simple it is."

"So Ellery showed you one of his tricks, did he?" chipped in Leroux.

"Ah, so you know about Ellery's magic too!"

"Know? He's been using me as a guinea pig this whole month. I had to keep it a secret until he got better at it. He can be rather childish at times."

"Leroux!" complained Ellery.

"What did you show her?" Leroux asked.

"Just one or two simple ones."

"So those were simple ones?" Agatha looked annoyed. "Then there's no harm telling me how they're done, right? Go on."

"It's precisely because they are so simple that I can't tell you how they were done. The first one I showed you, in particular, is a very elementary one—even children can learn it. But magic isn't just about the trick, it's about performance and misdirection."

"Performance?"

"Yes. For example…"

Ellery took his cup in his hand and took a sip of his black coffee.

"There's a scene in the movie *Magic* where Anthony Hopkins, who plays a magician, performs practically the same trick for his former love. But in the film it isn't presented as a normal magic trick, rather as an experiment in ESP. The magician seduced the girl by saying that if they were soulmates, they'd choose the same card."

"Oh. And you had no intention of seducing me with the same trick?"

"I wouldn't dare," said Ellery with a shrug and an attempt at a smile. "Alas, at the moment I don't have the courage to seduce our queen."

"That's a funny way of putting it."

"Thanks. By the way"—Ellery raised the cup of coffee he was holding and stared at it intently—"to change the subject: regarding that Nakamura Seiji we were talking about this afternoon, did you know he had more than his fair share of obsessions? I got the shivers when I took a close look at this cup earlier."

It was a fancy moss-green cup, part of the tableware which had been left in the kitchen. But it was its shape that was significant. Like the building, this cup, too, was decagonal.

"He probably had them specially made. This ashtray and the plates we used are all the same. Everything is a decagon. Any thoughts, Poe?"

"None."

Poe placed his half-smoked cigarette in the ashtray.

"Obviously, it's eccentric, but you know what the rich are like. They love to play around."

"Just the rich playing around, eh?"

Ellery clutched his cup with both hands and peered intently inside. Although it was a decagon, its small size made it appear almost round to the naked eye.

"Anyway," he went on, "I feel it was worth coming all the way to this island, even if only for this Decagon House. I almost want to drink a toast to those who died here."

"Ellery," said Agatha, "the Decagon House might be a hit with everyone, but there's nothing else on the island at all. Just a lot of dreary pine trees."

"You're mistaken there," Poe said. "There's a rocky stretch beneath the cliffs west of the ruins, and a staircase, so we can get all the way down to the sea. I might be able to do some fishing."

"Now you mention it," Leroux said, "I did notice you carrying some fishing gear earlier. With any luck we might be able to eat some freshly caught fish tomorrow."

He licked his lips.

"Don't expect too much of me," chuckled Poe, stroking his beard.

"Did you see that there are a couple of cherry-blossom trees right behind this house?" he went on. "The buds are ripe, so they might bloom in a couple of days."

"How wonderful!" cried Agatha. "Let's hold a cherry-blossom viewing party then!"

"Sounds good," agreed Leroux.

"Cherry blossoms, eh?" said Ellery. "What is it about cherry blossoms in the spring in Japan? Personally, I think peach and plum blossoms are much more pleasing to the eye."

"That's just because you never want to be like anyone else," countered Leroux.

"Is that right? Did you know that our exalted ancestors all preferred the plum to the cherry, Leroux?"

"Really?"

"Of course. I think I'm correct here. Orczy?"

Orczy shuddered at the shock of finding herself suddenly addressed. Her face flushed and she nodded hesitantly.

"Well?" Ellery prompted. "Care to explain?"

"Yes… all right," stammered Orczy. "In the poems of the *Manyōshū*, the plum and the Amur silver-grass are the plants mentioned the most often. There are more than a hundred poems about each of them, but only about forty about the cherry blossom."

Both Orczy and Leroux were second-year literature students. Her major was English literature, but she was also knowledgeable about classical Japanese literature.

"Well, I never heard about that," Agatha said, impressed. As a third-year pharmacy student, she knew nothing about the topic. "Tell us more, Orczy."

"A-all right," Orczy answered half-heartedly. "During the period the *Manyōshū* was compiled, the trend was to imitate the mainland—China—so it might have been a reflection of Chinese preferences. The number of poems on cherry blossoms only grew after the creation of the *Kokin Wakashū*... but many of them were about falling blossoms."

"The *Kokin Wakashū*, so that means the Heian period, I think?" Ellery asked.

"It was during the rule of Emperor Daigo. Early tenth century..."

"Could it be because of the pessimistic world view back then that there were a lot of poems about falling flowers?"

"I wonder. The period when cherry blossoms start to fall is also the season when epidemics thrive. They say that cherry blossoms attract illness, so they used to hold the *Hanashizume* festival every spring to ward off illnesses. So it might have been related to that..." Orczy trailed off.

"I see."

"What's the matter with you, Van?" said Poe. "You're so quiet."

Van was sitting next to Poe, his head hanging down.

"Not feeling well?"

"No, my head hurts a little."

"You don't look so good either. And you have a fever."

Van moved his shoulders around to loosen them up and took a deep breath.

"Sorry, but I think I'll go to bed now."

"Yes, that's probably best."

"OK. Well..."

Van placed both hands on the table and slowly rose from his seat.

"You can make as much noise as you want out here. I don't mind."

They said goodnight and Van retreated to his room. His door closed and, for a second, the dimly lit hall fell silent. They heard the metallic click of the lock being turned.

"Just like him," Carr said. Up until that moment he had been nervously jigging his knees in silence. His eyes were wide, as if he were anxious about something. "What a scaredy-cat. Who bothers to lock his door when he's staying with people he knows?"

"Tonight's a bright night."

Pretending not to hear Carr, Poe gazed up towards the decagonal skylight.

"I think it was full moon two days ago," Leroux observed. At that moment a beam of light swiftly crossed the sky. It came from the lighthouse in J— Cape, which reached all the way there.

"Look," said Agatha, "there's a halo around the moon. That means it's going to rain tomorrow."

"That's just superstition," scoffed Ellery.

"Don't be so rude, Ellery. Anyway, it's not just superstition. It has to do with the water vapour in the air."

"But the weather report said it would be clear the whole week," Ellery insisted.

"Hmm. Well, anyway," Agatha went on, "it's more scientific than all those stories about a rabbit on the moon."

"A rabbit!" Ellery snorted with laughter. "You know in the Miyako Islands they see a man carrying a bucket on the moon. Ever hear the story behind it?"

"Ah, I know that one." Leroux's youthful face brightened. "He was sent to the human world by God, carrying one bucket with the elixir of immortality and one with the elixir of death. But he mixed them up and he gave the snake the elixir of immortality and mankind the elixir of death. As a punishment, the man has to carry the bucket for all eternity."

"Quite."

"The Khoikhoi have a similar legend," Poe said. "But in their story it was a hare who was sent to earth. The hare failed to relay the words of the Moon God and, in his anger, the god threw a stick at it. That's when the hare ended up with a split lip."

"People tell the same stories all over the world." Ellery leant his long body on the blue backrest and crossed his arms. "The one about the rabbit on the moon is known in China, Central Asia, India…"

"As far away as India?" asked Poe.

"The Sanskrit word for 'moon' is *śaśin*, which translates as 'having the markings of a hare.'"

"Wow."

As he reached out for his cigarette case on the table, Poe looked up at the skylight once again. The bright-yellow moon floated in the sky.

Tsunojima, the Decagon House.

The shadows of those present were cast on the surrounding walls by the dim light of the lamp.

Slowly, the night advanced.

The First Day on the Mainland

1

My daughter Chiori was murdered by all of you.

Kawaminami Taka'aki frowned as he lay sprawled on the bed in the middle of his small room. It was eleven o'clock in the morning. He had found the letter in his mailbox just now on his return home.

He had stayed out all night playing mah-jong at a friend's place and come home with a drowsy mind, the noise of the tiles still echoing in his ears as usual, but the letter had awoken him immediately.

"Wha-what's this?"

Rubbing his eyes, he picked up the envelope that held the letter and took another good look at it. It was an ordinary brown envelope, postmarked yesterday—25th March. It had been posted from within O— City. The only thing peculiar about it was that everything on it had been written with a word processor.

There was no address for the sender. The back of the envelope only said "Nakamura Seiji".

"Nakamura Seiji."

He muttered the name. Never heard of him. No, wait, he had heard it somewhere.

He sat up, legs crossed, and looked again at the letter. It had also been written with a word processor. The paper was a high-grade B5.

"My daughter Chiori was *murdered* by all of you."

He remembered the name Chiori. The letter probably referred to Nakamura Chiori. And this Nakamura Seiji would be her father.

It had happened over a year ago, at the New Year's party of the K— University Mystery Club, of which Kawaminami had been a member at the time. Nakamura Chiori had been his junior, one year below him, so she was a first-year student. Kawaminami was a third-year now. He would become a fourth-year starting in April, but he had quit the Mystery Club in spring last year.

Because at the New Year's after-party, Nakamura Chiori had died.

Kawaminami had left the party early because of an appointment. The "accident" had happened after his departure. Acute alcohol poisoning, coupled with a chronic disease, had led to a heart attack. It had been too late by the time the ambulance had brought her to the hospital.

Kawaminami had also attended the funeral.

Chiori had been living in O— City with her grandfather on her mother's side. The ceremony was held there. But the name of the chief mourner wasn't Seiji. It was a much more old-fashioned name. It wasn't her father, but her grandfather. Now that he thought about it, he hadn't seen anybody that could have been Chiori's father there.

But why had someone calling himself Chiori's father sent him this letter—someone he had never seen or spoken to?

"Seiji" claimed in his letter that Chiori had been murdered. His daughter had died because of the alcohol she had been made to drink at the party. Kawaminami could understand that, in his eyes, his daughter had been killed. But what was he thinking, writing this letter over a year after it happened?

53

Kawaminami straightened up suddenly.

Nakamura Seiji... Aha!

He had found the correct thread among his memories.

He jumped up, went over to the steel rack leaning against the wall and pulled some folders out. They were full of interesting newspaper clippings he had collected.

I think it was around September last year...

After searching for a while he found the article.

THE BLUE MANSION ON TSUNOJIMA IN FLAMES. A MYSTERIOUS QUADRUPLE MURDER?

Kawaminami sat down on the floor and opened the folder. He tapped his fingers on the big characters of the headline.

"An accusation made by a dead man?"

"Excuse me, is this the Higashi residence? My name is Kawaminami of K— University. Is Hajime there?"

"Kawaminami, you say?"

The woman on the other end of the phone was probably Hajime's mother.

"Hajime left on a trip this morning. With some friends in his club."

"The Mystery Club?"

"Yes. He said he was going to an uninhabited island."

"An uninhabited island? Do you happen to know the name?"

"Err, I think it was Tsunojima. Somewhere near S— Town."

"Tsunojima..."

Kawaminami felt his breathing cease and he grasped the receiver tightly.

"Did Hajime get a letter, by any chance?"

54

"A letter?"

"A letter from someone called Nakamura Seiji."

"I don't…"

She hesitated for a moment, but she seemed to sense the urgency in Kawaminami's voice. She asked him to wait a minute and left the phone. The sound of organ music reached his ears. After a while she returned and said, somewhat anxiously:

"Yes, a letter from a Nakamura Seiji has been delivered. Is there something wrong?"

"It's there? It's really there?"

"Yes."

He suddenly felt his strength draining out of him. His shoulders sagged and he was not sure what to do.

"Oh, yes, thank you—it's nothing. Sorry for bothering you."

Kawaminami replaced the receiver and leant against the wall. It was an old building and the walls would creak if you put too much weight on them. Through the badly made window he could hear the droning of an almost-broken washing machine.

A letter from Nakamura Seiji was also delivered to Higashi's place.

He blinked his bloodshot eyes several times.

Could it be just a prank?

He looked up the club's address list, made a note of all the members who had been at the after-party and made several calls. They had all gone away and, since most of them had been boarding students, he was unable to find out whether they had received letters too. Now they were all on a trip together. To Tsunojima of all places, the site of that horrific incident. Was it just a coincidence?

After a moment of reflection, he picked up the address list again and looked up the phone number of the deceased Nakamura Chiori.

2

O— City was a thirty-minute bus ride and another forty-minute train journey away from S— Town, from where the Mystery Club members had left for Tsunojima. The distance between the towns was less than forty kilometres as the crow flies. Kawaminami got out of the train at Kamegawa, four stations after O— City, and walked briskly up the road leading to the mountains.

He had called the home of Nakamura Chiori's grandfather. A friendly middle-aged woman, probably the housekeeper, had answered the phone and Kawaminami had introduced himself as a friend of Chiori from university.

It would have been awkward for him to call out of the blue and immediately start to grill the woman, but, with tact and patience, he had managed to get confirmation that Chiori's father was indeed the Nakamura Seiji of the Tsunojima incident, and had also managed to obtain the address of Nakamura Kōjirō, Seiji's younger brother. He'd learnt of the existence of Kōjirō while going through newspaper articles about the incident.

Kōjirō was living in the Kannawa district in Beppu. He was a teacher at a high school there and, because it was the spring holiday, he would probably be at home.

Kawaminami's family home also used to be in Beppu. He could easily find his way there, he thought, as his curiosity grew.

He didn't even consider making a phone call first, but decided to head for Kōjirō's house immediately.

Kannawa is home to several of Beppu's famous hot springs, known as "Hells". In the wide clear sky he could see white plumes of steam rising from the rows of houses and the gutters of the sloping roads. To the left he could see the black foothills of Mount Tsurumi.

Past a small shopping area, the streets quickly became silent. The neighbourhood was full of inns, hostels and rental villas for both short- and long-term visitors, who came to the hot springs for medical purposes. As he had been given the exact address on the phone, he managed to find his destination without any trouble.

It was a nice one-storey house. On the other side of a low hedge, flowers like yellow broom, white meadowsweet and pink quince were already showing the colours of spring.

Kawaminami went through the lattice-windowed gate and followed the stone steps through the front garden. He took a deep breath and pushed the doorbell. Moments later, a round baritone voice came from the other side of the door.

"Who is it?"

The man who appeared did not fit this traditional Japanese house at all. He wore a white open-necked shirt under a brown cardigan and charcoal-grey trousers. His hair had been brushed back casually and was streaked with grey.

"Excuse me, are you Nakamura Kōjirō?"

"Yes."

"Er… My name is Kawaminami. I was in the same college club as Nakamura Chiori. I'm sorry for coming here like this out of the blue."

Behind his horn-rimmed glasses, Kōjirō's clean-cut face softened.

"A member of K— University's Mystery Club? And you're here because?…"

"I received this curious letter today."

Kōjirō took the letter. After scanning the orderly row of characters that spelt the sender's name, his eyebrows shot up and he took another look at Kawaminami.

"By all means come inside. A friend is here, but don't mind him. I'm afraid, since I live here alone, I can't offer you very much in the way of food."

Kawaminami was led to a traditional *tatami* mat room towards the rear of the house. The room was L-shaped, consisting of two six-*tatami* rooms joined together. The paper wall panels that had originally separated the rooms had been removed to form a twelve-*tatami* room. The part in front was used as a living room and reception area. On a dark-green carpet stood a sofa set of the same colour. The part in the back overlooked a garden to the right and was being used as a study. Kawaminami could see several bookcases reaching to the ceiling and a big desk. The rooms were so tidy it was hard to believe a single man lived there.

"Shimada, we have a guest."

The friend Kōjirō addressed was sitting on a rattan rocking chair in the front room, facing out towards the garden.

"This is Kawaminami from K— U.'s detective-fiction club. And this is my friend Shimada Kiyoshi."

"Detective fiction?" Shimada asked and he jumped up from his seat. In the process the rocking chair struck his legs and, groaning softly, he fell back into it.

"Er, I actually quit the club last year."

"Hmm."

Shimada rubbed his legs with a grimace and said:

"So what brings you here to dear old Kō?"

"This," said Kōjirō, and he passed Kawaminami's letter to Shimada, who stopped rubbing his legs when he saw the name of the sender and took a hard look at Kawaminami.

"Mind if I read it?"

"Not at all."

"To tell you the truth," Kōjirō said, "I've received a similar letter."

"What?!"

Kōjirō walked to the study desk in the back, picked up a letter lying on top of a red-brown desk mat and passed it to Kawaminami.

Kawaminami studied the front and back of the envelope. The same envelope, the same postmark, the same typed letters as appeared on the one he had received. And the sender was "Nakamura Seiji" as well.

"May I look inside?"

Kōjirō nodded in silence.

Chiori was murdered.

That was all. Although the text was different, it had also been typed using a word processor on the same high-grade B5-sized paper.

Kawaminami, his eyes fixed on the letter, was at a loss for words. A mysterious letter from the dead. He had guessed that every member who had been present at last year's after-party had been sent the same letter, but even this man, Nakamura Kōjirō, had received one.

"What could it mean?"

"I've no idea," Kōjirō replied. "I'm as shocked as you are. I was just saying to Shimada that it must be a practical joke in very bad taste, and how some people have too much time on their hands. And then you turn up."

"It's not just me. Other club members also got the letter."

"Well, well."

"Is it possible that this Nakamura Seiji—excuse me, your brother—is still alive?"

59

"Impossible." Kōjirō shook his head decisively. "As you know, my brother died last autumn. I was the one who had to identify the body. It was horrible—sorry, but I don't want to talk about it."

"So does that mean that this letter is really just a prank?"

"I can't think of any other explanation. My brother died six months ago. That's the honest truth. And I'm afraid I don't believe in ghosts."

"What do you think about the contents of the letter?"

"Well, I…"

A worried look came over Kōjirō's face.

"I know what happened to Chiori, but as far as I'm concerned it was just an unfortunate accident. She was my little niece, so of course it feels as though she was taken from us unfairly, but I don't hate you for what happened. What I really can't forgive, though, is that someone is using the name of my brother and sending these letters around as some sort of sick joke."

"Is it really just a joke?" muttered Kawaminami. He wasn't convinced of that. He nodded half-heartedly and stole a glance at Shimada, who was sitting in the rattan chair with one elbow on his crossed legs and, for some reason, looking at him with amusement.

"By the way," Kawaminami said as he returned the letter to Kōjirō, "did you know that some members of the Mystery Club are on Tsunojima right now?"

"No," replied Kōjirō, uninterested. "I inherited the island and the mansion after my brother's death, but I sold it to an estate agent in S— Town last month. He beat down the price a lot, but I had no intention of ever going to that place again anyway. Don't know what they did with it after that."

3

Kōjirō still had work to do that day, so Kawaminami felt obliged to leave.

Just before he left the room, Kawaminami asked about the full bookcases in the back that had caught his attention. Kōjirō explained that, beside his work as social studies teacher at a nearby high school, he was also doing research on Buddhism. With a shy smile, he explained he was researching the "emptiness of the heart" in early Mahayana Buddhism.

"'Emptiness of the heart'?" asked Kawaminami, puzzled.

Shimada got up from the rocking chair to explain.

"You've heard of the Heart Sutra, no doubt? The one that goes 'Form is Emptiness and Emptiness is Form'? Kō here is researching the meaning of that 'emptiness.'" He approached Kawaminami with a bouncy step and handed back the letter he had been scrutinizing.

"How do you write your family name with kanji, Kawaminami?" he asked.

"The character for 'river', as when you write 'the Yellow River', combined with the character for 'south.'"

"Aha, so *kawa* and *minami*—that's a wonderful name. Kō, I'm going to leave you alone, too. Let's leave together, Kawaminami."

The two left Kōjirō's house and walked down the empty street. Shimada clasped his fingers together and stretched his arms. He wore a black sweater and jeans, which made his lean body look even taller and slimmer.

"*Conan*. Yes, that is really a wonderful name," Shimada said as he raised his arms behind his head. He was using the alternative readings for the characters *kawa* and *minami* to read the name Kawaminami as *Conan*.

"Why did you quit the Mystery Club? At a guess, I'd say the culture didn't suit you."

"You're right. Good guess."

"I could read it in your face." Shimada grinned. "So it wasn't because you lost interest in mystery fiction, then?"

"No, I still enjoy reading detective novels."

"That's good. I like a good mystery too, more than I do Buddhist texts. Nothing as clear-cut as a detective story. Well, Conan, what about having have a coffee with me somewhere?"

"All right," replied Kawaminami, and laughed.

The road sloped gently downwards. The light breeze blowing from the seafront was filled with the spirit of spring.

"You're an interesting man, Conan."

"I am?"

"You came all the way here just because of a letter that might well have been nothing more than a prank."

"It wasn't that far."

"Hm. Actually, I would have done the same if I'd been in your shoes. I have a lot of spare time, you see."

Shimada put both hands in the pockets of his black jeans and grinned.

"And you? Do you think it's all just an elaborate joke?"

"Kōjirō seems to think it is, but it doesn't add up," Kawaminami replied. "Of course, I'm not saying that a ghost wrote those letters. Someone is using the name of the dead man. But there's been just too much effort put into all of this for it to be a simple hoax."

"Like what, for example?"

"For example, all the letters were typed on a word processor. Getting hold of a word processor just for a joke seems a bit—"

"But the writer might simply have their own word processor. They have become popular in the last couple of years. Kō also has one at his place. He only bought the machine this year, but he's become quite skilled at it."

"It's true they've become popular. Quite a few of my friends have them too. And there's one in every office room at the university for students to use freely. But I still don't think it's all that common to use a word processor to write letters."

"That's true."

"A word processor avoids leaving handwriting samples, but why would you need to avoid handwriting if it was just a prank? And the text. It was just that one line. Don't you think it's too short? If you were out to scare people, you'd come up with more alarming things to say. Kōjirō's letter was like that too. So I can't help but feel there's a deeper meaning behind it all."

"A deeper meaning, eh?"

Reaching the end of the slope, they arrived at a promenade. Boats of all sizes were making their way across the sea, which glistened in the sunlight.

"Over there," Shimada pointed. "Let's go there. It's a nice place."

Across the road was a red roof with a weathervane. "Mother Goose" was written on the cafe's signboard in fancy lettering. Kawaminami couldn't help smiling at the sight.

4

After they sat down opposite each other at a table near the window, Kawaminami took another good look at the man he had just met.

He looked over thirty—quite a bit more than that, probably.

His cheeks appeared even hollower than they actually were because of his soft, shoulder-length hair. Kawaminami was tall and thin himself, but Shimada towered over him. A hooked nose decorated his swarthy face and his eyes drooped a little.

He was the sort of man who seemed strange on first meeting. He looked dark and bad-tempered, but the peculiar mismatch between his appearance and his way of talking was something Kawaminami found quite agreeable. He even thought it felt familiar in some way.

It was already past four in the afternoon. Kawaminami remembered he had not eaten anything since the morning, so he ordered pizza toast with coffee.

He took a look through the large window at the blue sea, which formed a giant arc on the other side of National Route 10. It was Beppu Bay. The shop was the kind of cosy little place you'd expect to find on the outskirts of a town filled with students. The Mother Goose-inspired paintings and dolls spread around the shop were probably a hobby of the owner.

"So, Conan, let's continue our conversation," Shimada said casually as he poured a cup of Earl Grey from the pot that had just arrived.

"You mean about the letters?"

"Of course."

"But I've already told you all my thoughts—mind if I smoke?"

"Not at all."

"Thanks."

He lit a cigarette and the smoke stung his eyes.

"As I just said, I don't think it's all just a prank. But if you ask me what it's about, I don't have any answers. To be honest, I can't think of any reason why anyone would do it. But…"

"But?"

"I might take a guess."

"Pray do."

"Well, if I look at the letter sent to me, for example, and try to read the sender's intention from it, I think can detect about three different messages.

"First, the letter is above all an accusation: 'Chiori was murdered.' The second message follows from the first: I hate you, I'll take revenge on you because you killed Chiori. So therefore a threat. The name 'Nakamura Seiji' was used to sign the accusation-cum-threat because he would have the best reason for doing so."

"I see. And the third message?"

"For the third message, we have to look at the letter from a different angle: the hidden meaning behind sending the letters, so to speak."

"The hidden meaning?"

"Yes. Why is the sender using the name of Nakamura Seiji, a deceased man, now? It might seem terrifying at first, but nobody in this day and age would really believe it. Can you imagine a ghost using a word processor? So I think it might be telling us in a roundabout way to take a good look at the incident that happened a year ago on Tsunojima. Or could I be overthinking this?"

"No, it's very interesting."

Shimada's eyes shone in amusement and he reached for his cup.

"Truly interesting. Another look at the Tsunojima incident. I do think that case needs more consideration. What do you know about it, Conan?"

"Only what I read in the newspapers."

"So I'd better tell you what I know first."

"Please do."

"You remember the outline of the case, I assume? It happened in September of last year. Location: the house known as the Blue Mansion on Tsunojima. The four victims were Nakamura Seiji, his wife Kazue and the servant couple. The gardener disappeared. The fire that broke out after the murders destroyed the mansion. The murderer has not been caught."

"I believe the police had the gardener as their prime suspect?"

"Yes, but there was no conclusive evidence. I think he was considered suspicious simply because he'd disappeared. And now for the details of the case…"

Shimada spoke in a low voice.

"First, I have to tell you more about the master of the mansion, Nakamura Seiji. He was three years older than Kō, so he was forty-six at the time. He'd retired by then, but before that he was a genius architect, highly regarded by those in the know.

"Nakamura Seiji was the first child of the Nakamuras, a family of considerable means living in Usa in the Ōita Prefecture. After graduating from high school, Seiji moved on his own to Tokyo. He won a prize at a national-level contest while he was studying architecture at T— University and drew the attention of everyone in his field. After he graduated, his supervising professor strongly advised him to enter graduate school, but the sudden death of his father forced him to return home.

"His father had left the Nakamura family a great fortune. Having inherited the money together with his brother Kōjirō, Seiji proceeded to build a mansion of his own design on Tsunojima and basically retired there.

"His wife Kazue—her maiden name was Hanabusa—had been his childhood friend during his time in Usa. They say their parents had arranged for the two to be married early on. They married around the time Seiji left for Tsunojima."

"Did he do any architectural work after that?"

"A little, but Kō said Seiji mostly did it for his own entertainment. He only took on requests that interested him, and then only when he felt like it. He had a peculiar love for designing the most bizarre buildings. But those buildings were loved in turn by other people with unusual tastes. Many clients came from afar to the island. But Seiji had been refusing nearly all requests for the last ten years and he seldom left his island."

"Quite a character."

"Kō himself is a bit strange too, studying Buddhism as a hobby, but even he agrees his brother was odd. Then again, I got the impression the two didn't get along very well.

"Anyway, the Kitamura couple—the servants—also lived in the mansion on Tsunojima. The husband did odd jobs around the house and piloted the motorboat that connected the island to the mainland. His wife did all the housekeeping. And then we have that gardener. His name was Yoshikawa Sei'ichi and he lived in Ajimu. He would come over once a month and stay several days. He happened to have arrived on the island three days before the fire. And that's it for my introduction to the cast of characters.

"Now for the circumstances of the case. Four bodies were discovered in total. They had been burnt black because of the fire, so forensics had quite some trouble with them. They eventually discovered the following facts:

"The Kitamura couple had died in their bedroom with their heads bashed in. The murder weapon was very likely the axe found in the same room. Both bodies showed signs of having been tied with rope. The estimated time of death for both of them was the afternoon of 19th September—the day before the fire.

"Nakamura Kazue had been strangled to death, on the bed in her bedroom, with a rope-like object. The left hand of the body was missing from the wrist down, and had been cut off after death. The whereabouts of the hand are still unknown. Her estimated time of death is sometime between 17th and 18th of September.

"Nakamura Seiji had been completely doused in kerosene and burnt to death in the same room as Kazue. Large quantities of a sleeping drug were found inside his body, and this was also the case for the other three victims. Estimated time of death was the early morning of 20th September, when the fire broke out.

"The fire is thought to have started in the kitchen. The murderer had splashed kerosene all over the mansion and then set fire to it in the kitchen.

"As you know, the police have set their minds on the theory that the missing gardener is the murderer. But there are still points that remain unclear.

"For example, the problem of Kazue's left hand. What reason could Yoshikawa have had for cutting off the lady's hand and taking it with him? And there's the problem of his escape route. The only motorboat on the island was still in the inlet. He could have hardly killed four people and then gone swimming across the sea to the mainland in late September. The police, of course, also looked into the possibility of the murderer being someone from the outside, but that theory seemed to fit less and less the further they pursued it. The rough outline of the case as proposed by the police based on the 'Yoshikawa equals murderer' theory is… Don't mind me—please eat your meal."

"Wha… oh, yes."

Kawaminami's pizza toast and coffee had been brought during Shimada's explanation. It was not politeness that had prevented him from touching it. He had been so intrigued by Shimada's story he had forgotten to eat.

"Motives. They came up with two. The first was that he wanted Seiji's fortune, so: robbery. The other is that he had an obsession with Kazue, or that they had secretly had a relationship. It was probably a combination of the two.

"Yoshikawa first knocked everybody out with sleeping pills before he started his crime spree. He tied Kazue up, did the same to Seiji and locked him up somewhere else. He then took Kazue to the bedroom and satisfied himself with her. Kazue was the first to be killed, and her estimated time of death was one or two days earlier than that of the other three victims. While there is no definite proof, it appears that he raped Kazue after her death. The Kitamuras were murdered next. They were probably still asleep because of the drug. And Seiji was last. Yoshikawa doused Seiji with kerosene in his sleep and then went to the kitchen to start the fire."

"But, Mr Shimada," Kawaminami asked, pausing with his cold coffee in mid-air, "why did the murderer keep Seiji alive until then? The same for the Kitamura couple. If he was going to kill them anyway, wouldn't it have been safer to do it right away?"

"He might not have planned to kill them right from the start. He might have panicked after he killed Kazue. The fact he saved Seiji for last does support the idea that the motive was robbery."

"Why?"

"*Because of Nakamura Seiji's characteristics as an architect.*"

"How so?"

"Yes. I told you just now that Seiji was a bit peculiar. There is a certain monomania, a childish touch, a playfulness to all the buildings Nakamura Seiji designed, including the Blue Mansion and its annex, the Decagon House. They are all a showcase for his peculiar tastes. One of them being what you might call a *love of gimmicks.*"

"Gimmicks?"

"Yes. I can only take a guess at the number, but the burnt-down Blue Mansion was full of gimmicks like hidden rooms, cabinets and vaults. Only Nakamura Seiji knew the location of all of them."

"So if someone were looking for his money, he'd need to get that information out of Seiji."

"Yes. Therefore the gardener wouldn't have killed Seiji right away."

Shimada paused for a moment and placed one elbow on the table.

"And that's all that's known about the case and the investigation. The police are still looking for the missing gardener, Yoshikawa. It doesn't seem likely they will find him, though. Got any questions, my dear Conan?"

"Let me think."

Kawaminami drank the last few drops of his coffee in one gulp and became lost in thought.

Based on what Shimada had told him, the line of investigation the police were following did seem the best. But it was all just circumstantial conjecture. In other words, it was nothing more than an attempt to make sense out of the confused situation.

The biggest hurdle in the case was the fact that the Blue Mansion had burnt down completely. Because of that, the crime scene had even fewer hints to offer than usual. And there was nobody left alive to tell them what had happened during the incident, or the time leading up to it.

"You're looking very serious, Conan," said Shimada, licking his lips. "Now it's my turn to ask you a question. It's not directly connected to the case on Tsunojima, though."

"Yes?"

"I want to ask you about that girl, Chiori. I knew Kō had a niece and that she was staying at Kazue's parents' place because of school. I've also heard she died in an unfortunate accident last year, but I don't know any of the details. What kind of girl was Nakamura Chiori?"

Immediately, a look of sadness crossed Kawaminami's face.

"She was a quiet girl. She wasn't one to stand out and always had a sad aura about her. I hardly talked to her. But she was always very pleasant. She would happily help out with odd jobs during parties and suchlike."

"And how did she die?"

"It happened in January last year, at the Mystery Club's New Year's party. She died of acute alcohol poisoning."

As he recounted the events, Kawaminami's eyes unconsciously wandered to the window.

"Usually when we had parties, she would leave after the first session, but that night we had an after-party, and we nagged her to come along. We really were an awful lot. She always had a low tolerance for alcohol. But everyone got caught up in it and they made her drink too much..."

"*They* made her drink?"

"Yes. I went to the after-party myself, but I had some other business and I left early with a friend of mine, Morisu. The accident happened after that. No..."

Kawaminami silently put his hand on the letter in his jacket pocket.

"No, it wasn't an accident. We might really be the ones who killed her."

Thinking about Chiori's death, Kawaminami really did feel some responsibility. If he hadn't left early, he might have prevented the others from making Chiori drink too much.

71

"Are you free this evening?"

As if he had perceived the dark feelings in Kawaminami's heart, Shimada suddenly put the question in a cheerful tone.

"What about it? Let's have a bite and a drink somewhere."

"But—"

"My treat. But in return, I want to talk to you about mystery fiction. I don't have any friends to talk about that, sadly enough. Do me this favour."

"All right, gladly."

"OK. Let's go to O— City then."

"But Mr Shimada…"

"Yes?"

"I haven't asked you yet, but how did you and Kōjirō come to know each other?"

"Ah, that's right. Kō was my senior at university."

"University? You also studied Buddhism?"

"Well, in a way."

With an embarrassed look, Shimada scratched his nose.

"Actually, my family runs a Buddhist temple just outside O— City."

"Oh, so you're a Buddhist priest?"

"No, I'm the youngest of three brothers and even at this age I'm still just loafing around, so I can hardly go calling other people weird. My father is over sixty, but still full of energy, so the only time I can recite a sutra for the dead is when someone dies in a detective novel I'm reading," said Shimada, and he solemnly put his hands together.

5

My daughter Chiori was murdered by all of you.

Morisu Kyōichi took up the letter from the low glass table once more and let out another sigh. He was leaning against the side of his bed and his two tired legs were stretched out on the thick grey carpet.

"My daughter Chiori was *murdered* by all of you."

He read the neatly aligned letters written with a word processor. His thoughts were indescribable.

The after-party of the New Year's celebrations of the Mystery Club, January last year. Morisu and his classmate Kawaminami Taka'aki had left the party early. The death had happened after their departure.

The name of the sender on the back of the envelope said "Nakamura Seiji". The man who was murdered six months ago on Tsunojima. Someone Morisu had never even seen or spoken to.

Morisu's room was on the fifth floor of Tatsumi Heights, a single-room-apartment building just across the main street in front of O— City Station, near the harbour.

He put the letter back in the envelope and reached out for the Seven Stars on the table, as he shook his head lightly. Lately, he had not been enjoying his cigarettes as much as he used to. But the craving for nicotine had not stopped.

What could the gang on Tsunojima be doing at that very moment?

As the thought crossed his mind, Morisu looked across his neat room. Near the wall stood an easel with an oil painting in progress. Several stone Buddha statues staring into time, surrounded by trees with fading colours. He had discovered this view on the Kunisaki Peninsula, somewhere on a mountain that nobody visited. He had only just begun to add a little colour to the charcoal sketch.

The smoke irritated his throat. He almost choked and threw the cigarette he had only inhaled once or twice into the ashtray filled with water.

He had a bad feeling. As if something unexpected were about to happen.

At that moment, his phone rang.

He looked at the clock. It was almost midnight.

There's only one person who would call me at this hour...

After waiting several seconds, Morisu picked up the receiver.

"Hey, are you there, Morisu?"

It was the familiar voice of Kawaminami Taka'aki, as he had expected. Morisu felt relieved.

"Hey, Doyle."

"I told you to stop calling me that. I tried to call you this afternoon."

"I went for a ride on my motorbike to Kunisaki."

"Kunisaki?"

"Yes, I told you I was doing a painting there, didn't I?"

"Oh. By the way, Morisu, did you receive a strange letter today?"

"Sent by Nakamura Seiji? Yes. I rang your place about twenty minutes ago to ask you the same question."

"So you got one, too."

"Yep. Where are you now? Can you come over?"

"That's why I called. I'm in the neighbourhood. We need to talk about this letter. I need to pick your brains."

"I don't have enough brains to pick."

"Two heads are better than one, and three are even better. I mean, is it OK if I bring someone along?"

"Sure. I'll be waiting."

"I thought the letter was just a joke in very bad taste, though I didn't really get the meaning of it," Morisu said as he compared the two letters placed next to each other on the table. "But it did say 'all of you', so I had a suspicion I wasn't the only person to get one."

"Yours appears to be a copy. I think the one that came to my place is the original."

Kawaminami took up his own letter.

"A similar letter was delivered to Higashi's house. I've already checked that on the phone. And while the message was worded slightly differently, another letter signed by Nakamura Seiji was delivered to Nakamura Kōjirō."

"Nakamura Kōjirō?"

Morisu frowned.

"You mean Nakamura Seiji's younger brother?"

"Yes. His letter said 'Chiori was murdered.' I went to Beppu today to visit him. That was where I met Mr Shimada."

Morisu made another small bow to the man he had just become acquainted with. Kawaminami and Shimada had been drinking before they came and the latter's thin, swarthy face had turned quite red. Kawaminami also seemed to have drunk a lot, as his breathing was uneven and his eyes were crimson.

"Explain everything to me from the beginning," said Morisu. Kawaminami leant forward and quickly recounted what had happened that day. His breath reeked of alcohol.

"As always, you're like curiosity on wheels," said Morisu when

Kawaminami had finished, staring in amazement at him. "So you haven't slept at all since yesterday?"

"Now you mention it, no. Anyway, it's mysterious, right? Who wrote all these letters and for what purpose? Any ideas?"

Morisu put a hand to his forehead and closed his eyes.

"An accusation, a threat and a call to reconsider the Tsunojima case. Yes, I think you're on to something. Especially the part about the Tsunojima case. It feels a bit forced, but it certainly is interesting. I also think there's something more to be discovered there. Ex-excuse me, Mr Shimada."

Shimada had been dozing off, his body leaning against the wall. Woken by Morisu, he stood up and rubbed his face like a cat.

"Mr Shimada, there's one thing I want to ask you."

"Ah, yes. Pray ask."

"Where was Nakamura Kōjirō when the incident happened on Tsunojima?"

"You're asking for his alibi?" A grin appeared on Shimada's sleepy face. "Straight to the point, I see. Who would benefit most by the death of Seiji and his wife Kazue? Kō, of course."

"Yes. I'm sorry to have to say this, but I think that this Kōjirō is the first person we should suspect."

"But my dear Morisu, the police aren't stupid. It goes without saying that Kō's whereabouts were checked. But sadly for them, he was able to provide a perfect alibi."

"Namely?"

"From the night of 19th September until the following morning, Kō was in the company of yours truly. He had called and invited me for drinks, which was quite unusual for him. We drank through the night in Beppu and I stayed at his home. I was also there in the morning when he received the news about what had happened."

"A perfect alibi, as you say."

Shimada nodded.

"I would like to hear more of your ideas, Morisu."

"OK. This isn't something that occurred to me just now. It's something I've thought ever since I first read about the case in the newspapers."

"Yes?"

"I can't explain why, it's just something I felt instinctively."

Having warned the two in advance, Morisu continued:

"I think that the most important issue in this case is the left hand of Kazue, which went missing from the crime scene. I have the feeling we'll have solved everything when we find that hand."

"The hand, indeed."

Both Morisu and Shimada looked at their hands and kept silent.

"By the way, Morisu, did you know that many of the Mystery Club members have gone to Tsunojima?" asked Kawaminami.

"Yes." Morisu smiled drily. "I was also invited, but I said no. I'm not interested in such a gruesome place."

"When will they be back?"

"They said one week from today."

"A whole week. In tents?"

"They pulled a few strings. They're staying in the Decagon House."

"Kōjirō did say he had got rid of the island. But something doesn't feel right about all this: them heading for an island of the dead, just as a letter from the dead arrives."

"It would be a very bizarre coincidence."

"Do you believe it's a coincidence?"

"Probably not." Morisu closed his eyes once more. "But if we want to investigate this, we'll first need to check whether, besides

Higashi, the other people who were at the after-party have also received a letter."

"You're right."

"Are you going to do that?"

"Will do. It's the spring holiday, so I have nothing to do anyway. Can't do worse than playing detective."

"That's just like you. What if you take a look into the Tsunojima case, too, while you're at it?"

"A look into what, precisely?"

"For example, what about paying a visit to the family of Yoshikawa, the gardener who disappeared?"

"But—"

"Conan," Shimada chimed in, "that's actually a good idea. I told you Yoshikawa Sei'ichi lived in Ajimu, right? I believe his wife still lives there, and she used to work for the Nakamura family on Tsunojima. So she's the only living person who knows about the private lives of the Nakamuras. It's worth a try."

"Do you know her address?"

"It won't take me long to find it."

Shimada laughed joyfully as he patted his shallow cheeks.

"What about this, Conan? Tomorrow morning you check who else got the letters, and then we'll go to Ajimu in my car in the afternoon."

"All right. And you, Morisu, are you coming along too?"

"I'd like to, but I've got work to do. I told you I was doing this painting, didn't I?"

Morisu indicated the canvas on the easel.

"The Buddha statues of Kunisaki? You did tell me you liked them. Are you going to compete in an art contest?"

"No, nothing like that. I just wanted to paint that sight before the flowers bloom. I've been going up there the last few days now."

"Wow."

"And I've never been the active type like you. I don't even like talking to people I don't know. But will you come back tomorrow night? It doesn't matter how late you come. I'm interested in how the case turns out as well."

Morisu leant wearily against his bed and lit a cigarette he knew he wouldn't enjoy.

"For now, you'll have to allow me to take on the role of armchair detective."

THREE

The Second Day on the Island

1

She had barely slept by the time she woke up.

They had retreated to their rooms at two in the morning. She had gone to bed immediately, but she hadn't been able to get to sleep right away and instead had lain staring into the dark void. She just hadn't felt at ease. The events of the day had brought up bad memories which had coiled themselves around her mind and wouldn't let go.

Ellery, Van, Poe, Agatha, Leroux and Carr. It wasn't as if she didn't like these six. In fact, for the most part, she felt something akin to affection for all of them, even Carr. The only member of the party she felt no affection for was herself.

Usually, when she experienced something depressing she could find salvation simply by going back to her boarding house, to her own room. She needed only to flee to her own little world. She could imagine everything she wanted there and steep herself in it. There she would have her best friends, her ideal lover and even people who worshipped her no matter what.

But…

But this was the first time in her life that she had set foot on this island, in this building, in this room. Even though she was finally all alone now, her mind still felt uneasy.

She had regrets. She had known this would happen. Perhaps she shouldn't have come here.

But, for her, this trip had held a special meaning.

The Decagon House on Tsunojima—had the others noticed it?

She knew. She knew that this was the home of the girl who had died because of their irresponsibility.

Nakamura Chiori was the only friend she had ever had, and the only person to whom she felt she could have opened her heart. They were in the same faculty, had entered the same year and were the same age… She'd felt that they were alike the moment they'd first met in the classroom. She was convinced Chiori had felt the same way. And they got along very well. They had also visited each other's room several times.

"My father is strange and lives far away on an island called Tsunojima," Chiori had told her once. She had also told her it was something she didn't wish to be known.

Chiori had died. And now they had come here to this island, where she was born and where her parents died.

It's not an intrusion—I am paying my respects.

This she kept telling herself.

She had no intention of telling the others. It would be OK if it were just her, she thought. If she could just mourn Chiori's death alone; if she could just provide some comfort to Chiori's spirit.

But should she really be the one to do that? Wasn't that conceitedness? Wasn't it disrespectful to the dead to be coming to the island like this?

All the worrying eventually brought her a fitful sleep. She felt like she were having one dream after another, where reality and fantasy collided. The settings in her dreams were all images from the island she had seen today.

That's why she had barely slept by the time she woke up.

With only the weak light showing through the gap between the shutters as her aid, she looked around the room, but she couldn't judge whether she were still dreaming or had really woken up.

A blue carpet on the floor. The bed was fixed to the left of the window. On the wall to the right of the window stood a desk, a chest of drawers and a full-length mirror.

Orczy slowly raised herself up, got out of bed and opened the window.

The outside air felt chilly to the skin.

The sky was white with a few clouds. She could hear the peaceful sound of waves.

She looked at her wristwatch, which she had placed near her pillow. Eight o'clock.

She finally realized it was really morning.

She closed the window and got dressed.

A black skirt, a white blouse and, on top of that, a Bordeaux-red sweater with an Argyle pattern. As always, she only glanced briefly at the mirror. She did not like facing her own image.

Orczy got her toilet bag and went out of her room.

It didn't seem as though any of the others were awake yet. Silence reigned over the decagonal hall, as if last night's excitement had all just been a dream.

But then…

Orczy noticed that something she had not seen before had been placed on the table in the middle of the hall.

It reflected the light coming in from the skylight directly above, and blinded her for a moment.

Perplexed, Orczy walked slowly towards the table. As soon as she realized what had been placed there, she gasped and remained frozen to the spot.

...What is this?

She reached out to the table, but quickly pulled her arm back.

After a few moments of shock, she forgot about washing her face and ran to Agatha's room.

2

The First
Victim

The Second
Victim

The Third
Victim

The Fourth
Victim

The Last
Victim

The Detective

The Murderer

Seven milky-white plastic plates, fifteen centimetres wide, five centimetres high. Red characters had been printed on each of them.

"What kind of joke is this?"

Ellery blinked in surprise, but then a smile formed on his lips.

Only the women were already dressed. The five men had merely put something light on over their pyjamas. They had all just been woken up by Agatha.

"Very funny. Who's behind this?"

Ellery addressed the question to everyone.

"Wasn't it you, Ellery?"

"Not me, Leroux. Probably Carr or Agatha, right?"

"It wasn't me."

"Nor me." Agatha tensed, then continued: "What about you, Van?"

"I know nothing about this," said Van, rubbing his puffy eyelids.

"Was it you who found the plates, Agatha?"

"No, Orczy. But I can't believe she's the one behind it."

"It wasn't me."

Orczy looked away as if she wanted to flee. Everyone's eyes went to the one person remaining. But a frown appeared on Poe's bearded face.

"I'm telling you, I don't know anything about this either," he said.

"Well then, who is it?"

Ellery shrugged, and went on.

"A joke's fine and all that, but this has lasted long enough."

Nobody said anything.

The seven looked at each other in an uncomfortable silence.

"Ellery," said Poe, "if you ask me, the one of us most likely to spring this kind of prank is either you or Agatha."

"I told you, it wasn't me," protested Ellery.

"And I'll have you know it wasn't me either," said Agatha.

The hall turned silent once again in the morning light.

The silence became oppressive. Each was watching for a sign from one of the others, waiting for someone to break into laughter and admit to the deed.

A painfully long time passed, during which they could hear the distant sound of the waves.

"I swear I didn't do anything." Ellery finally spoke with a serious look on his face. "Is there really nobody who will admit to this? I'll ask once again. Van?"

"I don't know anything about it."

"Agatha?"

"I already said it wasn't me."

"Carr?"

"Nothing to do with it."

"Poe?"

"Nope."

"And Leroux?"

"You must be joking."

"Orczy?"

Orczy shook her head with a scared look.

Again the sound of waves reached the ears of the group. It resonated with and fomented the wave of anxiety that had taken hold of the motionless seven.

"All right then," said Ellery as he brushed the forelock from his brow. "The criminal—I can use the word, can't I?—has to be one of us here. Considering that nobody has admitted to the deed, we'll have to assume that someone is among us with devious intent—or perhaps multiple persons."

"What do you mean by devious intent?" asked Agatha.

"How should I know? Someone's plotting something," replied Ellery bluntly.

"Don't beat about the bush, Ellery." Carr spoke with a sneer. "Just come out with it. This is a murder warning."

"Don't jump the gun, Carr!"

To everyone's surprise, Ellery raised his voice, and glared at Carr.

"I'll ask once again. Is there really nobody who'll admit to having done this?"

They all shook their heads as they watched each other.

"Very well, then," said Ellery and he gathered the seven plates from the table and sat down on one of the chairs. "Let's all take a seat." He conjured up his usual smile as he watched everybody slowly sitting down. "Sorry, Agatha, could you make us some coffee?"

"Of course," said Agatha and went to the kitchen alone.

Ellery looked alternately at the faces of the other five around the table and the plates in his hands. Nobody seemed to have even an inkling of what to say.

After a short time, Agatha appeared with a tray with coffee for everyone.

Ellery selected one of the steamy decagon-shaped cups and took a sip.

"Well now…"

He put both hands into the pockets of the dark-green cardigan he was wearing over his pyjamas and turned to the group.

"The seven of us are the only people on the island. Therefore, the person who placed these plates here has to be one of us. Has to be. But we all claim to know nothing about them. That means one of us is intentionally hiding the fact that he or she has placed them here.

"As you can all see, these plates are made of plastic. The characters are printed in a Gothic typeface. The words appear to have been sprayed on with red paint, but none of that helps us to identify the culprit."

"But Ellery," said Leroux, "is such ornate lettering really so simple that anyone can do it? You have to have some experience, surely?"

"So that would mean that Orczy is the prime suspect."

"That's not what I meant."

"The only one among us with any experience in illustrating and lettering is Orczy. Anything to say, Orczy?"

"…It wasn't me."

"Sorry, but that's really not good enough."

Orczy put her hands to her red face and looked up.

"You can buy books anywhere nowadays with stencils for lettering. Anyone could have used one of those and some spray paint."

"Exactly," agreed Ellery. "Anyone with just a little feeling for the arts could have done this: me, or Poe, or even Van."

Ellery, still smiling, drank the rest of his steaming coffee.

"What about the plates themselves?" asked Leroux, reaching out and taking one of them. "The edges aren't really smooth."

"They didn't come off-the-shelf. They were probably cut to size with a jigsaw or similar kind of tool."

"Could they have been used for underlay or something?"

"The culprit probably paid a visit to the DIY corner in the local supermarket, Leroux. They have plastic boards of all sizes and colours."

Ellery took the plate back from Leroux and arranged it with the others, like a hand of playing cards.

"Let's put these away for now," he said, as he stood up and went over to the kitchen. The eyes of the six others followed as if tied to him by string.

Through the open double doors they could see Ellery standing in front of the cupboard. He found an open drawer and dumped all of the plates inside. He came back into the hall and yawned in the refined manner of a Siamese cat.

"My goodness, we all look really stupid."

He spread his arms and looked down at his body.

"We're all up, so let's get dressed."

So saying, Ellery disappeared into his room and, with that, the tension hanging in the air also dissipated.

With a few sighs, the other six stood up one by one. The four men went separately back to their rooms, while Agatha and Orczy withdrew together to Agatha's room.

They walked with anxious steps and there was not one of them who did not steal a look at the kitchen drawer containing the seven plates before leaving the hall.

Thursday, 27th March. Their second day on the island had begun.

3

It was past noon.

Nobody at the lunch table mentioned the events of that morning.

It had been too sinister to joke or talk lightly about. But it was also too bizarre to discuss seriously. Each of them still had the contents of the kitchen drawer in mind and none of them stopped trying to read the others' thoughts, but they all acted as if the whole event hadn't happened.

After eating the sandwiches Agatha and Orczy had made for lunch, they left the table one by one.

Carr was the first to get up. He went outside on his own, holding a couple of paperbacks and rubbing his long, freshly shaven chin. Poe and Van stood up in turn and went to Poe's room.

† † †

"And back to business," said Poe in his deep voice as he sat down on the floor.

The seven guest rooms in the Decagon House all had the same layout. In the centre of the blue carpet in Poe's room lay the scattered pieces of a jigsaw puzzle he had just started.

"Two thousand pieces? Can you finish it during our stay?"

Avoiding stepping on the puzzle, Van walked to the back of the room and sat down on the edge of the bed.

A smile appeared from behind Poe's long beard.

"Just wait and see. I'll finish it."

"But you also want to go fishing, don't you? And there's the story for the club magazine."

"There's more than enough time. But first, I need to find this guy's nose."

The outline of the puzzle had already been completed and took up almost one *tatami* mat, or one by two metres. Beside it lay the lid of the puzzle box with the illustration of the completed puzzle. Poe rummaged among the little pieces while staring at the illustration.

It was a photograph of six foxes playing in a field. A large vixen surrounded by five cute cubs. The nose of one of the five was the problem Poe was currently grappling with.

"Hmm? What's the matter, Van?" Poe asked anxiously, when he noticed that Van's head was hanging wearily and his hands were on his knees.

"Still feeling sick?"

"Yes, a little."

"I've got a thermometer in my bag. Take your temperature. You can lie down if you want."

"Thanks."

Van put the thermometer under his arm and allowed his slim

body to sink into the bed. He ran his hands through his brownish, soft hair as he looked at Poe.

"So. What do you think?"

"Hmm—ah, here it is. Got it," said Poe, and he grabbed a little piece of the puzzle. "Good, good. What did you say, Van?"

"What happened this morning. What do you think?"

Poe's hand stopped in mid-air. He sat up straight.

"You mean about that…"

"Was it really just a prank?"

"I think it was."

"So why didn't anybody admit to it then?"

"There may be more to follow."

"More?"

"Yes. The practical joke isn't over yet."

Poe's fingers disappeared into his beard as he stroked his jaw.

"It's just an idea I had. For example, tonight one of us might find their coffee spiked with salt. And that would be 'the First Victim.'"

"Aha."

"And with a sly smile on his face, our 'Murderer' will commit one crime after another. So, just a big murder game."

"Oh, a murder game."

"It might be a stupid idea, but it makes a lot more sense than us all cowering in fear because we think a series of actual murders have been announced ahead of time."

"True," agreed Van. "It's not as if we're characters in a story. Murders don't just happen like that. Yes, I'm sure you're right. But Poe, who do you think is behind this game then?"

"Well, the one most likely to come up with such a game is Ellery, of course. But he seems to be taking on the role of 'the Detective.'"

"Now you mention it, do you remember Ellery yelling 'Anybody want to challenge me?' yesterday? This might be an answer to that."

"I don't know about that," said Poe. "If you're right, that would mean that 'the Murderer' is one of the three people who were there when he said that: you, me or Leroux. But those plates this morning had to have been made in advance, didn't they?"

"I see what you mean. And the only people besides Ellery who might plan a prank like this are Leroux or Agatha…"

"But it still could be Ellery. Think of all those plots where the detective turns out to be the murderer."

"The way Ellery took control of the situation this morning was rather *too* impressive…"

"Hmm—and the thermometer, Van?"

"Ah, I'd forgotten about that."

Van sat up straight and took the thermometer out from under his cardigan. He looked at it, frowned and handed it to Poe.

"You really do have a fever."

Poe looked at Van's face.

"Your lips look dry as well. How's your head?"

"Hurts a little."

"You need rest today. Got any medicine?"

"I've got some over-the-counter drugs for a cold."

"They'll do. You'd better go to bed early today. You don't want it to get any worse while you're on a trip."

"I'll do as you say, Doctor," answered Van in a hoarse voice, as he fell back on the bed and stared vacantly at the ceiling.

Having cleaned up after lunch, Agatha and Orczy made themselves some tea and took a rest in the hall.

"Oof, will it be like this for six days? I can't believe cooking for seven is so much work."

91

Agatha leant back in her chair.

"Look, Orczy, my hands are all rough from the washing-up liquid."

"I've got some hand cream."

"Me too. I can't get enough of that stuff."

"You really have a lady's hands."

Agatha grinned and loosened the scarf that held her hair. Orczy gave her a slight smile back, grasped the decagonal cup in her small hands and took a sip.

"Orczy."

Agatha looked in the direction of the kitchen and suddenly changed the topic.

"What do you think those plates mean?"

Orczy shuddered and shook her head silently.

"It was really scary this morning," Agatha continued, "but after I thought about it, it really might just be a joke. What do you think?"

"I don't know." Orczy looked around anxiously. "Everyone says they don't know anything about it, even though there's nothing to hide if it's just a joke…"

"That's precisely it."

"Wha-?…"

"Maybe we just took it too seriously. In other words, the one who did it felt guilty about having pulled a prank."

"I don't know."

"Well, who do you think the culprit is?"

"…"

"It might be Ellery," Agatha went on. "But he isn't the type to feel guilty about anything, so we can rule him out. Maybe it's little Leroux."

"Leroux?"

"You know how he is. Leroux's head is always full of detective fiction. He probably thought it'd be funny to frighten us all with such a jape."

Orczy looked away, neither agreeing nor disagreeing. She shrank down uncomfortably into her chair.

"I'm scared," she mumbled, so quietly she could have been talking to herself.

Those were her true thoughts. Those plates—she simply couldn't believe it was just an innocent joke. She could sense some kind of malice behind them.

"We shouldn't have come to this island after all."

"Don't say such things."

Agatha laughed cheerfully.

"Let's go out and breathe in some fresh air after our tea. This hall is gloomy, even in the afternoon. There's a peculiar atmosphere here, because of these ten walls around us. It makes you worry more than necessary about little things."

Sitting on the pier in the inlet, Ellery stared down into the depths.

"I still think it's weird, don't you, Ellery?" said Leroux, who was standing next to him.

"What?"

"You know what I mean. Those plates this morning."

"Oh."

"You really weren't the one behind it?"

"Stop joking."

They had been like this for some time. Leroux would say something and Ellery would just answer vaguely, without even bothering to look at him.

"But it would be just like you to prepare those plates, even for 'the Detective' and 'the Murderer'."

"I know nothing about them."

"Don't act so cross. I was just saying it would be like you."

Leroux shrugged his round shoulders and crouched down.

"But it was probably just a prank. Don't you think so?"

"No," answered Ellery bluntly, and shoved his hands in his coat pockets. "I'd really like to think so, but I don't."

"So why do you think it wasn't?"

"Because nobody admitted to it."

"That's true."

"And too much effort went into it."

Ellery turned around and looked Leroux in the eye.

"It'd be different if they had been written in pencil on pieces of paper. But someone has gone to the effort of cutting those plastic plates to the same size, preparing forms for the lettering and spraying the plates with red paint. I wouldn't have done all that just to give you a little scare."

"But…" Leroux removed his glasses and started to wipe them clumsily. "Are you saying that there really will be murders?"

"I think there's a strong possibility."

"Bu… how can you say that so calmly? A murder… that means someone will die. Someone will be killed. And not just one person. If those plates are announcing all our murders in advance, then there'll be five victims. It's just unbelievable."

"Sounds ridiculous, doesn't it?"

"It is ridiculous. This isn't a film or a novel. Those plates have the same role as the infamous Indian figurines, right? If 'the Murderer' kills 'the Detective' and commits suicide at the end, then it'll be precisely like *And Then There Were None*."

"Apparently."

"And why should we be murdered anyway, Ellery?"

"Why ask me?"

After that, the two stared in silence at the waves crashing on the rocks. The waves were rougher and louder than the day before. The water was also darker.

Eventually, Ellery stood up.

"Leroux, I'm going back. It's cold out here."

4

The noise of waves resonated in the darkness overhead, sounding like the rough snoring of a giant. It served to increase their anxiety and their feeling of impending doom.

The gloomy decagonal hall where they had just finished their dinner was dim in the weak light of the oil lamp.

"They make me feel sick," Agatha said after she had given everyone coffee. "These walls. My eyes hurt just from looking at them."

The ten white walls gleamed in the light of a single lamp. They were theoretically at a 144-degree angle to one another, but, depending on the light, the angles sometimes appeared wider and sometimes narrower. In contrast, the table in the centre of the room always retained its decagonal shape, which made the walls seem even more distorted.

"Really, they make me dizzy."

Van rubbed his bloodshot eyes.

"Go to bed early, Van. You still don't look too well," Poe admonished him.

"Still feeling sick?" Agatha put a hand to Van's forehead. "You have a fever. You need to go to bed, Van."

"I'm OK. It's only seven o'clock."

"It's not OK. We're on an uninhabited island here. We don't have a real doctor with us. What if your fever turns worse?"

"…All right."

"Did you take some medicine?"

"I'll take it just before I go to bed. It makes you sleepy."

"Take it now and go to sleep then. Better safe than sorry."

"OK."

Van stood up reluctantly, like a child obeying his mother. Agatha brought a water jug and a glass from the kitchen and gave them to him.

"Well, goodnight," said Van, and he walked to the door of his room.

But then…

"What're you planning to do, hiding in your dark little room so early?"

It was Carr's low, deep voice. Van's hand, which was reaching for the doorknob, stopped in mid-air. He turned round.

"I'm going to sleep, Carr."

"Well. And there I was thinking you were going to sharpen your knife."

"What do you mean?"

Carr chuckled at Van's angry question.

"You know, I think that it was you who announced our murders this morning."

"Van, ignore him and go to sleep," said Ellery.

"Wait, Ellery," Carr continued in an ingratiating voice. "Considering the circumstances, don't you think that it's only normal to suspect Van?"

"Why?"

"Think about it. In cases where several people gather in one place and they get killed one by one, the person behind it is usually the host or organizer."

"That's just in mystery stories."

96

"And those plates announcing our murders were nothing more than props for this particular mystery story. He's the one behind it. He's our culprit. What's wrong with assuming that it's just like what happens in the books?"

Carr thrust out his chin.

"Anything to say, our dear host Van?"

"Enough of your jokes." Holding the jug and the glass in his hands, Van stamped his foot on the floor. "I didn't invite you all here. I only told you that my uncle bought the place. The first person to mention it was our upcoming editor-in-chief, Leroux."

"He's right. Leroux told me about it and I was the one who had the idea of us all coming here," Ellery said angrily. "If you want to suspect Van, you'll need to suspect me and Leroux too. Or else your reasoning lacks logic."

"Well, I don't like 'great detectives' who spout deductions only after someone has been killed," said Carr.

Ellery tutted disdainfully, and went on:

"And your theme of the host being the murderer is just too cliché. It certainly won't help you find a 'great criminal'. If I were the culprit, I'd just have made use of the invitation sent to all of us."

"What nonsense!" exclaimed Poe, stubbing his half-smoked cigarette out violently. "Great detectives, great criminals—can't you keep fiction separate from reality? Van, you don't have to listen to this kooky lot. Go to sleep."

"Kooky?" Carr's look hardened and he stamped his foot. "Who's kooky?!"

"Just try and use some common sense." With a sour look on his face, Poe lit a new cigarette. "First of all, this discussion is absolutely useless. This isn't the first time the seven of us have got together somewhere. Of course it's possible that Van's the culprit, and that he lured us all here using the delicious bait of the Decagon House. It could also have been Ellery or Leroux, who came up with the idea for the trip. Or you, Carr, might have been biding your time, waiting for the perfect chance to execute your plans. If we're just arguing possibilities, we could go on for ages."

"Poe's right," said Agatha. "This argument isn't going anywhere."

"Also," said Poe as he calmly puffed smoke out of his mouth, "you all assume that those plates were indicating a murder, but don't you think that's just nonsense? All of us love the game called mystery fiction and we're gathered on an island with a bloody backstory. Why can't you just consider those plates a part of the whole picture?"

Poe then expounded on the theory he'd proposed to Van in his room that afternoon.

"That's it, Poe!" Leroux clapped his hands excitedly.

"Salt in our coffee?" Ellery put both his hands on his head and leant backwards on his chair. "If this really ends with a pinch of salt, I'll take my hat off to our criminal for his sense of humour."

"Glad you all can still be so optimistic." Carr stood up with a sullen look and stormed back to his own room.

Van said "Goodnight" in a hoarse voice and then he, too, disappeared into his room.

"I'm curious as to the identity of our murderer." Agatha smiled at Orczy.

"Ye-yes," replied Orczy with downcast eyes.

Ellery took the blue bicycle cards out of his pocket and fanned them out on the table.

"All right, who will 'the First Victim' be? This game has become interesting."

It might have been simply a flight from fear. Every one of them had felt relieved by Poe's theory. The choking anxiety that had hung in the air since the morning had suddenly been dispersed.

However, there was one person on the island who knew that the words on the plates meant exactly what they said.

FOUR

The Second Day on the Mainland

1

The car went west on National Route 10.

Kawaminami would occasionally steal a glance at Shimada Kiyoshi, sitting in the driver's seat. With every glance, Kawaminami had to suppress the urge to burst out laughing. This eccentric third son of a Buddhist priest was driving a very ordinary red Familia. In contrast to the jeans and sweater outfit of yesterday, Shimada was wearing a dark-grey suit and sporting a pair of fancy saxe-blue sunglasses. Somehow Shimada's personality enabled him to pull off the mismatched combination.

The first name of the missing gardener's wife was Masako, and she was still living in Ajimu, according to Shimada. He had managed to find out her address that morning and had made an appointment with her for the same afternoon.

The car had left Beppu in the direction of the mountains and passed through the Myōban Hot Spring area.

Tent-like structures made of straw could be seen on both sides of the narrow road. Smoke rose through gaps in the straw. The inhabitants were looking for mineral salt left by dried-up hot springs. The salt, known as "hot water flowers", was used as a bathwater additive.

They finally reached the slope that would lead them down into the Usa district.

"And how did your work go, Conan?" asked Shimada.

"Ah, sorry, I haven't told you yet."

Kawaminami, who had been leaning on the passenger-side window watching the scenery go by, scratched his head and straightened up in his seat.

"There were some I couldn't get hold of, but I think we can safely assume that everyone who was at the after-party has received the letter."

"OK. And how many of them have gone to the island?"

"Some of them live on their own, so I'm not sure, but probably all of them except for Morisu and me, who left the party early."

"That suggests that something really is going on."

"I agree. But I think Morisu would challenge that assumption and say that we might be looking at it from the wrong end."

"The wrong end?"

"Yes. Because it's hardly a coincidence that the members who were present at the after-party are also the ones on the island. They're members who often meet together anyway, and that's why they went to the after-party and to the island together. So the fact they all got the letters and went on a trip to Tsunojima might mean nothing at all."

"That's a peculiar way to think about it."

"Morisu is always careful. And he's also very single-minded and that causes him to act even more cautiously, or something like that."

"But he gladly took on the role of detective last night."

"That's true. Which shows that even he was startled by the letters. But he's actually a very clever guy."

Kawaminami Taka'aki and Morisu Kyōichi had made a great team during the former's time in the club.

Kawaminami was always bursting with curiosity and energy. If something sparked his interest, he couldn't stay still. But he was also quite aware that his own abundant curiosity could often prevent him from considering situations deeply enough. He also knew that, while his enthusiasm could flare up in a flash, he could also lose interest just as fast.

Morisu, on the other hand, could feel passionate about things in a different way from Kawaminami, yet it was rare to see that side of him in his everyday life. He was the type who kept his thoughts to himself, thinking everything over until he was satisfied before taking any action. To Kawaminami, his friend Morisu was a wise advisor, who would stop him from making rash assumptions or jumping to wrong conclusions.

"For now, you'll have to allow me to take on the role of armchair detective," he'd said.

That was the perfect role for Morisu, Kawaminami thought. He wasn't one for false modesty, but he knew that the role of Watson fitted him better. Morisu would be the one playing Holmes.

Kawaminami took another look at Shimada Kiyoshi sitting next to him.

But this man wouldn't settle for the role of a Watson, or a Lestrade either.

The view from the window was stunning: slopes covered with long grass stretched to highlands in the far distance.

"The mountain on our left is Mount Tsurumi, right?" asked Kawaminami.

"Yes. It's been a popular spot for hang-gliders lately."

"How far is it to Ajimu?"

"We'll reach the Usa district at the bottom of this slope. Then we'll have to climb another one to reach Ajimu Plateau. It's half-past one now, so we should arrive there before three."

Kawaminami put both hands on his waist and stretched his back, yawning.

"Tired, Conan?"

"I'm a night person, so I had trouble getting up early today."

"You can sleep now. I'll wake you when we get there."

"Ah, sorry, if you don't mind."

Kawaminami reclined his seat and Shimada put his foot down on the accelerator.

2

The woman at the front door was not at all like the person Kawaminami had vaguely imagined. Yoshikawa Masako appeared to be a reserved but friendly woman, dressed in a *komon* kimono. Believing he was going to meet the wife of a man who had killed four people because of some sort of twisted love, Kawaminami had expected someone much more withdrawn.

She was in her early forties at the most, but worry had aged her features and left her looking worn out.

"My name is Shimada—I called you this morning. I apologize for contacting you out of the blue," said Shimada.

The gardener's wife bowed her head.

"You said you were a friend of Kōjirō. You must have come a long way."

"You seem to know Kō, I mean, Nakamura Kōjirō."

"Yes. I'm in much debt to him. As you probably know, I was working in the mansion on Tsunojima before I married my husband. I had been there ever since Nakamura Seiji moved to the island. It was Kōjirō who recommended me for that position."

103

"Ah, now I understand. So that's where you first met your husband?"

"Yes. My husband was also working at the mansion at the time."

"Is this his family home?"

"Yes. We lived in O— City for a while after our marriage, but we moved here because of his parents' health."

"So he had to travel quite a distance to work?"

"When we moved here, he quit all his jobs except for the ones at the mansion on Tsunojima and Kōjirō's home in Beppu."

"Oh, so your husband was also responsible for Kōjirō's garden?"

"Yes."

"The reason we came here today is this letter—it was sent to my friend Kawaminami here," said Shimada, showing her the letter Kawaminami had given him earlier.

"What is this?"

"It's a letter from someone using the name of the deceased Nakamura Seiji. A similar letter was sent to Kōjirō."

"How awful."

"We thought the letter might have something to do with what happened on Tsunojima. And we hoped you might tell us something that could help us."

Masako seemed perplexed, but eventually looked up at the two men.

"Come inside. And would you be so kind as to burn some incense for my husband…"

Shimada and Kawaminami were led to a badly lit *tatami* room. Through the open sliding paper door they could see a small family altar behind Masako, who had sat down opposite them in a traditional *seiza* position.

The new memorial tablet appeared to float in the dark.

"As you know, my husband went missing and was never found. Last month, with the new year, I finally gave up on him and we held a ceremony in private."

She fought back tears as she spoke.

"But isn't there a possibility your husband is still alive?"

"If he were still alive, he would have contacted me."

"But—"

"I will tell you this: my husband was absolutely incapable of doing something that atrocious. I know the rumours, but I don't believe any of it. Everybody who knew him says the same."

Masako's tone was defiant. Shimada nodded quietly:

"I heard that your husband left for the island three days before the mansion burned down. When exactly was that?"

"He left here in the early morning of 17th of September."

"And he didn't happen to make any calls to you between then and the morning of the 20th, when the fire broke out?"

"He did once, in the afternoon of the day he left."

"By phone?"

"Yes. He told me he'd arrived safely."

"Did he act any differently from usual?"

"He was the same as ever. But he did say that the mistress had been ill."

"Kazue?"

"My husband didn't see her around, so when he asked Seiji, he said the lady had been taken ill and was in bed."

"Aha."

Shimada pouted his lips slightly and scratched the bridge of his nose.

"I ask you this, knowing it to be very rude, but is there anything to the rumours of your husband having feelings for Kazue?…"

Masako went pale. "Both my husband and I were very devoted to the mistress," she replied, "but as I said before, my husband would never do the evil things some people suggest. The accusation that my husband was in love with the mistress is just nonsense. And what's more…"

"Yes?"

"The rumours my husband wanted to steal Seiji's fortune are also nothing but baseless accusations. There wasn't anything left."

"Nothing left? There was nothing to steal there any more?"

"I shouldn't have spoken."

"No, please. I understand that you are upset."

Shimada's deep-sunk eyes gleamed.

"So there was nothing left of Seiji's fortune?" he muttered. Then, as if he'd just remembered something, he added:

"I heard that Seiji and Kōjirō didn't get along as brothers. What are your views on that?"

"Hmm," Masako murmured vaguely. "Seiji could be a bit peculiar."

"Did Kōjirō ever visit the island?"

"He occasionally visited when I was still working there, but I heard he hardly went there after I left the job."

"During the time you were working there… I see."

"Excuse me."

Kawaminami, who had been listening in silence up to that point, interrupted.

"Do you know what happened to Nakamura Chiori? I knew her from university. That's why I got the letter Mr Shimada showed you."

"Miss Chiori?"

Masako looked down at the dark *tatami* mats.

"I still remember her from when she was a little girl. My husband occasionally told me about her after I'd left the island—the poor girl. She was still so young when it happened."

"Up to what age did Chiori live on the island?" queried Shimada.

"I think she moved to her grandfather's place when she started kindergarten. My husband said that she only returned sporadically to the island and it was her mother who usually went out to O— City to meet her. The mistress really loved her daughter."

"And Seiji?"

Shimada leant slightly forward.

"How did Seiji treat his daughter?"

"He..."

Masako had trouble voicing her thoughts.

"I think he was probably not very fond of children."

3

All in all, they talked for almost two hours.

They left the Yoshikawa residence in Ajimu after five. On the way back they stopped for dinner, so by the time they got back to Beppu it was already past nine.

Shimada was naturally tired because of the long journey. From time to time he would click his tongue at the lights of the oncoming traffic.

"Is it all right if we make a detour via Kō's place?" he asked suddenly.

"I don't mind," answered Kawaminami, although he didn't really feel like it. He'd felt dispirited ever since they'd left Ajimu.

This was mostly because of lack of sleep and physical fatigue. But he was also feeling disappointed and he felt mentally exhausted, too.

Even though they'd gone all that way, they hadn't managed to discover anything significant, he thought. He hadn't expected to find a clear-cut answer, but he'd hoped for at least some new information.

For example…

And he hated himself for hoping so.

I would have been satisfied if Yoshikawa Masako had also received a letter signed by Nakamura Seiji.

He knew he was quick to get fired up, and quick to lose interest. In a way, he was still just a child. Like a child who always wanted new toys, he too was always on the search for some new stimulus. And when the initial excitement wore off, he would get bored and give up.

They finally arrived at Kōjirō's home in Kannawa.

It was a quiet night. The sky was filled with thin clouds. The moon shone as pale as bone in the darkness.

Shimada rang the bell. They could faintly hear it ringing inside, but even after a long wait, there was no reply.

"That's strange. The lights are still on."

Shimada coughed and rang the bell again a couple of times and also knocked on the door once or twice.

"Maybe he's already gone to bed?"

Shimada started to go round to the back entrance, but, seeing Kawaminami leaning with his back to the gatepost and his head hanging down, he changed his mind.

"Oh, forget it. We'll come back another day. Sorry, Conan, for bringing you all this way for nothing. You look very tired. Come on, let's go."

† † †

They got back on the National Route heading for O— City.

Shimada opened the window a little. The evening wind blew into the car, carrying with it the smell of the sea.

"Cold, Conan?"

"No, not really."

He was still feeling dispirited and upset with himself.

"Sorry, I've had you going up and down since this morning."

"No, I'm the one who should be sorry… Slumped here like this."

"That's OK. You're just tired."

Shimada didn't seem to mind at all. He took his left hand off the steering wheel and massaged his temple.

"I think that, on the one hand, it didn't turn out quite as we'd hoped, but on the other, we did manage to get hold of some significant information."

"What do you mean?"

"Of course we'd hoped to learn more about the whereabouts of Yoshikawa Sei'ichi. If he were still alive somehow, he might well have been in contact with his wife. But that didn't seem to be the case."

"But Mr Shimada, don't you think that there's something strange about the fact that they've already held a funeral ceremony, even though only six months have passed since his disappearance?"

"Maybe, but I don't think that Masako is the type who would lie. She appeared to be a nice, honest woman."

"Oh."

Shimada grinned.

"I've a good eye for people, you know. Call it a priest's instinct. Anyway, that didn't turn out as we wanted, but… Conan, could you pass me a cigarette?"

"A cigarette?" Kawaminami reacted in surprise. He hadn't seen Shimada smoke even once before now.

"I've got Seven Stars," he said and passed Shimada the pack. Keeping his eyes on the road ahead, Shimada skilfully pulled a cigarette out of the case using just one hand.

"I was a heavy smoker up until a few years back. But my lungs got bad and I practically stopped smoking then. One a day now. I may lead a loose and lazy life, but that's the one rule I try to stick to."

He lit the cigarette and blew some smoke into the air contentedly.

"As for the fruits of our labour: first of all, the fact that not much of Seiji's fortune was left. If that's true, then yes, the 'Yoshikawa equals murderer' theory is seriously weakened."

"And what about him being in love with Kazue?"

"I didn't believe in that theory from the start. It felt forced. I once talked with Kō and he said that Kazue wasn't the kind of woman who would go around seducing gardeners. He was also of the same opinion as Masako, that the gardener was an honest man who would never even think of falling in love with a married woman."

"So you don't think that Yoshikawa is the murderer."

"I don't think it's very likely."

With some regret, Shimada crushed the cigarette he had consumed in no time into the ashtray.

"And from what we heard today, I have the feeling that the reason the two brothers didn't get along was Kazue."

"Kazue?"

"If Kazue was having an affair, maybe she wasn't having one with the gardener, but with Kō."

"Kōjirō and Kazue?"

"Yes. I remember now: last year, after the incident happened, Kō stayed cooped up in his house for a week or two and was a total wreck. I suspect now that it wasn't because of the death of Seiji, but because of the death of Kazue."

"But Mr Shimada, that would mean that the murderer is—"

"I have a little idea. I'll tell you later, but first you'll have to report today's progress to Morisu, right?"

"Now you mention it, yes."

Kawaminami took a look at the dashboard clock. 10.40 p.m.

The coastal National Route in the direction of O— City was less busy now. Among the scattered red tail lights ahead was the black body of a truck. And on the railway running parallel to the road a brightly lit train ran by...

"He told us to call, but since we're driving anyway, let's just go round there."

Shimada's suggestions had perked Kawaminami up a little. As if sensing that, Shimada smiled.

"Morisu. Yes, he has a wonderful name too."

4

"Knowing you, I expected you'd have had enough of playing detective after one day," said Morisu mockingly, as he poured hot water from the pot into cups with teabags. "But you don't appear to have, to my surprise. Maybe it's because you were accompanied by Mr Shimada?"

"How did you guess?" Kawaminami laughed in embarrassment.

"So, please give me the report on your investigations, Mr Detective."

Kawaminami briefed Morisu on the facts they had discovered that day.

"So that's what you've been up to."

Morisu poured himself a second cup of tea and, without adding sugar, drank it in a single gulp.

"And? What are your plans for tomorrow, Watson?"

"I wonder."

Kawaminami stretched out on the floor then sat up wearily with his head resting on his knees.

"To be honest, I am feeling a bit down right now. The spring holiday is long, you know. And I've been spending every night playing mah-jong. And then that letter from the dead came. I just couldn't ignore it. And, as always, I got all fired up, but now…"

"Spare us your self-analysis. You're boring Mr Shimada."

But Shimada was just smiling as he stroked his pointed chin.

"I don't think there's anything wrong with being at a loose end from time to time. It's much more healthy than allowing your imagination to wither because of the hectic life you lead. I'm like Conan. If I hadn't had time on my hands, a man of my age would never have become involved in something like this. But then again, I'm an inquisitive guy at heart. By the way, Morisu…"

"Yes?"

"I should like to know what our 'armchair detective' is thinking."

"I thought you'd never ask."

Morisu wet his dry lips with his tongue and smiled.

"Actually, I've had a little idea ever since you told me everything last night. But this isn't a deduction, just a hunch, so don't take it too seriously."

"As Conan said, you're a careful man."

"For someone careful, this is a pretty wild idea, though. I even suspect that you, Mr Shimada, might have been thinking the same."

"Possibly."

"OK, this is it."

Morisu looked from Shimada to Kawaminami.

"I think it's quite surprising you didn't think of it. Basically, isn't the case on Tsunojima the same as what Francis Nevins Jr calls the 'Birlstone gambit'?"

Kawaminami yelled out. "You mean that one of the supposed murder victims is still alive?"

"I don't claim it's true. I only point out the possibility. And I believe it could only be Seiji."

Morisu continued his explanation slowly, while he poured his third cup of tea.

"The heads of the bodies identified as the Kitamuras had been smashed in with an axe, but even after the remains had been burnt, I don't think one of them could have got away with passing off another's body for their own. There were simply too many identifying marks remaining. The same goes for Kazue's body. That would have been identifiable too, despite her missing left hand. That only leaves the body thought to be that of Seiji.

"Think about it. The corpse had been doused with kerosene and gone up in flames. The face was, of course, unrecognizable, but old wounds or traces of surgery wouldn't have been easy to find either. I don't know how the police identified the body, but there's a possibility it was someone other than Seiji. And then we have the disappearance of the gardener who'd been on the island at the time... Mr Shimada?"

"Yes, Detective?"

"Did you happen to check whether Seiji and Yoshikawa Sei'ichi were of similar age and build?"

"Haha. You're sharp." Shimada laughed cheerfully. "Yoshikawa was the same age as Seiji, forty-six. Both were of medium height and build. And both had blood type A. The burnt body naturally also had blood type A."

"How did you find all of that out?" Kawaminami asked in surprise, to which Shimada scratched his cheek in embarrassment.

"Ah, didn't I tell you? I know some people in the police. Morisu, supposing Nakamura Seiji and Yoshikawa Sei'ichi really switched places, how do you explain the events of the case?"

Morisu placed his hand on his forehead and stared into space.

"Kazue was the first to be murdered. Her estimated time of death was between the 17th and 18th. The gardener had arrived on the island and called his wife Masako in the afternoon of the 17th, so Kazue had probably already been killed by then. When the gardener thought it strange he hadn't seen Kazue, Seiji told him his wife was sick and in bed. In truth, he'd already given her a sleeping draught and then strangled her.

"So, fearing he might be found out, Seiji decided to murder the Kitamuras and Yoshikawa too. He drugged all three of them and tied them up. He killed the couple with an axe on the 19th. He then moved Yoshikawa, who was still sleeping because of the drug, to the room where he had killed Kazue earlier. He untied Yoshikawa, dressed him in his own clothes and poured kerosene over him. And then he set fire to the mansion and fled the island.

"And so the switch of the murderer Nakamura Seiji and the victim Yoshikawa Sei'ichi was complete. A textbook example of what is known in crime fiction circles as the 'headless corpse' trick. But even this theory leaves some questions unanswered. I can come up with four, just off the top of my head."

"Oh? And they would be?…" Shimada urged him.

"First of all, motive. What reason could Seiji have had to kill the woman who had been at his side for over twenty years? You could simply say he was mad, but even madmen have their own reasons.

"Second—and I already mentioned this last night—is the missing left hand. Why would Seiji cut off the left hand of his wife? And what did he do with it?

"Third is the time gap between the murders. He killed his wife first on the 17th and finally the gardener in the early morning of the 20th. What was Seiji doing during those three days?

"And finally, how did Seiji flee from the island after committing these crimes? And where has he been hiding since then?"

"I was thinking along almost the exact same lines on our way over here," said Shimada, "and I think that, of the questions you just listed, I can at least provide an answer to the first."

"A motive for killing Kazue?"

"Yes. Of course, as you said, this is nothing but a wild guess."

"Jealousy?" tried Morisu carefully. Shimada pursed his lips and nodded.

"Even normal emotions can turn into madness if they manage to dwell long enough in the heart of a genius like Seiji."

Shimada turned to Conan.

"What do you mean?" asked the latter.

"Do you remember what Yoshikawa Masako said about Nakamura Chiori?"

"Yes, of course."

"She said that Chiori seldom returned to the island. She also said that Kazue adored her daughter, but when we asked about Seiji…"

"She said something about Seiji not being fond of kids."

"Precisely. Seiji didn't love his daughter very much."

"And I remember that, at Chiori's funeral, he wasn't the chief mourner."

"You understand what I'm trying to tell you, don't you?"

Kawaminami looked alternately at Morisu and Shimada. The latter nodded gently. Morisu frowned and looked away.

"You suspect that Chiori wasn't Seiji's daughter."

"That's correct, Conan."

"But then whose daughter was she?"

"Nakamura Kōjirō's. According to Masako, Kō occasionally visited the island when she was working there and before she married Yoshikawa. That means there hadn't always been bad blood between the brothers. And I think the period when Kō stopped going to the island dates from the time Chiori was born. What do you think, Morisu?"

"I've no idea."

Morisu reached out for the cigarettes on the table.

"So that's why we went by Kōjirō's house on the way back," said Kawaminami.

"Yes. I wanted to see what I could get out of Kō."

"Mr Shimada," interrupted Morisu. "I think you had better reconsider that."

"Oh, and why?" Shimada was taken aback.

"It might be none of my business, but even if you and Kōjirō are good friends, I don't think much good can come of you prying into rather private affairs."

Morisu looked silently at Shimada.

"There's nothing wrong with us talking about the case here. But I don't think it's right to act purely on guesswork and invade other people's privacy, especially when it involves a secret as delicate as that."

"But Morisu, it was you who suggested we visit Yoshikawa's wife," retorted Kawaminami. Morisu sighed gently.

"All day today I've been regretting saying something as careless as that. But even I make mistakes when my curiosity clashes with my conscience. And last night, I was caught up in the moment. But I shouldn't have said that merely because I found the case intriguing. I felt even worse thinking about it while facing the stone Buddhas."

He looked at the easel near the wall. Thick colour had been applied to the picture on the canvas with a palette knife.

"It might be selfish of me, Mr Shimada, but I'm getting out of the game at this point. I've explained my deductions and I'm now resigning as 'armchair detective'," said Morisu.

Shimada didn't seem to be offended at all. "So your final conclusion is that Seiji is still alive?"

"Conclusion is too strong a word. I merely pointed out a possibility which may not have been given enough attention before. If you ask me whether I really think Seiji is still alive, then I'll have to answer with a no."

"And the letter? What do you make of that?"

"Probably just a joke by one of those who've gone to the island—would you like some more tea?"

"No, thanks."

Morisu poured himself a fourth cup.

"Suppose Seiji were really still among the living, would he be making accusations about the death of Chiori, a daughter he didn't love, and possibly even hated?"

"Hmm."

"And I also think that keeping an extreme feeling—like the urge to murder someone—burning for a long time is much more difficult than you make it out to be.

"If Seiji had been responsible for the incident six months ago and he wanted to kill not only Kazue, but also the persons responsible for Chiori's death, as well as his brother Kōjirō, wouldn't he have gone after Kōjirō and the others right after killing Kazue? I don't think that his urge to kill could have been all that strong if he went into hiding for six months first, and then restarted his revenge by sending a bunch of threatening letters."

"..."

"Do you have some more hot water for me?" asked Kawaminami, trying to help Shimada, who seemed at a loss for words.

"There's no more left. I'll boil some."

"No, that's OK. I've had enough anyway."

Kawaminami lay down on his back and crossed his arms.

"Mr Shimada and I have too much free time, so while you're entitled to your own opinion, of course, I think we'll continue digging a bit more."

"Look, I'm not telling you to stop."

Morisu's face softened.

"But I do think you should avoid trampling over the secrets people have been trying to keep hidden, without any regard for their feelings."

"All right."

Kawaminami yawned and muttered.

"I wonder how the guys on Tsunojima are doing."

They of course had no idea.

No idea that, on the little island not far across the sea from the mainland, the parade of death was about to begin.

FIVE

The Third Day on the Island

1

It was almost noon when Agatha woke up. She had overslept because she had lain awake almost the whole night, finally falling asleep only in the morning.

She took one look at the clock and sat bolt upright. But, after listening carefully, she realized the others hadn't got up either.

She covered herself with the blanket again and lay restlessly on her stomach.

She had gone to bed at three in the morning. Except for Van and Carr, who had gone to bed early, she guessed the others had turned in at around the same time.

At first Agatha felt ashamed of getting up so late, even if she was on holiday, but when she realized she wasn't the only one, she reached out for the cigarettes on her bedside table.

She had low blood pressure. It would take a good hour before she could get up and get ready for the daily routine.

That's odd, thought Agatha… *Is Orczy still in bed?*

Even though they had gone to bed so late last night, it was unlike Orczy to lie in this long. Maybe she had already got up, but had returned to her room when the others didn't appear. Or…

With vacant eyes she followed the drifting cigarette smoke. She enjoyed smoking, but refrained from it in the company of others.

After starting on her second cigarette, she slowly pulled her weary body out of bed.

She put on a beige jumper over a black blouse and stood in front of the mirror. Making sure her clothes were in tip-top order, she collected her toilet bag and make-up pouch and exited the room.

The empty decagonal hall was as gloomy as ever despite the noon hour. The table in the centre was like a white spot floating in the darkness. The ten-sided patch of sky visible through the skylight was as grey as yesterday.

Agatha walked straight to the bathroom, washed her face quickly and applied her make-up. Returning to the hall, she started cleaning the cups, glasses and ashtrays full of stubs that had been left lying on the table last night.

And then she caught a flash of red out of the corner of her eye…

What's that?

She turned her head and immediately remembered where she had seen that red before. She could feel herself turn as white as a sheet. It was hanging on one of the plain wooden doors.

The First
Victim

At first only a faint sound came from her lips, but in the next moment Agatha was screaming at the top of her lungs.

A door behind her swung open and Carr became the first to jump out into the hall. He was already up and dressed.

He caught sight of the petrified Agatha and then saw the object she was staring at.

"Whose room is that?" he shouted.

Agatha was unable to speak. The plate with the red characters was covering the name on the door.

Door after door opened and the others came out.

"Whose room is it, Agatha?" repeated Carr.

"O-Orczy's."

"What?"

It was Poe who darted to the door. Still dressed in his pyjamas, his hair shaggy from disturbed sleep, he grabbed the doorknob furiously.

The door wasn't locked.

It was almost anticlimactic how easily the door opened.

A dark room. A beam of light coming in through the gap between the shutters, cutting through the darkness like a sharp-edged sword.

"Orczy."

Poe called out to her in a trembling voice.

"Orczy."

The bed against the wall was grey in the darkness. She was lying there peacefully, her blanket covering her neatly up to her chest. Her own dark-blue cardigan had been pulled over her head…

"Orczy!"

Poe let out a roar and rushed into the room. The body lying on the bed, however, did not move at all.

"What happened? Orczy…"

Lifting the cardigan that covered Orczy's face with his powerful, trembling hands, Poe felt his whole body shiver. The other five, who had followed him and were now standing in the entrance, tried to push inside.

"Don't come in," implored Poe, his arms raised to discourage them. "I beg you. She wouldn't want you to see her like this…"

Hearing these words, the five stayed where they were.

Poe took a deep breath, raising his shoulders. He carefully lifted the blanket and started to examine the body of poor Orczy, who would never move or feel embarrassed again.

After he was done, Poe replaced the blanket and cardigan. He got up sluggishly, stared up at the ceiling and let out a long, groaning sigh.

"Let's get out." He turned to the others. "This is a crime scene. We'd better lock it. Where's the key?"

"It's here." Before anyone could react, Ellery stepped into the room and picked up the key from the desk by the wall. "The window's unlatched. What about that?"

"Better lock it too. Let's get out, Ellery."

"But what happened to Orczy?" Van asked. Poe grasped the key Ellery had given him and said in a quiet voice:

"She's dead—strangled."

"No!" screamed Agatha.

"I'm sorry, Agatha."

"No… Poe, I want to see Orczy."

"I can't let you."

Poe closed his eyes and shook his head sadly.

"Orczy was strangled to death, Agatha. Please, don't look at her. Even if she's dead now, she still deserves some dignity."

Agatha instantly understood what Poe meant. He was talking about the horrible sight of a strangled body. She nodded and was led away from the room.

And just when Poe was reaching to close the door, someone stepped in front of him to block his way.

"Aren't you trying a bit too hard to get us away from the room?"

It was Carr. He looked up at Poe and, with a grim smile on his face, said: "You could say we're all experts on murder here. And we all want to find the person who did this to Orczy. So give us a chance to investigate the crime scene and the body."

"Damn you!"

Poe's face turned pale, and his whole body trembled as he yelled.

"Are you going to use the death of a friend as a source of amusement? This is work for the police."

"What are you blathering about? When will the police come? How are we going to let them know? Remember what the plastic plates said. By the time the police arrive, we might all be dead except for 'the Murderer' and 'the Detective'."

Poe pushed harder in an attempt to close the door. Carr, in turn, used his bony yellow hands to push Poe's away.

"Think about it more carefully and don't be so stupid, Poe. The next to be murdered might be none other than yourself, you know."

"Move away, Carr."

"Or is there something else? Why are you so confident that you alone won't be killed? The only person who can be sure of that is the murderer himself."

"What?"

"Oh, now I've got it!"

"You bastard!"

"Stop it, you two."

Poe was ready to jump at Carr. The look on Carr's face showed he was ready to take Poe on, too. But Van grasped Carr's arm and pulled him away from the door.

"What're you doing, you piece of scum?!"

Carr's face was crimson with fury as he screamed the words. Taking advantage of the moment, Poe closed the door quickly and locked it.

"That was unseemly of you, Carr," said Ellery, who had just

come back from the kitchen unobserved and was holding the remaining six plates in his hands. "Poe's right. Unfortunately."

2

"It's unbelievable. This has to be a sick joke by someone. This kind of thing doesn't happen in real life."

"Leroux."

"A murder is no joke! This has to be a nightmare. It just doesn't make sense."

"Leroux, stop it."

Agatha's shrill voice made Leroux start, his round shoulders shuddering. He looked up.

"Sorry," he muttered softly and stared down at the floor.

The six were all sitting around the table in the hall. Not one of them looked into any of the others' faces. The empty seat that, until last night, had been occupied by the girl with the short hair and downcast eyes stood out painfully now.

"Who killed Orczy?"

The question came from Agatha's rose-pink lips, but it sounded more like a curse and hung trembling in the cold air.

"Nobody's going to just come out and say, 'It was me,'" replied Ellery.

"But the murderer has to be one of us. One of us six. Who killed Orczy? Why not stop pretending you don't know anything about it, you murderer?"

"I told you, nobody's going to kill someone and then confess to it just like that."

"But Ellery—"

"I know, Agatha. I know."

Ellery banged his fist lightly on the table.

"We need to find out who the murderer is. What about it, Poe? Won't you tell us what you found out?"

After a moment's hesitation, Poe pursed his lips and nodded solemnly.

"I already told you just now, but she… Orczy was strangled to death. A length of nylon cord, the sort you can get anywhere, was still wound around her neck and ligature marks were clearly visible beneath it. There's no doubt this was murder."

"Any sign of Orczy having fought back?"

"No. She was probably attacked in her sleep, or when she was off guard. I couldn't find any sign of her being hit on the head, so she wasn't knocked out first. There was one thing I couldn't make sense of, though."

"Which was?"

"You all saw it too. I don't know why, but the murderer arranged the body in a kind of dignified pose. Orczy was lying on her back with her pyjamas in order and her cardigan covering her face. That might have been the murderer's conscience at work I guess. But one more thing…"

Poe frowned deeply.

"Orczy was missing her left hand."

"What?"

"What do you mean, Poe?" cried Agatha.

"Her left hand had been cut off."

Poe looked around the group, placed both his arms on the table and turned them over, palms up. On his fingers were several dark-red bloodstains.

"A big, sharp instrument like a kitchen knife was used. The murderer must have found it difficult to do. The cut was horribly clumsy."

"It was cut off after the murder, of course," said Ellery.

"I can't say with certainty, but I think it's correct to assume that. If it had been done while the heart was still active, there would have been a lot more blood than there actually was."

"And you didn't see such an instrument in the room?"

"No. I couldn't find the cut-off hand either."

"So the murderer took it with him," muttered Ellery to himself, as he clasped his thin fingers together. "Why would he do that?"

"He must be insane," Agatha shrieked.

Ellery snorted lightly.

"He must be, or he must love bad jokes. It's an allusion—to the incident that happened on this island last year."

"Ah."

"The quadruple murder in the Blue Mansion. One of the victims, Nakamura Kazue, was strangled, after which her left hand was cut off."

"But why, Ellery?" Agatha asked.

"You mean what was the intention behind the allusion? Who knows?" Ellery shrugged. "Let's go on—Poe, can you give an estimate of the time of death?"

"There were some signs of *livor mortis*. I noticed that *rigor mortis* had just started when I checked for Orczy's pulse. I could open the clenched fingers of her right hand relatively easily, so *rigor mortis* hadn't reached her joints yet. Also, considering the coagulation of the blood… I'd say it was four or five hours after death. Orczy died between seven and eight this morning, or with a wider range, between six and nine. But I'm just an amateur, so don't take it as read."

"I believe you."

Carr cackled like a monkey, his teeth sticking out of his mouth.

"You're the star of our beloved K— University's medical faculty. We can trust what you say… Unless, of course, you yourself are the murderer…"

Poe remained silent and didn't even look at Carr.

"Does anybody have an alibi for between six and nine this morning?" Ellery posed the question to all of them. "Anybody notice anything that could be relevant to the case?"

Nobody reacted.

"Anyone with an idea about the motive, then?"

Leroux's, Van's and Agatha's eyes all slowly turned to look at Carr.

"I see." Ellery seemed exasperated. "You all think Carr had a motive. Rather obvious, though, isn't it?"

"What? Why me?" exclaimed Carr.

"Orczy turned you down, didn't she?"

Carr gasped and clamped his mouth shut.

"But Ellery, if Carr was the murderer, he would never have arranged her body in such a dignified way," Agatha cried out in a sardonic tone… "Carr's the only one who wouldn't have done that."

3

"Damn them."

Carr sat down on the rocks and spat on the ground as he looked at Cat Island, floating in the sea before his eyes. He grabbed some nearby weeds and tore off the leaves.

"Damn them," he repeated angrily.

The leaves he had gathered were carried by the wind and danced out to sea.

They always go their separate ways, except when they're out to get me—only then do they work together. That Poe, too, with his pretentious talk... And I'm sure I wasn't the only one who wanted to take a better look at Orczy's body and the inside of the room.

Ellery in particular was all ready to investigate. Leroux, too. Van as well. We allowed Poe to do it all. Don't they realize how dangerous that might be?

Even the tumult of the waves below started to get on his nerves. He spat on the ground once more, pursed his lips and hit his knee with his fist.

It's all Orczy's fault. Turned down? I was just bored and had a little chat with her. Hmph. She thought I was serious and got all high and mighty... Stupid woman. Who did she think she was? Hmph. As if I would kill someone because of that...

Carr stared at the scenery in front of him, his whole being filled with anger and humiliation.

"There's not a boat to be found here. And we don't have the tools to cut down trees and make a raft. Even if we could improvise one, I doubt we could make it all the way to the mainland—want a smoke, Van?"

In search of a way to communicate with the mainland, the group—except for Carr—had decided to split up into two teams and explore the island. Poe, Van and Agatha formed one team. They were exploring the area between the southern and eastern coasts.

Poe gave Van a cigarette, took one himself and then crossed his arms in silence.

"The only thing we can do is to start a fire and hope they find us."

"Would they really notice something like that? Also..." Van

gazed up at the sky as he lit a cigarette. "The clouds don't look so good. It might rain tonight."

"That's bad. Why didn't we think of a method of making contact before we came out here, just in case?"

"It's too late now. Who would have expected something like this?" Van's shoulders sagged. "And my fever had just dropped too. I can't believe this is happening…"

"I haven't seen a single fishing boat this whole time," said Agatha, plainly distressed.

The heavily overcast sky threw a dark shadow across the sea.

"But a boat might come eventually," said Poe. "We'd better have someone on watch here. Teams of two, in three shifts."

"Poe, no!" Agatha cried. "I don't want to be left alone with someone who might be the murderer."

"Teams of three, then," offered Van.

"We might as well come all together then," said Poe. "The only time a boat will pass by here is when it leaves or returns to the harbour, so probably around dusk or dawn."

"But there's a chance they might pass by at other times," said Van.

"Maybe, but if you ask me the chance is very small. The old boatman told us that when we came here. The fishing grounds in this area are further south, so boats hardly come this way at all."

"But there's not much else we can do," said Van. "Do we have something we can use as firewood to light a signal fire?"

"That might be a problem." Poe looked back at the forest. "Just pine trees. They don't burn well when fresh. We could gather dry, fallen pine needles and burn them, but there aren't that many, so they wouldn't be able to see the fire from the mainland. The only thing we can do is wait for a boat to pass by."

"What's going to happen to us?"

Agatha looked terrified.

"We'll be all right. Somehow."

Poe placed his hand on Agatha's shoulder and smiled awkwardly through his beard. But Agatha seemed unconvinced.

"You say that, but for all I know you, or perhaps Van, might be the one who killed Orczy."

Poe took out a new cigarette in silence.

"Or Carr, or Leroux, or Ellery…"

Agatha was deathly white and was visibly trembling.

"One of you killed Orczy. Killed her and then cut off her hand."

"But you're one of the suspects too, Agatha," Van said with a solemn look, unusual for him.

"It wasn't me."

Agatha turned back towards the forest and buried her head in her hands.

"Aah, I can't believe it. Is this real? Van, Poe? Is Orczy really dead? Is there really a murderer among us?"

"You know, Leroux, I was thinking of another possibility."

"Another one?"

"It's obvious. There might be someone besides us on this island."

"What?"

Ellery and Leroux had first gone to the inlet with the pier, then to the rocky area near the burnt-down Blue Mansion, and were now walking along the little path through the grove. They were heading for the northern cliffs that overlooked Cat Island.

Leroux stopped in his tracks and asked again.

"What do you mean, Ellery?"

"There's a possibility the murder was committed by an outside party." Ellery smiled. "Or do you prefer to think that one of us is the murderer?"

"D-don't make jokes about that. But who could be hiding on the island?"

"Oh, if you ask me…" Ellery said nonchalantly, "I'd say Nakamura Seiji."

"Oh!"

"Why so surprised?"

"But Ellery, Nakamura Seiji was murdered last year."

"So they say, but I think that a mistake was made there. Have you never considered it, Leroux? The body of Nakamura Seiji, which was found six months ago, was the textbook example of a 'headless corpse'. And then there's that gardener who disappeared at the same time."

"You mean that Seiji was the murderer and the body thought to be his was actually the gardener's?"

"Precisely. A simple switch."

"And so Seiji is still alive and has now come to the island."

"A possibility. Though perhaps he actually lives on the island."

"He's living here?"

"Remember the story the old fisherman told us two days ago? That sometimes the lights of the Decagon House are on? Seiji might've been the one who lit them."

"You can't believe all those ghost stories. The island was crawling with police and media after the murders. Where do you suppose Seiji was hiding then, and where is he hiding now?"

"That's why we're exploring. We just took a look at the little boathouse in the inlet, but there was nothing suspicious there. Of course our first priority is to find a way to contact the mainland, but I think we should look for traces of someone living on the

131

island too. That's also why I said we need to take a look at Cat Island."

"But still, I can't believe that Seiji's the murderer."

"Really? Don't you remember that the window in Orczy's room wasn't locked? Isn't it reasonable to suppose she forgot to lock her window and that someone came in from outside?"

"Then why was the door also unlocked?"

"The murderer opened it from the inside after the murder. To get into the hall and glue the plastic plate on the door."

"But that doesn't make sense. How could anyone from the outside know that you'd placed the plates in the kitchen drawer?"

"The one who left those plastic plates could have been someone from the outside in the first place, couldn't he? The lock on the front door is broken, so anyone can go in and out as they please. Yesterday morning Seiji could have left those plates on the table, waited until we got up and observed us through the kitchen window. Or someone among us might be working with him."

"That's impossible."

"I'm just discussing theories, Leroux. For a big fan of mystery fiction, you're not showing much imagination."

"Ellery, mystery novels and reality are two different things. Anyway, what motive could Nakamura Seiji have for wanting to kill us?"

"Who knows?"

They had reached the end of the path and come out on the cliffs where Carr was sitting. Seeing them, Carr stood up and looked the other way.

"Hey, you'd better not go off alone all the time."

Ellery was speaking to Carr, who had not said a word. He ignored Ellery and walked off into the grove.

"Difficult guy."

Ellery clicked his tongue lightly.

"Everybody's on edge right now. I'm afraid I might've said too much, too. But he seems to be holding a grudge against me personally."

"I think I know what's bothering him," said Leroux, and he glanced to where Carr had vanished. "Even at a time like this, you always remain so calm, Ellery, as if you're observing us normal people from a place far away."

"That's how I appear to you?"

"Yes. I'm not sure whether it's a compliment, but I do feel some kind of respect for you for that. Carr is the opposite, and I think he's jealous."

"So that's all it is?"

With an uninterested look, Ellery walked in the direction of the sea.

"There are too many shrubs here. Not a good place to view the island."

He was talking about Cat Island, which lay in front of them. Leroux stood next to Ellery and said, while paying attention to where he put his feet: "It does seem like two or three people could hide there. But then there's this cliff."

"He might have a boat. It's not far, a rubber dinghy is probably enough. Leaving from the rocky area over there and then… Hey, look, Leroux."

Ellery pointed.

"That slope on the island, do you think it's climbable?"

"Yes, I think so."

Staring at the dark Cat Island floating on the white waves, Leroux tried to make sense of all the thoughts inside his confused mind.

True, the possibility of another party being present on this island could not be dismissed altogether, as Ellery had pointed out. Someone else could be out there, hiding, and after their lives. But to assume that person was Nakamura Seiji would be jumping to conclusions. What were the chances of Nakamura Seiji still being alive? Even if he were, why would he want them dead?

It's just impossible.

Leroux slowly shook his head.

It's just impossible, he thought.

But there was something in his memory that nagged at him. There was something he needed to remember.

The waves washing the cliffs at his feet also washed his mind. Every time a fragment of memory appeared, the waves immediately took it away.

Leroux gave up thinking and looked at Ellery next to him. Ellery had nothing more to say and was looking coolly at the sea.

The wind brought the scent of dusk.

4

"...Due to low pressure, the sky will become cloudy over a large region, starting tonight and lasting until tomorrow night, but it will stay dry. The weather will recover, starting the day after tomorrow. And now, the weather forecast for each area in Kyūshū..."

Eventually, the voice coming out of Leroux's radio cassette player was drowned out by a loud female DJ.

"I've had enough. Switch it off, Leroux, I don't want to listen to it any more," said Agatha irritably. Leroux hastened to comply.

Their simple dinner had been conducted in a heavy silence, illuminated by the oil lamp. The six were sitting around the table, all avoiding the spot directly across from the door of Orczy's room. The plate with "The First Victim" was still on the door. It appeared to have been stuck there with strong glue, and they couldn't get it off.

Agatha said in a deliberately cheery voice: "Hey Ellery, show us another of your magic tricks."

"Hmm? Oh, sure."

Ellery, who had been playing with his cards in silence, did a riffle shuffle, gathered the cards into a case and put the deck in his coat pocket.

"Why are you putting them away when I asked you to show me a trick?"

"Easy there, Agatha. I put them in my pocket *because* you want to see a magic trick."

"What do you mean?"

"This is how the trick starts."

Ellery coughed softly, and then peered into Agatha's eyes.

"OK, ready, Agatha? Think of any of the fifty-two cards, any one you want, except for the joker."

"Just think of it?"

"Yes. Don't say it out loud—done?"

"Yes."

"OK…"

Ellery took the case from his coat pocket again and put it on the table. It was the blue bicycle deck.

"Now take a good look at this case. Then think really hard of the card you chose and repeat the name of the card in your head."

"OK," said Agatha. "Just think of it hard, right?"

"Yes. That's enough."

Ellery picked up the card case with his left hand.

"Now Agatha, what card did you think of?"

"I can tell you now?"

"Yes."

"Queen of Diamonds."

"Heh. Let's take a look at the case then."

Ellery opened the lid of the case and took the cards out face up. He slowly fanned them out between his hands.

"Queen of Diamonds, right? Oh!"

Ellery stopped fanning out the cards and directed Agatha's attention to one of them with his eyes. One single card was facing the other way round.

"One card is the other way round, you see."

"Yes."

"Could you take it out and show us the face?"

"Yes—but it can't be…"

With a doubtful look, Agatha took out the card and placed it on the table face up. It was, without any question, the Queen of Diamonds.

"Unbelievable!"

Agatha was surprised.

"Neat trick, don't you think?" Ellery smiled, put the cards back in the case and the case in his pocket.

"Ellery, that was really impressive."

"Haven't I shown it to you before, Leroux?"

"First time I've seen it."

"It's one of my best card-guessing tricks."

"Agatha wasn't in on this, right?"

"I wasn't, Leroux," she said.

"Really?"

"There was no set-up here," insisted Ellery. "And I'll also tell you that this wasn't a probability trick, betting on the fifty-two-to-one chance that Agatha would choose the Queen of Diamonds."

Ellery lit a Salem cigarette and took a slow drag.

"Let's do a little riddle now. I need to write this one down."

He produced a pencil and a piece of paper from his pocket and wrote: *WHAT'S AT THE TOP OF A TREE AND THE BOTTOM OF A WELL?* Then he held the message up and showed it to the group.

"Why couldn't you just say it out loud?" asked Leroux, but Ellery merely raised an eyebrow in reply.

"Got it."

Agatha clapped her hands together.

"A horizontal line! Of the T and L?"

"We've got a winner," cried Ellery.

"Oh, I get it now," said Leroux. "The horizontal line of the letters T and L when you write the words 'tree' and 'well' out in capitals."

"Indeed," confirmed Ellery. "Now here's another one: what has four letters, sometimes has nine letters, but never has five letters."

The group sat in silence for a few moments.

"This time I really have no idea," said Agatha.

"Oh, I'll put you out of your misery," said Poe, as he put a new packet of Lark cigarettes into his birchwood case. "I heard this one at university a while back. There's no riddle, just a trick. Ellery was merely making a series of statements: the word 'what' has four letters, 'sometimes' has nine letters, and so on."

Leroux groaned.

"That's terrible."

"Not fair," agreed Agatha.

Ellery shrugged.

"It's a hard one. I'll give you that."

"You always have to pay attention to the phrasing of a riddle. The language is like a secret code," said Poe.

"Speaking of codes," cut in Ellery, "did you know that the first book featuring a secret code is the Old Testament? I think it was the Book of Daniel."

"That long ago?" asked Leroux.

"Yes, even here in Japan we've been using secret codes for quite a long time, you know. There's that famous question-and-answer poem between Yoshida Kenkō and Ton'a in the *Shoku Sōanshū*. Didn't you learn about it in high school?"

"No, what kind of code is it?" Agatha asked.

"Kenkō's poem to Ton'a went:

"The night is cool
Oh, the harvested rice ears when I wake
My hand for a pillow
Even both my sleeves in autumn
Blow in the unrelenting wind.

"Take the first letters of each line of the original text and it says *yonetamahe*, or 'Rice please'. He was asking for food. And if you take the last letters of each line and read them the other way around, you get *zenimohoshi*, or 'Also need money'."

"That's a miserable story," said Agatha.

"And the Buddhist priest Ton'a replied:

"Night is depressing
My dear friend
You did not come
But something will work out
So come around for a while.

"Take the first and last letters again, and you get the message *yonewanashi, zenisukoshi*: 'No rice, little money'."

"They must have spent quite a bit of time thinking that up."

"I think there was another famous secret code in a question-and-answer poem in the *Essays in Idleness*. What was it again, Orczy?"

They had been relaxing as they talked, but at the sound of the name they all caught their breath and froze.

"I—I'm sorry. It just slipped out."

So even Ellery could lose his head. Such a mistake was unlike him.

There had been a tacit understanding between them since dinner that they would not mention what happened to Orczy, but Ellery's slip immediately brought them all back to the inescapable reality. An oppressive silence filled the room.

"Ellery, don't you have any other stories?" said Leroux, trying to help Ellery, who was at a loss for words.

"Ah, yes—"

Cruelly interrupting Ellery, who was trying his best to conjure up his usual smile, Carr hit the table.

"Agatha, how about some coffee?" he said, casting Ellery a scornful look. Ellery started to say something, but Agatha immediately cut him off.

"Yes, good idea. I'll make some coffee. I'm sure everybody would like some."

She stood up hurriedly and went to the kitchen alone.

"Hey."

Carr glared at the faces of the remaining four in turn.

"We're holding a wake for poor Orczy tonight, right? So stop pretending nothing has happened and let's all be nice to each other."

139

"And here you are. Sugar and milk as well."

Agatha put the tray with six moss-green cups down on the table.

"Sorry we ask you to do it every time," Ellery said, as he took the cup closest to him. The others also reached out for cups. Agatha took one for herself and pushed the tray with the last remaining cup to Van, who was sitting next to her.

"Ah, thanks."

Van placed his half-smoked Seven Stars cigarette in the ashtray and held the cup in his hands, warming himself.

"How's your cold, Van?"

"Ah, much better, thanks. Ellery, we didn't really talk it over, but is there really no way of contacting the mainland?"

"There doesn't appear to be one."

Ellery drank his coffee black.

"There's a lighthouse on J— Cape, so I thought we could try waving a white flag from here. But I suspect it's unmanned."

"Yes, I think you're right."

"Then one of us would need to risk his own life to swim to the mainland, or we could make some sort of raft."

"Neither of those plans sounds much good."

"We could make a signal fire," Poe said.

"I don't think a few burning pine needles would be enough to attract the attention of the outside world," countered Ellery.

"We could set fire to the Decagon House if necessary," insisted Poe.

"I think that would be going too far," cut in Van.

"It would be stupid and dangerous. But you know, Poe, Leroux and I weren't just looking for a means of communication with the mainland when we went around the island earlier."

"What else were you looking for?" said Poe.

"Something that we failed to find, even though we searched pretty much the whole island… No, wait."

"What?"

"The Blue Mansion—we didn't search the ruins of the Blue Mansion," Ellery muttered, touching his fingers to his forehead. "There might be an underground room there."

"An underground room?"

It happened just at that moment.

Interrupting Poe and Ellery's discussion, someone fell on the table, groaning horribly.

"What's wrong?" Agatha screamed.

Everyone stood up. The table trembled. Brown liquid flew from the half-drunk cups. He thrashed about and kicked his chair to the floor as his legs jerked like a broken mechanical doll's. His upper body finally slipped off the table onto the blue-tiled floor.

"Carr!" Poe shouted and ran to his side.

Thrust aside by Poe, Leroux stumbled and knocked over his own chair.

"What's happened to Carr?" Ellery exclaimed.

Poe examined Carr's eyes and shook his head. "I don't know. Does Carr have any medical issues that anyone knows of?"

Nobody answered.

"This is bad," said Poe.

Carr continued to breathe weakly, making a shrill wheezing sound. Poe put his large arm around Carr's shoulders.

"Help me, Ellery. We need to make him throw up. I think it's poison."

Carr's body convulsed strongly, pushing Poe's arm away. Only the whites of his eyes were visible as he lay on the floor, curled up like a shrimp. After a while there was another heavy convulsion.

141

Brown vomit came out of Carr's mouth, accompanied by a terrible cry.

"He will live, won't he?" Agatha asked Poe with a terrified look.

"I don't know."

"Can't you help him?"

"I don't know what poison it is. But even if I knew, there's little I could do here. We can only hope it wasn't a fatal dose."

The same night, half-past two in the morning.

Carr died lying on the bed in his room.

5

Everybody was too exhausted to say anything. It wasn't fatigue they were suffering from, it was something closer to paralysis.

It was different from what had happened to Orczy: this time someone had suffered, collapsed and died a horrible death in front of their eyes. The visceral, vicious breakdown of everyday life had numbed their senses.

Agatha and Leroux stared into space with half-opened mouths, their minds elsewhere. Van kept sighing, his head resting on his hands. Poe, his eyes fixed on the window, didn't once reach for his cigarette case. The look on Ellery's face never changed, like a Noh mask with its eyes closed.

No moonlight came in from the skylight.

Occasionally the beam from the lighthouse lit up the patch of dark sky visible above. The light of the oil lamp flickered as if it were alive. The monotonous rhythm of the waves could be heard, coming and going, coming and going.

"Let's get this over with," said Ellery. "I want to sleep."

He was barely able to keep his sleepy eyes open.

"Agreed," Poe replied sluggishly, which seemed to wake the other three from their stupors.

"The only thing I can tell you," Poe went on, "is that some kind of poison was used. I don't know what type."

"Can't you make a rough guess?" asked Ellery.

"Well, maybe." Poe frowned deeply. "Based on how fast it acted, I think it's a very strong poison. It caused shortness of breath and convulsions, so there is a good chance it was a neuro-toxin. Common poisons that fall under that category are potassium cyanide, strychnine and atropine. It might also have been nicotine, arsenic or arsenous acid. But atropine and nicotine would cause dilation of the pupils, and I didn't see that. Cyanide would have caused a unique smell—you know, the so-called bitter almond smell. But I didn't detect that either. So it was probably strychnine, or some sort of arsenic or arsenous acid."

The six half-drunk cups were still on the table. Agatha had been staring at them while listening to Poe's explanation, but now she suddenly burst out laughing.

"So it was in the coffee. That means that I'm the prime suspect."

"Yes, Agatha," Ellery replied drily. "Was it really you?"

"Would you believe me if I told you it wasn't?"

"Well, no. That would be illogical."

"I guessed as much."

The two laughed silently. They were as aware as everyone else of the bizarre, abnormal tone of their conversation.

"Would you two stop it?" reprimanded Poe in a low, grim voice, after which he put a cigarette in his mouth and offered his birchwood case to Ellery.

"We need to think about this seriously."

"I know. We're not joking around just for the hell of it."

Ellery pushed Poe's cigarette case back and took his own Salem pack from the breast pocket of his shirt. He took out a cigarette and tapped the filter on the table to pack the tobacco down.

"Let's start by going over the facts," he said. "It was Carr himself who asked for coffee. While Agatha was in the kitchen, the rest of us remained here. It took about fifteen minutes for Agatha to boil some water, make the coffee and return with the cups on the tray. Agatha placed the tray on the table. To be precise, the tray contained six coffee cups, the sugar jar, the jar of powdered milk and seven spoons placed on a saucer, one of them to be used for the milk. Is that correct, Agatha?"

She nodded meekly.

"Regarding the order in which the cups were taken," continued Ellery. "I took the first cup. Who was next?"

"I was," said Leroux. "I took mine almost at the same time as Carr."

"I was next after that, I think," said Poe.

"And then I took one and placed the tray in front of Van," said Agatha. "Right, Van?"

"Yes, that's right."

"OK. To sum up, it went: me, Leroux and Carr, Poe, Agatha, and finally Van."

Ellery put his cigarette in his mouth and lit it.

"Let's think about who had a chance to put the poison in Carr's cup. First of all, Agatha."

"But the cups were all identical—I could have ended up taking the poisoned cup myself. Even if I knew what cup the poison was in, there's no way I could have arranged for Carr to pick that particular one," Agatha countered with a cool voice. "If I were the murderer, I would have handed out the cups myself."

"Now that you mention it, you've always handed out the cups to us before. Why didn't you do so this one time?"

"I just didn't feel like it this time."

"Ah. But I will tell you this, Agatha: the murderer might not have been targeting Carr in particular. The murderer's end goal is to kill all of us, but it doesn't really matter who 'the Second Victim' is."

"So you think that Carr just happened to draw the short straw?"

"I think that's the most logical approach to take. Nobody was sitting on either side of Carr, correct? Nobody could have put poison in his coffee after it had been brought here. So it could only have been you."

"But the poison could already have been in the sugar or the milk."

"But you yourself also took milk, remember? Besides, Carr took his coffee black, without sugar. So he didn't even use a spoon to stir it with."

"Ellery, wait," Leroux chimed in. "I saw Agatha while she was making coffee. The kitchen doors were open and my chair was right opposite, so I had a clear view of Agatha's hands. The counter was also well lit because of the candle on top of it. She didn't do anything suspicious."

"Glad you told us that, but I'm afraid that doesn't constitute conclusive evidence. Considering the distance between this table and the kitchen counter, it's possible you might have overlooked something. It isn't like you were keeping a watch on her from start to finish."

"I'm sorry," stammered Leroux.

"Nothing to be sorry about. You weren't to know what would happen."

"No, I mean, I *was* keeping a watch on Agatha all the time."

"Leroux!"

Agatha's eyes widened in surprise. Leroux looked away and repeated "I'm sorry" in a timid voice.

"But it was the natural thing to do," he continued. "One of us killed Orczy this morning, and it might have been Agatha. Even our dinner of crackers, canned food and juice was a horror to me. Actually, I think your behaviour was the strangest, Ellery. You were the first to try the food, tucking in as if everything were perfectly normal."

"Is that so?" A faint smile appeared on Ellery's lips. "So, Leroux, you are absolutely positive that Agatha isn't the murderer."

"Well, that's—"

"Carr is dead. Poisoned. Surely you don't think his death was a suicide?"

"No—"

"But as I just said to you, Ellery," Agatha broke in. "If I were the murderer, how could I have avoided winding up with the poisoned cup myself? I drank my coffee."

Ellery blinked slowly as he put out his Salem in the decagon-shaped ashtray.

"There were only six cups. You could easily have remembered the position of the poisoned cup. You picked your own cup and gave the last to Van. If the poisoned cup had been among the last two cups, you could have simply passed that cup on to Van. Even if you had ended up with the poisoned cup, you could simply not have drunk from it."

"I'm telling you, it wasn't me."

Agatha's long hair swung wildly around as she shook her head. Her hands, holding the edge of the table, trembled.

"Ellery," Van said weakly, "if Agatha were the murderer, would she really have chosen to kill Carr like this, in a way that makes her the most obvious suspect? She's not that stupid. What do you think, Poe?"

"I agree with you," said Poe, and turned to Ellery. "The only light in this hall is the lamp on the table. And I don't think any of us was watching everyone else as we took our cups of coffee from the tray."

"What do you mean, Poe?" asked Ellery.

"You were the first to pick up a cup. You could easily have had some poison hidden in your hand, and dropped it into one of the other cups. What about it, magician?"

"Haha. Very good." A bitter smile appeared on Ellery's calm face. "All I can say is that I didn't do that."

"And of course, we can't just take your word for it. But there are other possibilities, too. The poison could have been given to Carr before the coffee, for example."

"A slowly dissolving capsule?"

"Precisely."

"Yes, but regardless of how the poison was administered, surely suspicion falls on you, Doctor. If you think about it, no amateur could easily get his hands on poisons like arsenic and strychnine… Perhaps Van of the science faculty or Agatha of the pharmacy faculty, but Leroux and I are from the humanities. We don't have anything to do with labs full of dangerous drugs and strong poisons."

"Anyone could steal some poison if they really wanted to," objected Poe. "The security of the labs and experiment rooms at our university is laughable. It's the same with the agriculture and engineering faculties. If you just pretend you belong there, you can walk right on in. Also, it was none other than you, Ellery, who once said he had relatives in O— City who ran a pharmacy."

Ellery gave a little whistle.

"That's a good memory you have."

"Basically, it's pointless for us to sit here discussing where the poison came from."

Poe leant forward slowly.

"And there's still another possibility as to how the poison was administered. I can't believe it hasn't occurred to you. It could have been smeared on one of the cups beforehand. Then any one of us could have done it."

"Precisely."

Ellery brushed back his unruly lock of hair and smiled. Agatha stared at him, perplexed.

"You thought of that, Ellery?"

"Of course. Don't think I'm stupid."

"Yet you still accused me of being the murderer."

"I was also planning to go after the others and tease them a bit."

"Well, I think you're horrible."

"We're not in a normal situation here, so you can't expect me to act normally."

"You—"

"By the way, Agatha, there's something I want to ask you."

"What now?"

"Tell me, did you wash the cups before you made the coffee?"

"No, I didn't."

"And when were they last washed?"

"We drank tea after we came back from exploring the island, remember? They were washed then. I placed the washed cups on the counter."

"Together with the seventh cup, Orczy's?"

"No, I put Orczy's cup back in the cupboard. I just couldn't look at it any more."

"Hm. That's all right. That makes it more plausible that the cup was poisoned beforehand. You'd just have to go into the kitchen in the evening and smear some poison in one of them. Anyone could have done that."

"But Ellery," Leroux said, "how would the murderer then know which of the cups was poisoned? There was nobody here who didn't put their lips to their cup."

"There must have been some sort of mark."

"A mark?"

"Yes. A chip or a scratch or something," said Ellery. He picked up Carr's moss-green cup and began to examine it.

"Anything?"

"Wait a sec… Oh, that's strange."

Ellery cocked his head in surprise and passed the cup to Leroux.

"You take a look. I don't think it looks any different from the others, though."

"Really?"

"Not even a small crack?" Agatha asked.

"Nothing at all. Maybe you'll find a little crack under a microscope."

"Stop joking. Give me that."

The cup was passed to Agatha.

"You're right. There's nothing here that could serve as a mark."

"So does that mean that the cup wasn't poisoned beforehand?" Ellery stroked his hair with a dissatisfied look on his face. "Here are the three current theories: Agatha's the murderer, or I'm the murderer, or someone who made Carr swallow a poisoned capsule is the murderer."

"Whoever it is, we won't be able to determine the method and the identity of the murderer here," Poe said. Ellery reached out for Carr's cup, which Agatha had placed on the table and contemplated it.

"If it was someone from outside, then it wouldn't matter whether there was a mark or not."

"What did you say, Ellery?" asked Poe.

"Nothing…" Ellery looked away. "What bothers me is the motive. I think we can assume that the person who killed Orczy and Carr and the person who arranged those plates are one and the same. That means that he, or she, is serious about taking the lives of at least five of us here on the island. Five, assuming that 'the Detective' won't end up as 'the Sixth Victim' too."

"But a motive for that…" muttered Leroux, shaking his head weakly.

"There has to be one," Ellery said decisively, "however weird it might be."

"The murderer must be mad, insane!" Agatha shrieked. "How can we understand the thoughts of a madman?!"

"Insane…" repeated Ellery, and he lifted his left hand to look at his watch. "It's almost morning. What should we do?"

"We need to sleep. We won't get any answers if we just keep discussing while we're all as tired as this."

"I agree, Poe. I can't go on much longer either."

Ellery rubbed his eyes, got up unsteadily and walked to his room.

"Wait, Ellery." Poe stopped him. "Wouldn't it better if we all slept together here?"

"I don't want to!" Agatha looked at everybody with frightened eyes. "What if the person next to you is the murderer? He could just reach out with his arms and strangle you. That thought alone is enough to frighten me."

"I doubt the murderer would do something as stupid as strangling the person next to him. He'd get caught immediately."

"Can you be absolutely sure, Poe? What if he kills us all in our sleep?"

Agatha almost burst into tears as she stood up, knocking her chair over.

"Agatha, wait."

"No! I can't trust any of you."

She fled to her room. Poe let out a long sigh.

"She's in bad shape."

"It's only natural," said Ellery with a shrug. "To be honest, I feel the same as Agatha. I'll sleep alone, too."

"Me too," added Leroux. The eyes behind his glasses were red. Van followed as well, leaving Poe, who was running his hands through his hair, alone.

"Make sure you lock your doors, everyone."

"Oh we will," said Ellery, looking briefly at the front entrance. "Even I'm afraid to die."

SIX

The Third Day on the Mainland

Dusk was approaching.

The sea was turning dark. Kawaminami was standing on an embankment, peering at the faraway shape of an island floating in the sea. Shimada's lean body was crouching on a flight of steps leading down to the water. He was chatting to some children who were fishing there.

They had finally come here—to S— Town.

Could Nakamura Seiji still be alive? They had come in the hope of finding a clue that could support the theory they had arrived at last night. They had also wanted to take a look at Tsunojima.

But after half a day spent questioning local people and fishermen, all they had unearthed was a bunch of ghost stories. Having discovered nothing that could further their investigation, the two had come to this place down by the harbour to relax a little.

Kawaminami put a cigarette to his lips, sat down and stretched his legs. He watched Shimada and listened to the waves rolling in. Dressed in blue jeans and a green bomber jacket, casting with the fishing rod lent to him by the kids, laughing in his childish voice, Shimada didn't seem like a man in his late thirties at all.

Strange guy, Kawaminami thought. Then he recalled how the discussion last night between Shimada and Morisu had unexpectedly taken an awkward turn, and let out a deep sigh.

Shimada and Morisu had completely opposite personalities, in a way. If Morisu was yin, then Shimada was yang. In the eyes of the serious and introverted Morisu, Shimada, who simply followed his own interests and instincts, must have seemed an inconsiderate busybody. And Shimada was a lot older than Kawaminami and Morisu. That must have rubbed him up the wrong way, too. Shimada in turn seemed to be disappointed by Morisu's goody-two-shoes act, which threatened to spoil his fun.

"Mr Shimada, isn't it about time to go?" Kawaminami stood up and yelled to him. "The trip back will probably take another hour."

"Let's go then."

Shimada gave the children their fishing rod back and waved goodbye. His long legs brought him back to Kawaminami in a few steps.

"You seem to like children."

"Well, yes," Shimada said without any hesitation. "Don't you think it's wonderful to be young?"

The two walked side by side along the path next to the embankment.

"We didn't discover anything today," said Kawaminami.

"Oh, really?"

Shimada grinned.

"We gathered some ghost stories, didn't we?"

"Those are just the sort of rumours you hear everywhere. Stories like that always go round when people die under unusual circumstances."

"I disagree. No matter how strange it may sound, I think that the truth might be hidden somewhere in those stories."

A swarthy, well-built young man was repairing a net on the side of the road with expert fingers. He was probably not even twenty. There was something childlike about his enthusiasm for the job in hand.

"You know, Conan," Shimada said, "I can only hope that your comrades—no, ex-comrades—don't fall under the spell of the Tsunojima ghost."

"What do you mean?"

"I mean that the ghost of Tsunojima might well be none other than the man thought to be dead, Nakamura Seiji. Perhaps Seiji is still alive and on the island. And your ex-comrades unwittingly paid him a visit."

"But that's—"

"Sorry." A voice they didn't know interrupted them. Surprised, they turned around. It was that of the young man repairing the net.

"You friends of those students who went to the island?" the young man asked in a loud voice, his hands still holding the net.

"Yes," answered Shimada immediately. He walked up to the man. "Do you know them?"

"Father and I took them to the island. We're going to pick them up again next Tuesday."

"That's interesting," said Shimada enthusiastically, and crouched down next to the man. "Was there anything strange about the group that went to the island?"

"Not really. They were all excited to be going out there. Don't know what's so interesting about that island though."

The young man spoke bluntly, but his eyes, fixed on Shimada, seemed friendly. He ran his hand through his short hair and spoke again, showing his bright white teeth.

"You trying to find something about them ghost stories?"

"Ah, yes. Something like that. Have you seen the ghost?"

"No. That's just a rumour. I don't believe in no monsters."

"Ghosts and monsters are different things."

"That so?"

"You know who the ghost is?"

"That Nakamura Seiji guy, right? They say his wife's haunting the place too."

"Well then, have you never considered the possibility that Seiji might still be living on the island?"

The young man raised an eyebrow in surprise.

"Still living? Didn't he die? That's why he's a ghost."

"He might not have died," Shimada said gravely. "For example, that story about the lights going on in the Decagon House: it might be Seiji himself who puts on the lights there. Those stories of people seeing Seiji—isn't it more sensible to suppose that he's really still alive, rather than that they saw his ghost? I also heard a motorboat sank near the island. What if Seiji killed those fishermen and sank the boat because he had been seen?"

"You're a funny lot." The young man chuckled in amusement. "But you're wrong about the boat. 'Cause I saw the boat get turned over."

"What?"

"The waves that day were high, you see, and I happened to be here when they were getting ready to go out, so I warned them. I told them it was dangerous and there was nothing but small fish to find around that island. But they didn't listen and went off. And they had just left here and hadn't even come close to the island when a high wave caught them. Old folk might say a ghost sank the boat, but that was just an accident.

"And you said the ghost killed the fishermen, but in truth nobody died. All the men on the boat were saved."

Kawaminami, who was standing listening to the two men, suddenly burst out laughing. Shimada pouted his lips.

"Then I'll take back the thing about the boat. But still, I think that Seiji might be alive."

"Alive and living on the island, you mean?" asked Kawaminami. "What's he eating, then?"

"He could have a motorboat hidden somewhere. He could leave the island sometimes to get provisions."

"Well now," the young man looked doubtful.

"You think it's impossible?"

"I guess it's possible if he came up at the other side of J— Cape in the night. Nobody goes out there. But if he just tied his boat there, somebody might discover it, don't you reckon?"

"He probably hides the boat somehow. Anyway, as long as there's no storm you could get to shore in a motorboat, couldn't you?"

"Yeah. With the weather right now, you could manage with a dinghy with an outboard motor, even."

"I see, I see."

Shimada hummed happily and jumped up.

"Thank you very much. Yes, I learnt something good."

"Really? You're a funny one," laughed the man.

Shimada waved to the young man and walked to the car parked further down the road. Kawaminami ran after him.

Shimada grinned. "Great catch we made, don't you think, Conan?"

Kawaminami was not sure what part of Shimada's discussion with the fisherman could be called a "great catch". But he was sure Shimada wasn't ready to abandon the theory of Nakamura Seiji still being alive.

"Yes, right," he agreed half-heartedly.

But whatever he's thinking, Kawaminami thought, looking at the lingering sun above the sea on the other side of the embankment, *they're out there on that island now. Ah well, what's the worst that could happen?*

The black shadow of Tsunojima melted silently into the twilight.

SEVEN

The Fourth Day on the Island

1

The sound of people talking.

The voices were not loud, nor did they come from close by. Familiar tones, familiar intonations. And, as background music, the constant pounding of waves. Waves? Yes, the sound of waves…

Slowly, he was dragged out of sleep. And then…

He opened his eyes and awoke on top of the hard bed. His hands searched for his glasses and he turned to lie on his back. He put the glasses on and a white ceiling came into focus. He sighed wearily.

I'm in the Decagon House.

His throbbing temples ached. With each beat, things he didn't care to remember flashed through his mind.

Moving his tender head slowly, he got out of bed and put on his clothes, fumbling with the buttons on his shirt. Then he went over to the window and untied the belt that held both handles in place. He unlocked the window and pushed it open, together with the shutters.

The overgrown lawn. The leaning pine trees. The dark, inky sky.

He stretched his arms and managed to take a deep breath. After inhaling some fresh air he closed the window, locked it once again and tied the belt around the handles. Then he finally left his room.

Ellery and Van were the people he had heard talking in the hall. Agatha and Poe were also already up and standing in the kitchen.

"Morning, Leroux. I'm glad to see you're all right," Ellery said without any hint of humour, pointing at something behind Leroux.

"What?"

Leroux turned round, pushed his glasses up his nose and saw, to his surprise:

The Second
Victim

The plate was on the door of Carr's room.

It was hanging at eye level, covering Carr's own nameplate, exactly like the one on Orczy's door.

"Our murderer is a reliable fellow," said Ellery. "Glad he went to all that trouble for us."

Leroux backed away, turned around, and looked at Ellery, who was sitting on one of the chairs with his long legs crossed.

"You returned the remaining plates to the cupboard drawer, I assume?" Leroux asked.

"Yes," replied Ellery. "You're going to suggest we get rid of them, I suppose?"

Ellery put the plates from the drawer on the table and slid them towards Leroux. There were six of them.

"But…"

"Yes, as you can see, the plate of 'the Second Victim' is still there. The murderer seems to be well prepared. Figured we'd keep an eye on these plates after the first murder. Probably has another set of the same plates. Also—keep this a secret from Agatha…"

Ellery lowered his voice to a whisper and beckoned Leroux to come closer.

"A secret?" Leroux muttered. "Why?"

"She might become very agitated if we don't break it to her gently. We found it before she got up, so Van, Poe and I talked it over and decided to hide it."

"Hide what?"

"What do you think?"

"I've no idea."

"It was Poe who found it. He woke up around noon and, after washing his face, he happened to take a look at the bath unit in the back…"

"There was something there?"

"Yes. Inside the bathtub. A hand covered in blood."

"What?!"

Leroux clapped his hand to his mouth.

"O-Orczy's?"

"No, you're wrong there. It wasn't Orczy's hand."

"But then whose?"

"It was Carr's. Carr's left hand was cut off and placed there."

"No way."

"The murderer probably waited for all of us to fall asleep and did it this morning. We didn't lock the door to Carr's room. Anyone could have sneaked in and cut off the hand."

"And where's the hand now?"

"We put it back in Carr's bed. We can't count on the police coming here any time soon and we couldn't just leave it there either."

"But why…" Leroux put his fingers to his throbbing temples. "But why would the murderer do such a thing?"

"Why indeed."

"Is it an 'allusion' again? But even so…"

Agatha and Poe came out of the kitchen and prepared the table. Spaghetti, potato salad and soup.

Leroux sat down and looked at his wristwatch. It was already three o'clock in the afternoon.

He had only eaten once yesterday. He should have been starving, but he had no appetite at all.

"Leroux, Poe kept an eye on me all the time, so you can just enjoy your meal without any worries. I also washed all of the tableware again. Or do you think Poe and I are in this together?" said Agatha sarcastically. She had probably hardly slept. Her lightly made-up face showed signs of fatigue. Her rose-pink lips, too, had lost their usual colour.

2

After lunch the five headed out to the ruins of the Blue Mansion together.

The plot on which the mansion had stood was about eighteen metres along each side and completely black, being covered with ashes and bricks.

It was surrounded by dark-green pines interspersed with dead brown trees. The sky was thick with clouds and the dark, shadowy sea came and went down below.

The place was as dark and gloomy as something out of a scary fairy tale.

The cliff to the west of the Blue Mansion overlooking J— Cape was not very high. The line of pine trees around the mansion was broken by a small path leading to a narrow concrete flight of steps, which in turn led down to a rocky area beneath the cliff.

Four of the group stood at the crest, looking out for boats passing near the island, while the fifth member of the party walked around the ashes and bricks on his own. It was Ellery. As he walked, he poked at the bricks scattered here and there with his feet, inspecting the debris. Then he crouched down suddenly.

"What're you doing, Ellery?" Van called over to him. Ellery raised his head and smiled.

"Looking for something."

"Looking for what?"

"I told you last night, didn't I? An underground room. I was just thinking that there might be one here."

The others exchanged quizzical glances, then slowly walked towards Ellery, who was still crouching amid the bricks.

"There," Ellery murmured as he placed his hand on a filthy pitch-black piece of wood about one metre square. "It looks as though this has been moved."

It appeared to have been part of the burnt wall once, and some parts of it were still covered by blue tiles. Ellery tried to lift it and it came up surprisingly easily.

"Found it," Ellery cried out joyfully.

There it was, a square black hole. A narrow, concrete staircase led down into darkness. This was certainly the entrance to the underground room of the burnt-down Blue Mansion.

Ellery flipped the piece of wood over, impatiently grabbed the torch he had brought from the pocket of his jacket and stepped into the tunnel.

"Watch out. It might collapse," said Poe anxiously.

"I know, I'll be ca—"

Ellery's answer was cut short. His body suddenly jerked forward. With a brief cry he fell down, as if he were being sucked into the darkness.

"Ellery!"

"Ellery?"

"Ellery!"

"You all right, Ellery?"

The remaining four cried out simultaneously. Van jumped forward and made to follow Ellery into the hole.

"Wait, Van. It's dangerous going in like that."

Poe held him back firmly.

"But Poe—"

"I'll go first."

Poe threw away the cigarette between his fingers, searched the pocket of his jacket and pulled out a penlight. He put his foot on the staircase, carefully illuminating the inside of the hole.

"Ellery!"

He yelled, but there was no reply. He bent his large body forward and went down two steps. He stopped suddenly.

"But this is…" Poe growled. "There's a thread strung across here. Ellery must have tripped over it."

The thin, strong thread was approximately at shin height to an adult, strung between what appeared to be pipes running down both sides of the steps. It was almost invisible unless you looked very carefully.

Poe cautiously stepped over the obstacle and hastened down the staircase. In the dark in front of him he could see a yellow halo. It was Ellery's torch.

"Van, Leroux, come down here. Be careful of the thread—Ellery?"

Ellery was lying at the foot of the stairs. Poe picked up the torch lying on the floor and shone it on the feet of the two coming down after him.

"Ellery, are you all right?"

"I'm OK," answered Ellery, still stretched out on the concrete floor. But then he groaned and grabbed his right ankle.

"I think it's sprained."

"Did you hit your head?"

"Don't know."

Van and Leroux joined them.

"Give me a hand," Poe ordered them, and took Ellery's arm.

"Wait, Poe," said Ellery as he got up gingerly. "I'm fine, honestly. Let's just take a look at this underground room."

Leroux took the torch from Poe and scanned the room.

The underground room was big—about fifty square metres. The four walls, the ceiling and the floor were all just bare concrete, with pipes running along them. In the back stood a big machine, probably a generator, but there was nothing of interest besides that. Some wooden planks of all sizes, dirty bottles and cans, a bucket, some rags… The room contained only junk.

"As you can see, Ellery, nothing out of the ordinary here," said Leroux.

"Nothing at all?" Ellery muttered. He stood supported by Poe and Van and had followed the light of the torch with his eyes. He appeared to have made a swift recovery.

"There can't be nothing. Check the floor, Leroux."

Leroux did as he was told and cast the light on the floor again.

"Ah, look at that."

They were looking at an arc-like area of two metres' radius, near the staircase where the four were standing. It was completely free of any of the junk that lay in the rest of the room. And, curiously, there was no dust or ash inside the arc either.

"Now that's what I call odd. As if somebody wiped this part clean."

A strange smile appeared on Ellery's pale face.

"Someone was here."

3

"Doesn't appear to be that bad. And you don't seem to have hit your head," said Poe as he treated Ellery's right ankle. "A sprained ankle and some bruises and scratches. One night with a poultice should do the trick. Unbelievable, how lucky you are. You could have been killed."

"I must have instinctively broken my fall," said Ellery, biting his lip. "But it was a real blunder on my part. I was too careless. I walked straight into *his* trap."

The five had returned to the Decagon House.

Ellery was sitting with his back against the wall, his leg outstretched on the floor as Poe treated the ankle. The other three watched, too nervous to simply sit down in their chairs.

"We'd better fasten the hall doors from the inside. And nobody should go outside, especially after dark. Someone is out there, trying to get us."

"But Ellery, I simply can't believe it."

Agatha seemed confused. She'd been told Ellery's theory of Nakamura Seiji being the murderer when they arrived back from the Blue Mansion.

"Can Nakamura Seiji really still be alive?"

"The underground room just now is enough evidence, I think. At least, it proves someone was there until recently. He guessed that we would find out about the underground room and try to enter it. That's why he laid a trap like that on the stairs. If I hadn't been so lucky, I'd be the 'the Third Victim' by now."

"OK, all done, Ellery."

Poe tapped Ellery's freshly bandaged ankle lightly.

"Don't move about too much tonight."

"Thanks, Doctor… Where are you going?"

"There's just something I want to check."

Poe walked across the main hall and disappeared through the doors leading to the entrance hall. He was back within a minute.

"Precisely as I thought. Sorry," he said to Ellery with a grim voice.

"What's the matter?"

"That thread. Turns out it's mine."

"Yours? What do you mean?"

"Fishing line. My fishing gear has been in the entrance hall since the first day. A roll of my stoutest line is gone."

"Oh, so that's what it was." Ellery leant back against the wall, clasping his arms around his raised knee. "There's no lock on the front door. So anyone, whether it's Seiji or anyone else, can come and go whenever they want. Nothing easier than for them to steal a roll of fishing line."

"But Ellery…" Poe sat down on a chair and lit a cigarette. "I don't think you should assume that Seiji is alive and that he's the murderer."

"You think I'm wrong?"

"I don't say your theory is completely impossible, but at the moment, I don't think we can judge whether the murderer is someone from outside or not. That's my objection."

"Hmm."

Still leaning against the wall, Ellery looked up at Poe's bearded face.

"It seems like our Doctor Poe hopes the murderer is one of us."

"I don't hope anything. But I do think that it's more likely. That's why, Ellery, I suggest going over all of our rooms together."

"An inspection of personal belongings, eh?"

"Yes. We know the murderer must be in possession of another set of those plates, Orczy's left hand, some kind of knife and maybe some remaining poison."

"Good suggestion. But Poe, if you were the murderer, would you hide incriminating stuff like that in your own room? There are plenty of safer hiding places elsewhere."

"But still, just to be sure."

"Hey, Poe," Van said. "Wouldn't it be even more dangerous if we made a search?"

"Dangerous?"

"Suppose the murderer is really one of us five, then he would be with us as we searched the rooms. We'd be giving the murderer an easy chance to get into the others' rooms."

"Van's right." Agatha spoke up. "I don't want anyone to come inside my room. The murderer might hide those plates or something else in one of the rooms. Or lay some kind of trap."

"Leroux, what do you think?" Poe asked with a grimace.

"I just can't stand this Decagon House any longer."

Leroux stared down at the floor, shaking his head slowly.

"It's like someone said earlier. That their eyes hurt just from looking at the walls. It's not just the eyes. My head gets all dizzy looking at them…"

"Are you after the salt? You just put it over there," said Van to Agatha, who, having tasted the soup, was looking around with a small plate in her hands.

"You keep such a good eye on me," replied Agatha, wide-eyed. "Nothing gets past you!"

She had replied sarcastically, but there was no strength in her voice. The bags beneath her eyes were getting bigger.

They were in the kitchen of the Decagon House.

Dimly lit by the lamp they had brought from the hall, Agatha was busy preparing a meal, while Van watched over her every movement. The other three were in the hall, occasionally glancing at the kitchen through the open doors.

Agatha bustled around the kitchen, trying to get the business of the murderer out of her head, but she was finding it hard to concentrate. She was looking around the kitchen again.

"The sugar's over here, Agatha," said Van finally. Agatha shuddered and glared at him.

"That's enough," she cried, putting her hands to the scarf that tied her hair. "If you're so afraid to eat what I cook, you can go eat from a can for all I care."

"Agatha, I didn't mean it like that."

"Enough!"

Agatha picked up a small plate and threw it at Van. The plate grazed his arm and hit the refrigerator behind him, breaking into pieces. The disturbance brought the other three running to the kitchen.

"I know I'm not the murderer," Agatha cried, both fists clenched tight and shaking like a leaf. "The murderer is one of you four, I know it. But you still have someone watch me? I tell you, I'm not the murderer!"

"Agatha!"

Ellery and Poe raised their voices simultaneously.

"What? Even with your guard posted here, if someone is poisoned again you'll all blame me anyway! You're all here to make a murderer out of me!"

"Calm down, Agatha," said Poe sternly as he took a step towards her. "Nobody wants to do that. Pull yourself together."

"Don't come any closer."

Agatha stepped back, her eyes flashing with fear.

"Stay away—I get it, you're all in this together. The four of you killed Orczy and Carr. And now it's my turn!"

"Agatha, come to your senses."

"If that's what you want, I'll become your murderer. Yes. If I'm 'the Murderer', I won't become a victim. Ah, poor Orczy, wretched Carr—yes, yes, I am the murderer. I killed the two of them. And now I'll kill the rest of you!"

It took the four of them to hold her down. Agatha had completely lost control and was swinging her arms and kicking her legs wildly. They dragged her back to the hall and put her on a chair.

"I can't take any more of this."

Agatha's shoulders sagged and she stared into space with dead eyes. Her trembling body slumped down on the table.

"I beg of you, I want to go home. I'm tired. I—I want to go back home."

"Agatha."

"I'm going. I'm going home. I'll swim back…"

"Agatha, stay calm. Take a deep breath." Poe put his large hand on Agatha's back and tried to calm her.

"Agatha, nobody is accusing you of murder. Nobody is going to kill you."

Like an unwilling child, Agatha was still resting her head on the table. Gradually her mumbling of "I'm going home, I'm going home" died away and turned to sobbing.

After a long while, she suddenly raised her head. And, in a monotone, husky voice, said: "I need to finish the dinner."

"That's OK. Somebody else will do it. You go and rest."

"No." Agatha pushed Poe's hand away. "I'm not the murderer."

5

Nobody spoke during the meal.

If anybody had opened their mouth, they would inevitably have talked about the case. The silence was an escape from the threatening reality. Perhaps the silence was also born out of fear of provoking Agatha, who was still in a state of shock.

"We'll clean up, so go and rest, Agatha," said Poe softly. Agatha usually avoided smoking in front of other people, but now she was staring blankly at the smoke rising from her cigarette.

"I've got some tablets if you have trouble sleeping. Just take them and go to bed."

Wariness flashed in Agatha's eyes.

"Tablets? No way!"

"It's OK, it's just sleeping pills."

"No, I won't take them."

"OK then—watch carefully, Agatha."

Poe opened the leather bag which was hanging from the back of his chair, and took out a little medicine bottle. He dropped two white tablets into the open palm of his hand, broke them in half, then gave half of each tablet to Agatha.

"Now I'll take the remaining two halves right in front of your eyes. Then will you trust me?"

Agatha stared silently at the tablets in her hand and finally nodded slowly.

"OK, great."

A clumsy smile appeared on Poe's bearded face and he swallowed the tablets in his hand.

"See, nothing wrong with me. Now you too, Agatha."

"I just can't sleep. I just can't."

"It's natural—it's because you're all worked up now."

"This morning I could still hear Carr's cry in my mind. I had finally started to doze off, when I heard something strange from the room beside mine, from Carr's room."

"I know. Just take those tablets, you'll have a good rest tonight."

"Really?"

"Yes, really. You'll fall asleep in no time."

Agatha finally put the tablets in her mouth, closed her eyes and swallowed them.

"Thank you."

Her lifeless eyes looked at Poe.

"Goodnight, Agatha. Don't forget to lock your door and window."

"Yes. Thanks, Poe."

After Agatha had disappeared into her room, the remaining four collectively uttered something resembling a sigh of relief.

"Impressive bedside manner, Poe. You'll make a great doctor."

Ellery smiled, waving the hand which held a cigarette between his thin fingers.

"How surprising to see someone like our Dame Agatha act that way. Maybe one of us will become your patient, too, tomorrow."

"Shut up, Ellery. You're taking this too lightly."

171

"I need to take this lightly." Ellery shrugged. "If I take it too seriously, I might be the next to lose it. I was nearly killed today, remember?"

"What if that was all just a one-man performance?"

"What do you... Ah, I guess there's no point getting all worked up over it. But of course, Agatha could be acting too."

"If the murderer is among us, they could be anyone," said Van, biting his nails.

"Only each one of us knows whether they're guilty or not. So we need to look out for ourselves."

"Yes, you're right... Why did all this happen anyway?" Leroux threw his glasses on the table and held his head.

"Hey, you're not going to get all hysterical on us as well, I hope?"

"I don't have the energy for that, Ellery. But why did the murderer start this insanity? Whether the murderer is one of us or Nakamura Seiji, what in Heaven's name could the motive be?"

Leroux's face, with its small round eyes, was full of despair.

"The motive, eh?" Ellery muttered. "There has to be something."

"I don't believe the 'Seiji equals murderer' theory," said Van irritably. "Nakamura Seiji is only alive inside Ellery's imagination. Even if it were true, it's like Leroux says, what motive could he have for killing us? This isn't a game."

"Seiji," whispered Leroux. Every time he heard or spoke the name he could feel a strange sense of creeping uneasiness. It had been with him ever since Ellery told him yesterday that Seiji might still be alive.

The reflection of the lamp flame danced in his glasses, which were lying on the table. Staring at them, he tried to retrieve *something* from this feeling of uneasiness.

A memory.

But he couldn't remember. And before long, another, more recent memory started to nag at him too, which perturbed him even more.

What was it? Leroux kept asking himself.

The newer memory had to be about something occurring after they had arrived on the island. He had seen something somewhere, subconsciously, something extremely important…

"Poe."

The headache he had endured since waking up was still throbbing.

Let's give up for today and go to sleep, Leroux thought.

"Could I have a sleeping tablet too?"

"Sure. It's just seven—already going to bed?"

"Yes, I have a headache."

"I should go too."

Poe gave the whole bottle of tablets to Leroux and casually stood up with a cigarette in his mouth.

"I'm starting to feel the tablets I took just now, too."

"Could I have one as well?" asked Van, slowly getting up from his chair.

"Sure. One's enough. They're quite strong. And you, Ellery?"

"Don't need them. I can fall asleep all by myself."

And after a little while the lamp on the table went out, and darkness descended upon the hall of the Decagon House.

EIGHT

The Fourth Day on the Mainland

1

"Is it really all right for me to come along?" asked Kawaminami again.

They were sitting in the car heading from O— City to Kamegawa. Shimada, who was holding the steering wheel, kept his eyes front as he nodded several times.

"Really. You knew Chiori and you're also one of the 'victims' of those threat letters. Besides, having come this far, you wouldn't want to be left out of the investigation, would you?"

"That's true."

He couldn't forget about the warning Morisu Kyōichi had given them two nights earlier.

Was it all right for them to invade other people's privacy just to satisfy their own curiosity?

Shimada said that he and Kōjirō were much closer than Kawaminami and Morisu seemed to think. He added that Morisu's ideas and attitude might be a bit too stuffy.

Kawaminami knew what Shimada thought. To be honest, Kawaminami didn't like Morisu's sudden change of attitude either, despite the help he'd happily provided at the start of their deduction game. Nevertheless, Kawaminami felt reluctant and even guilty about making such an informal visit to Kōjirō once again, a mere three days after his first.

"If you're really so against this, Conan, then just pretend we became best of friends these last three days. So now you're doing this for your best friend, even though you don't want to. Is that better?" said Shimada with a straight face. *He's really a strange person*, thought Kawaminami.

It wasn't just that he was brimming with curiosity. Kawaminami was certain that this man had powers of observation and insight that far surpassed his own. When Morisu had advanced the theory that Nakamura Seiji was still alive, it appeared that Shimada had already thoroughly considered the possibility.

The decisive difference between Morisu and Shimada was that while Morisu was, in a way, a strangely conservative realist, Shimada was like a dream-gazing child, a sort of romantic. He would let his imagination run wild on any real case that interested him and if he found a possibility he thought interesting, he'd start to weave it into his dream. At least that was how it seemed to Kawaminami.

And perhaps that was why, to Shimada, the question of whether his "dream" corresponded to reality was of secondary, even tertiary, importance.

The car left the National Route and they drove through familiar city streets.

The characteristic smell of hot springs mingled with the wind flowing in through the half-open window of the passenger side. It was often described as "the smell of rotten eggs", but Kawaminami didn't mind the smell of hydrogen sulphide.

They arrived at Kōjirō's house just after three o'clock in the afternoon.

"He should be here today," Shimada muttered, standing in front of the gate. "The high school he works at is already on spring holiday and besides, it's Saturday. He doesn't go out much in his free time either."

"Didn't you call him to say we're coming?" asked Kawaminami, to which Shimada shook his head.

"Kō, you know, he likes surprise visits."

"Oh."

"Odd, right? Depends on who's coming, of course. But as I'm a close friend..." Shimada winked and laughed.

The garden that Yoshikawa Sei'ichi had so often come from Ajimu to tend was still full of blooming flowers. Above the roof, branches with buds of cherry blossom were visible from behind the house. As they walked up the stone steps, the brittle petals of a spiraea sprinkled their shoulders.

This time, the doorbell was answered immediately.

"Oh, it's you, Shimada. And you too... Kawaminami, if I remember correctly?"

Kōjirō was dressed sharply today as well. Black slacks, a shirt with black stripes and a light coffee-brown Aran cardigan.

Kōjirō led the two of them to the same sitting space in the back, with no sign of surprise at Kawaminami's presence.

Shimada dropped down into the rattan chair on the veranda. Kawaminami waited for Kōjirō to offer him a seat, and let his body sink into one of the sofas.

"So what's up today?" Kōjirō asked while he was preparing tea.

"There was something we wanted to ask you."

Shimada leant forward in the rocking chair, his elbows on his knees.

"But before I do that, where were you two days ago?"

"Two days ago?" Kōjirō looked questioningly at Shimada. "I've been home every day the last few days. School's on vacation."

"Really? We stopped by two days ago, on the night of the 27th, but you didn't answer the door."

"Ah, I have to apologize for that. I have a deadline for a thesis and I've been pretending not to be at home to visitors and people who call on the phone alike these past two or three days."

"Is that any way to treat a friend?"

"Sorry—if I had known it was you, I would have let you in."

Kōjirō handed them the teacups and sat down on the sofa across from Kawaminami.

"And what did you have to ask me? Kawaminami is here too, so I assume it's connected to those prank letters signed with my brother's name?"

"Yes. But today we're here on a slightly different matter."

Shimada took a breath and continued.

"Actually, we want to ask something private about the late Chiori."

The hand that held Kōjirō's cup of tea stopped in mid-air.

"About Chiori?"

"I'm going to ask you a very weird question, Kō. You can punch me if you think it's unforgivable."

And then Shimada asked straight out.

"Was Chiori perhaps your daughter?"

"Nonsense. What kind of question is that?"

Kōjirō replied instantly, but Kawaminami had noticed that for one brief moment his face had turned pale.

"So I'm wrong."

"Of course you are."

"Hmm."

Shimada stood up from the rattan chair and moved to a seat next to Kawaminami. Kōjirō, still angry, crossed his arms. Shimada's eyes stayed fixed on him as he continued:

"I know it's an insulting question. You're angry, of course. But Kō, I need to know. Chiori was your and Kazue's daughter, wasn't she?"

"That's enough of your nonsense. Where's your evidence?"

"I don't have any evidence. But all sort of facts are whispering it to me."

"Stop it."

"I went to Ajimu with Conan here two days ago. To meet with the wife of the missing Yoshikawa Sei'ichi."

"Yoshikawa's wife? What for?"

"Those threatening letters incited us to find out more about the incident that happened on Tsunojima last year. And the conclusion we finally arrived at is that Nakamura Seiji is still alive and the one behind it all."

"Impossible. My brother is dead. I saw the body."

"A completely burnt body, I think?"

"Yes."

"That was Yoshikawa Sei'ichi's body. Seiji was the real murderer and, after he had killed Kazue and the Kitamura couple, he burned Yoshikawa's body in place of his own. Seiji's still alive."

"You're as imaginative as always. And I guess it was this imagination of yours that linked me with my sister-in-law?"

"Yes," Shimada continued without reservation. "Supposing Seiji was the murderer, what could it have been that drove him to commit those murders? You once told me, Kō, that your brother loved Kazue passionately, but his fixation on her was not normal. You said that the real reason he had withdrawn to the island at such a young age was that he wanted to keep Kazue all for himself, that *he wanted to keep her on the island*. For him to kill the wife he loved so much, there's only one motive I can think of: *jealousy*."

"But why jump to the conclusion that my sister-in-law and I had an affair?"

"Yoshikawa's wife told us that Seiji didn't love his daughter all that much. But it's a fact he loved Kazue very passionately. So why

178

didn't he love Chiori, the fruit of his and Kazue's marriage? It's a contradiction. Isn't that evidence that Seiji at least suspected he wasn't Chiori's father?"

"My brother could be a bit strange."

"Even if he was strange, he was still a person who loved his wife. There had to be a reason for him not to love the daughter his wife bore him," said Shimada decisively, before continuing: "And so, if we assume this hypothesis to be true, then who is Chiori's real father? Several facts point to you, Kō. A young man who could come into contact with Kazue even though she was confined to the island. And there's the fact that you and your brother had a falling out around the time of Chiori's birth—"

"You're completely wrong. I've had enough of you, Shimada. I deny everything. Nothing like that ever happened," said Kōjirō angrily, as he removed his horn-rimmed glasses. "And I'll say this again: my brother isn't alive. He's dead. And I have nothing to do with that case."

Kōjirō said this resolutely, but his eyes avoided Shimada's gaze and the hand on his knee was trembling slightly.

"Then I have one more thing to ask you, Kō," said Shimada. "On the 19th of September of last year, the day before the Blue Mansion went up in flames—do you remember?—you called me to have a drink, even though you hardly ever touch alcohol. We went from one bar to another and you got dead drunk. To me, you seemed like a man trying to drink away his pain."

"So? What are you trying to say?"

"You were completely drunk and, finally, you started to cry. You probably don't remember any more. I got you back home, and we both fell asleep on these sofas here. Kō, you were muttering as you cried, 'Kazue, forgive me, forgive me' over and over."

"No..."

The colour in Kōjirō's face changed visibly. Shimada didn't stop.

"I didn't think too much of it at the time. I'd had quite a few drinks myself. And even after I learnt about what happened on Tsunojima, I didn't immediately think back to that night because I was involved with something troublesome of my own at the time. But now that I do look back…"

Shimada sighed heavily once again.

"*Kō, on the night of the 19th of September, you already knew that something had happened on Tsunojima.*"

"But how…" Kōjirō turned away from Shimada's gaze. "How could I have known something like that?"

"The murderer himself, Seiji, told you."

Shimada's intense gaze remained fixed on Kōjirō.

"Kazue's body was missing the left hand. Seiji had cut it off. I think he sent it to you, Kō. You probably received it on the 19th. You couldn't call the police because you were afraid of scandal, so you tried to drink everything away."

"I, I—"

"I don't know the details about how you and Kazue found each other. I don't need to know. Even if you two were the reason Seiji went mad, I don't think anyone has the right to blame you. But Kō, if you had called the police on the 19th, the lives of the Kitamuras and Yoshikawa might have been saved. Your silence that day was a crime."

"A crime?" muttered Kōjirō, and he suddenly stood up.

"Kō."

"It's OK, Shimada. I've had enough."

Kōjirō turned away from Shimada's gaze and walked to the veranda with dull, lifeless steps.

"That over there," he said and he pointed at the wisteria pavilion in the garden. "I planted that the year Chiori was born."

2

Kawaminami didn't appear to have returned home yet. The lights in his room were out.

Morisu Kyōichi looked at his watch. 10.10 p.m. His friend probably hadn't gone to bed yet though.

He parked his motorbike near the entrance of the apartment building and went into the coffee house on the other side of the road.

The shop was open until 2.00 a.m. At this time of night it was usually full of students who lived nearby but, because of the spring holiday, there were only a few customers dotted about the place.

He took a seat near the window overlooking the road.

He sipped his black coffee and considered leaving once it was finished. After all, it wasn't as if he had to see him. He could always make a call later.

He's always quick to get all fired up, and then lose interest again. By now he's probably had enough of playing detective.

Morisu put a cigarette in his mouth and started to reflect.

It had been the "letter from the dead" that had sparked Kawaminami's interest. The letter was all it had taken to get him started. And, once he had found out that the members of the Mystery Club had gone to the island, he naturally couldn't just sit still. Kawaminami had gone all the way to Beppu to visit Kōjirō and come to him, Morisu, to ask for advice. Usually, the Kawaminami he knew would have started to lose interest around this point. However, it was different this time.

Shimada Kiyoshi's face appeared in his mind.

He wasn't just some curiosity seeker. Shimada had a sharp mind—Morisu could admit that. But his insensitive inquisitiveness, which Shimada seemed to think was acceptable, was something Morisu just couldn't stand.

Of course it was normal to be intrigued by those curious letters. And, considering Shimada's love of detective fiction, it was also natural he would dig into that case that happened last year.

Still, Morisu regretted suggesting a visit to Yoshikawa Sei'ichi's wife. He had made the suggestion without thinking it through. What must Yoshikawa Masako have thought when she was suddenly visited by strangers asking her this and that about her missing husband—whom they also suspected of murder?

Morisu had proposed the theory that Nakamura Seiji might be alive, but realistically speaking it was impossible. It was just a hypothesis he had posed to put an end to a silly detective game being played by a couple of mystery addicts. But then Shimada had turned his attention to the motive behind the Tsunojima incident. He'd focused on the relationship between Kazue and Kōjirō and even suggested that Chiori might have been Kōjirō's daughter. What's more, he was planning to confront Kōjirō himself with that theory.

The smoke in his throat almost hurt. With a gloomy feeling, Morisu took another sip of his bitter coffee.

Thirty minutes had gone by when, just as Morisu was about to leave, a car stopped in front of Kawaminami's building. It was a red Familia. Recognizing the silhouette of the person who got out, Morisu stood up.

"Kawaminami."

He stepped out of the shop and yelled, and Kawaminami waved to him.

"So it was you. I thought the bike looked familiar. There's nobody in my building with anything off-road like that." Kawaminami was looking at the dirty, mud-covered motorbike— a Yamaha XT250—parked by the side of the road. "You came all the way to visit me?"

"No, I was just passing by anyway," Morisu answered, tapping the knapsack hanging from his shoulder and pointing with his chin at the canvas holder set on the bike's rear carrier rack. "I went to Kunisaki again today. On my way home now."

"How's the painting going?"

"I think tomorrow will be the last day. Come and see it when it's finished."

"Hello, Morisu."

Shimada had emerged from the driver's seat and was looking at Morisu with a friendly smile. Morisu's tone suddenly became solemn.

"Good evening. Where did you go today?"

"Just a visit to Kō... No, a little drive to Beppu. You know, I'm getting along so well with Conan. We were planning to have some drinks in his room now."

Morisu and Shimada followed Kawaminami up to his room. He quickly put away the futon which was still lying on the floor, took out his folding table and prepared drinks.

"Morisu, you too?"

"No, I'm fine. I'm on my bike, remember?"

Shimada had headed straight for the bookcase and was looking at the spines of the tightly arranged books.

Watching Kawaminami preparing ice in his glass, Morisu asked:

"And how's the case going?"

"Hmm," Kawaminami answered with a long face. "We went to S— Town yesterday, but we were only able to see Tsunojima from the beach, and to hear a couple of ghost stories."

"Ghost stories?"

"The usual rumours, the ghost of Seiji roaming the island, that sort of thing."

"Oh. And today? You didn't just go up there for a drive, I assume?"

A troubled look appeared on Kawaminami's face and he grimaced.

"Well actually…"

"So you did go to see Kōjirō?"

"Yes. Sorry for ignoring your warning."

Kawaminami stopped mixing the whisky and water and looked down at his friend apologetically. Morisu sighed briefly and leant forward.

"And the result?"

"We know most of what happened last year. Kōjirō told us. Mr Shimada, your drink is ready."

"You mean you know the truth behind the case?" Morisu asked in surprise.

Kawaminami nodded and gulped down his whisky and water.

"And the truth is?"

"*It was a murder–suicide planned by Seiji.*"

And Kawaminami started to talk.

3

"I planted that the year Chiori was born," said Kōjirō, and he shivered slightly.

"The wisteria?"

Shimada cocked his head, puzzled.

"But why?" he started, but then he mumbled "I see" to himself. He turned to Kawaminami, who hadn't understood any of the exchange.

"It's a reference to *The Tale of Genji*, Conan."

"*The Tale of Genji*?"

"Yes—I'm correct, I think?" Shimada asked Kōjirō, who was standing on the veranda. Kōjirō nodded, and Shimada went on.

"Hikaru Genji, who had been deeply in love with his father's wife, Lady Fujitsubo, for many years, finally slept with her for one single night. But she became pregnant, and the two of them had to keep on betraying and deceiving their father and husband after that."

Kōjirō had considered his brother's wife, Kazue, his Lady Fujitsubo.

Chiori, the child born of sin. The birth had brought the two of them closer, but had also torn them apart. His heart, still longing for Kazue, had made him plant that wisteria, because Fujitsubo meant "wisteria pavilion". Lady Fujitsubo never forgot about the sin she had committed with Hikaru Genji, nor did she ever forgive herself. And neither would Kōjirō's lover...

"You always did like that story."

Shimada stood up from the sofa and walked up behind Kōjirō.

"Seiji found out about you, didn't he?"

"No, I think my brother only had suspicions. I think half of him knew something had happened and the other half was trying to deny it," answered Kōjirō, his eyes still fixed on the garden. "My brother had incredible talents, but as a human being, he was lacking something. He loved my sister-in-law passionately, but it was—how to put it—a twisted love, which had been overcome by a longing, a mad desire to keep her all for himself. That's how I looked at it.

"I think my brother knew that himself. He knew that he wasn't a good husband to her. That's why he was always afraid, always suspecting her. I think he felt something close to fear for Chiori. But part of him still tried to believe, wanted to believe

185

Chiori was his own daughter. That part of him that still believed in his bond with his wife was what kept his mind balanced those twenty years.

"But then Chiori died. With the sudden death of his daughter—whom he had always tried to believe in, despite his fears—he lost the one bond that tied him to his wife. My brother was thrown back into a sea of suspicion. He suspected his wife didn't love him, that her heart was elsewhere, that it lay with his own brother. And he brooded, suffered and finally broke… My brother killed her with his own hands."

Kōjirō, his eyes fixed on the new leaves that had grown on the wisteria pavilion, didn't move a muscle.

"What happened on Tsunojima—that was a forced suicide planned by my brother."

"A forced suicide?"

"Yes. That day, on the afternoon of 19th September, I did indeed receive a package from my brother, just as you said. Inside was a bloody left hand, sealed inside a plastic bag. I recognized the ring on the ring finger. I instantly realized what had happened.

"I telephoned the Blue Mansion. My brother answered, as if he had been waiting for me. He said, with neither laughter nor sorrow in his voice: 'The Kitamuras and Yoshikawa died for me too. As a farewell gift for the two of us…'

"He'd gone completely mad. That was all I understood. He didn't listen to anything I said and was talking about how the two of them were heading for a new stage, something about the blessings of the grand darkness, that I needed to take good care of the present he'd sent me. And after going through all that, he hung up the phone.

"There's no way my brother is still alive. Even if the physical evidence says there is a possibility, I say the psychology doesn't allow for it. *He didn't die* because *he had killed my sister-in-law. He couldn't bear to live any more and decided to take her with him.*"

"But Kō—"

"Listen, Shimada, and you too, Kawaminami. Nakamura Seiji is dead. He set himself on fire. The couple of days between him murdering his wife and his own death weren't just to give him time to send her hand to me, for revenge and to have me suffer. They were so he could hold in his arms the body of the wife who had always been too far away to reach in life."

Kōjirō didn't speak again. Looking at his back, it appeared he had become smaller and older.

This figure staring motionlessly at the garden—what, Kawaminami asked himself, was he projecting upon the wisteria pavilion? The image of the murdered woman he had loved? The face of her murderer, his own brother? Or the image of his daughter, who had died in a tragic accident?

It was just as Shimada had said: Kōjirō had been the father of the deceased Chiori. *So the person who had reason to hate the students who drove her to her death was…*

"Kō, I want to ask you one more thing."

Shimada broke the heavy silence.

"What did you do with Kazue's hand? Where is it now?"

Kōjirō didn't say a word.

"Kō, I—"

"I know, you just want to know what really happened. You'll say that you won't tell the police, right? I know, Shimada."

And Kōjirō pointed to the wisteria pavilion once again.

"There. Her hand is buried beneath that tree."

"It was just as you said, Morisu."

Kawaminami put away another whisky and water.

"It may sound rude to Mr Shimada, but we asked things we should never have asked about, I think. It doesn't feel right."

Morisu kept smoking silently.

"Kōjirō said that Nakamura Seiji is dead. I think that's the truth. Now the only problem left is the letters."

"What are your thoughts about the whereabouts of Yoshikawa Sei'ichi?" asked Morisu, also including Shimada in the question.

"Mr Shimada seems to be interested in his disappearance too, but as the body hasn't been found, I think he just fell into the sea and was washed away," replied Kawaminami, and he looked at Shimada, who was sitting with his back leaning on the wall. He was reading a book he had taken from the bookcase, his glass in one hand. Had he, or had he not, been listening to their discussion?

"Anyway"—cheeks red from the alcohol, Kawaminami clapped his two hands softly together—"this is the end of playing detective. Maybe we'll find out who wrote those strange letters when the gang returns from the island next Tuesday."

NINE

The Fifth Day

1

He felt as though he had seen one nightmare after another last night. He couldn't remember what the dreams were about, but he knew he'd cried out in his sleep.

He'd kicked away his blanket, which lay next to his bed now. His shirt had become wrinkled from his restless sleep: he hadn't undressed before getting into bed last night. His body was covered in perspiration, but his throat was completely dry. His lips were cracked and painful.

Leroux sat upright and, arms clutched around his torso, rocked his head slowly from side to side.

His headache had calmed somewhat. But in return, his mind appeared to have stopped working. A light mist seemed to be covering his whole consciousness. The distance between his body and the faculties which commanded it felt further than usual. No sense of reality.

The light that leaked through the gap between the shutters told him that the night was over.

Leroux's heavy arms lifted the blanket up and put it on his lap.

A square screen came down in his foggy head. The four corners were black, the centre white, like an exposed film. On the screen were close-ups of all of the friends with whom he had arrived on the island four days ago.

Ellery, Poe, Carr, Van, Agatha and Orczy. All seven of them, including himself, had been enjoying the prospect of this little adventure, each in their own way. At least, that's how Leroux had felt. Freedom on an uninhabited island. A cold case to pick over. A bit of a thrill. Even if they did have some trouble on the island, it would just add to the fun and make the week pass more quickly, he'd thought. Things had turned out differently though.

Short, thin hair. Big, shifty eyes beneath thin but wide eyebrows. Red cheeks with freckles. Her face suddenly became bloated and purple, it trembled, it twisted and finally her features went slack. The thin cord wrapped around her neck changed into a poisonous, slithering black snake.

Oh, Orczy, Orczy, Orczy...

Leroux clenched his fists and hit himself on the head. *I don't want to remember anything any more.*

But as if someone else were in control, the projector started rolling again. The screen wouldn't go black.

A sardonic laugh, the corners of a mouth twitched into a smile. A badly shaven chin. Big, hollow eyes. Carr was next. His big-boned body twisted in pain. The shaking table. A chair kicked over. The violent convulsions, the vomit and, finally, it was all over.

"Why?"

He whispered.

"Why all of this?"

Ellery falling into the darkness of the underground room. Poe's grim voice. Van's pale face. Agatha's hysterics.

And still there was a murderer among the surviving friends. Or could someone else be hiding on the island?

Ellery had suggested that Nakamura Seiji might still be alive.

Why would a man they'd never met, a man whose face they'd never seen, start killing them?

A black shadow appeared on the screen in his mind. The figure's outline was vague, rippling as if under water.

Nakamura Seiji—the man who had built the Decagon House. The man thought to have been burnt in the Blue Mansion in September of last year. If he were still alive, he would be the one behind the murders now.

Nakamura Seiji... Nakamura... Nakamura.

"Ah."

A gasp escaped from his mouth.

"Nakamura?"

Slowly, the black shadow started to take form. He searched for a thread tied to his memories within the maze of his blurry, half-sleeping mind and the shadow finally changed into a small, fair-skinned woman.

No, it can't be.

Was he still dreaming? Could it really be possible that Nakamura Chiori was the daughter of Nakamura Seiji?

Leroux hit himself with his fists again.

The city at night. The hustle and bustle. The cold wind. The bar of the after-party. The light reflecting from their glasses. The sound of ice. The smell of alcohol. Cheers. Intoxication. Cacophony. Insanity. And then... A sudden lurch from comedy to drama. Confusion. The sound of sirens. The revolving red lights.

"It just can't be," he said more loudly.

He wanted to drown out the threatening hum that grew louder and louder in his ears.

But the hum didn't lessen, only increased in volume until it was a furious buzz. His restless anxiety and impatience made his

191

whole body perspire. The red lights flashed and the sirens wailed, hammering nails into his nerves.

Leroux held his head in his hands. He couldn't handle it any more, he wanted to scream.

Suddenly a different scene was projected on the screen. The noise and light disappeared.

What's this? thought Leroux, regarding the scene from afar.

What's this? Where is this? It's the sea. He could hear the sound. Close by. The smell of the tide. The rippling surface. The waves climbing the black rocks and receding again, leaving behind a white line. This is, this is…

…This happened yesterday.

Leroux pushed his blanket away. His fear had gone, as if the heavy curtains that covered that part of his mind had been lifted.

I saw this yesterday. They were all standing on the cliffs near to the Blue Mansion, looking out for boats. It was the rocky area he had seen then, beneath the cliffs. He had climbed down there with Ellery two days ago, too. If he remembered correctly, at that time he also…

He felt like something had taken possession of him.

He knew he was not completely conscious yet. *It's dangerous to go alone*, he thought for a second, but that thought was quickly engulfed by the fog in his mind.

Leroux slowly got out of bed.

Agatha carefully opened the door and peeked into the hall.

Nobody there. It didn't seem as though anyone was up yet.

She'd had a good night's rest, thanks to Poe's sleeping tablets, sleeping like the dead until she'd woken up moments ago. She didn't remember having any dreams. It had been a satisfying sleep, almost bafflingly so, considering the dangerous situation they were in.

Her body felt rested. Her nerves had also calmed down.

I should thank Poe.

Agatha slowly tiptoed into the hall.

Hugging the wall, she quietly made her way to the bathroom. Her eyes scanned the space carefully, her ears alert for any noise.

Even in the morning light, the hall of the Decagon House appeared distorted. Her eyes were drawn to the strange shadows covering the white walls, preventing her from taking a good look around.

It really seemed as though no one was up yet. She could hear nothing but the relentless noise of the waves.

She entered the bathroom and left the door half open, not forgetting to check the toilet and the bath unit in the back for any surprises.

She stood in front of the dressing table and stared into the mirror. In the gloomy darkness, she saw herself dressed in a white one-piece dress.

The circles beneath her eyes had become less dark. But since coming to the island, her cheeks had become visibly hollow and she looked pale. Coupled with her dull, dry hair, it even made her doubt whether she was really looking at herself.

Agatha sighed as she brushed her hair. Recalling not only the murders but also her own unseemly behaviour the previous night, she sighed again.

She wanted always to be beautiful and dignified. Always, no matter what happened, no matter where she found herself. She had always prided herself on being such a woman.

But the face she had just washed, looking back at her in the mirror…

It wasn't beautiful. Not a hint of dignity.

Nothing to save her.

I should use some brighter make-up, Agatha thought as she opened her make-up pouch. Abnormal murders, abnormal circumstances, abnormal ideas. This was the only consolation she had within this maddening, abnormal reality.

Today I won't use my rose-pink lipstick, but the red one.

She didn't care how the others looked at her any more. All she had on her mind was what she could see in the mirror.

2

Van was woken by the alarm of his wristwatch.

Ten in the morning? Got to get up.

His shoulders were stiff and his joints hurt. He hadn't had as much sleep as he'd hoped. He put his fingers to the eyelids of his puffy eyes. He felt nausea in his stomach.

Are the others still asleep?

He sat upright and listened for any noise as he lit a cigarette. He felt dizzy when the smoke reached his lungs. He knew both his body and mind were completely drained.

Will I be able to make it back home safely?

He stared aimlessly into nothing as he thought the case over in his mind.

If he was honest, he was scared. Incredibly afraid. If he could, he would have burst into tears like a little child and run away back home.

A shudder went through his body, after which Van put his cigarette out and got up.

He went out into the hall and noticed that a door to his left, three rooms away, was half open. It was the bathroom, one door before the kitchen.

Someone's up already, he thought.

But even so, I don't hear anything. Someone probably went to the toilet and forgot to close the door.

The door opened away from the kitchen. Van approached the door from the right, circling the centre table. He couldn't hear anything.

He put his left hand on the back of each of the blue chairs that surrounded the table. He could hear the beat of his heart grow louder. As he came closer, he could see more of the bathroom through the half-open door. And then he saw it.

"Ah!"

Van let out a faint cry, as if he was being strangled. He felt his whole body tremble. He was frozen to the spot.

A white figure was lying beyond the door to the bathroom.

A delicate lace one-piece dress. A thin, lifeless arm extended. Black hair spread across the floor. It was the body of Agatha, totally lifeless.

"A… A…"

Van stood still, his right hand to his mouth. In the back of his throat, the impulse to yell out and the urge to throw up were competing. His voice wouldn't follow his command.

He put a hand on a chair, his body bent double. Then with shaky legs he desperately made his way to Poe's room.

The violent beating on his door made Poe sit up.

"What? What's the matter?"

It only took a moment for him to banish sleep, push his blanket away, roll out of bed and rush to the door.

"Who is it? What's happened?"

There was no answer.

The beating on the door stopped and in its place came a soft whimpering noise. Poe unlocked the door quickly and turned the knob. But something was blocking the door.

"Hello, who's there?"

He put his body weight against the door and pushed it open with his shoulders. He managed to squeeze into the hall through the gap he made.

It was Van who was leaning against the door. Both hands were pressed against his mouth and his back trembled pitifully.

"What's the matter, Van? You OK?"

Poe placed his hand on Van's back. Holding one hand to his mouth, Van pointed with the other hand towards the door of the bathroom adjacent to Poe's room.

"Hmm?"

The door was half open. He couldn't see inside from where he was.

"What is it?"

"A-Agatha…"

Van had not even finished what he was trying to say when Poe cried out, removing his hand from Van's back.

"Agatha? But Van, are you OK?"

Van nodded, still whimpering painfully. Poe reached the bathroom. He peered inside through the half-open door.

"Ellery! Leroux! Wake up! Get up now!" Poe bellowed.

Ellery was awakened by the violent beating on someone's door.

It wasn't his door. He had guessed that something had happened when a deep voice cried out.

That's Poe. That means…

Ellery quickly got out of bed and grabbed his cardigan. His right ankle wrapped in bandages no longer felt as painful as before.

He could still hear Poe. It seemed as if he were talking to Van. Then he then heard him crying out even louder.

"Agatha?"

Even as Ellery put his hand on the doorknob, he could hear Leroux's and his name being called.

"What's the matter?" answered Ellery as he opened the door.

Van was on all fours in front of Poe's room. The door to the right, the door of the bathroom, precisely opposite Ellery's own, was completely open. Was it Agatha who was lying there face down? Poe was beside her, crouching on one knee.

"Has Agatha been murdered?"

"It appears so."

Poe turned around to Ellery.

"Van is feeling bad. Help him throw up."

"Got it."

Ellery went to Van, helped him get up and took him to the kitchen.

"You haven't been poisoned, have you?"

"No, I just suddenly... when I found Agatha..." Van groaned, his head over the sink. Ellery rubbed his back.

"Drink some water. Your stomach is all empty now. There's nothing to throw up."

"I-I'm all right. I'll get it myself. You'd better go to the bathroom."

"OK."

Ellery turned, left the kitchen, and went to Poe in the bathroom.

"Is she dead, Poe?"

Poe closed his eyes and nodded.

"Poison again. Prussic acid, I think."

Poe had turned Agatha's body face upwards. Her eyes were wide open. The expression frozen on her slightly open mouth was one not of pain, but of surprise.

Poe put his hands to her eyelids and closed her eyes, which gave her face an improbably peaceful look. She appeared to have just finished putting on her make-up. Her coloured cheeks gave the illusion of life. Her reds lips seemed as if they would start talking at any moment. The faint, bitter smell hanging in the air was what had led Poe to his suspicion.

"Ah…" Ellery frowned deeply. "So this is the infamous smell of almonds."

"Yes. Anyway, let's carry her to her room."

Van came stumbling from the kitchen just as Poe reached for the body's shoulders. He put his back to the wall and looked across the hall with a blood-drained face.

"Hey, where's Leroux?"

"Leroux?"

"Now you mention him…"

Ellery and Poe noticed the door to Leroux's room for the first time and cried out simultaneously.

┌─────────────────┐
│   The Third   │
│   Victim   │
└─────────────────┘

Attached to the door, the plate with the red characters seemed to be mocking them.

3

"What the!… So Agatha is the *fourth* victim? Leroux!"

Ellery dashed to the door to Leroux's room.

"Leroux, Leroux! No use. Door's locked. Van, don't you have a master key or something?"

"This isn't a hotel, you know."

"Then we'll have to break it down. Ellery, move."

"Wait."

Ellery stopped Poe with a wave of his hand.

"The door opens into the hall. It won't go down easily even if we shoulder-charge it. It's faster to go outside and break the window."

"You're right. Let's take a chair with us."

Poe turned to Van.

"You come too."

"Look, you two," said Ellery, who was on his way to the front entrance. "The rope tied to the doors has been unfastened."

He pointed to the double doors that led to the entrance hall. The rope they had tied to the handles last night had been untied and was hanging down.

"Somebody went outside," said Poe, picking up a chair.

"Perhaps it was Leroux," suggested Van.

"Who knows what's going on?" asked Poe.

Ellery shook his head sombrely.

"Anyway, let's go. There's nothing we can do until we've taken a look inside his room."

Poe raised the chair and swung it with all his might. The shutters had looked sturdy, but after a few blows they managed to pull them out of the wall, hinges and all, and then break the glass window. After that, it was easy to put their hands through the hole and release the latch. But the handles inside the room had also been tied together with a belt and it took them some effort to untie them.

The window was at Van's chest level, and he was of average height. Poe, the tallest of them, stood on top of the broken chair

and went into the room with a nimble dive surprising for someone of such large build. Ellery went next. Van stood beneath the
window, both hands clutching his stomach.

But Leroux was not to be found in his room.

He had gone out and not come back.

The air was damp and sticky. It appeared to have rained during
the night. The grass at their feet was moist and soft.

Poe and Ellery jumped down from the window, their shoulders
heaving as they panted with exertion.

"Let's split up and look for him. I'm afraid we might not find
him alive, though," said Ellery. He crouched with one knee on the
ground, patting the bandages around his right ankle.

"But your ankle…" Poe started. He'd cut the back of his right
hand on some fragments of glass when he'd broken the window.

"I'm fine. I can even run."

Ellery stood up and took a look at Van. Van was crouching
down on the grass, his body shaking.

"Van, you stay here at the entrance until we call for you. You
need to calm down first."

Ellery straightened up and calmly gave out orders.

"Poe, you go down to the inlet. I'll search around here and
the Blue Mansion."

After Ellery and Poe had run off, Van stood up sluggishly and
walked to the entrance of the Decagon House. The sour, bitter
taste of what he had just thrown up was still clinging to his tongue
and wouldn't go away. The need to vomit had receded, but he still
felt something stuck in his chest.

The sky was lead-grey. There was no wind and it was not cold,
yet the shivering of his body underneath his sweater wouldn't stop.

Van's tired feet finally brought him to the front entrance. He sat down on the steps, which were wet from the rain, and curled up, hugging his knees. He took several deep breaths. The feeling in his chest finally went away, but his body kept shuddering occasionally. He stared at the melancholy scenery of shadowy pine trees for a while.

"Van! Poe!"

He could hear Ellery's voice from afar. It came from the right, from the direction of the burnt-down Blue Mansion.

Van got up and, while his legs didn't seem to respond to his wishes, he still managed to force himself into a brief run. He saw how Poe came sprinting from the direction of the inlet. The two met at the opening in the line of pine trees surrounding the burn site.

"Poe, Van, over here."

The two went through the arch of pine trees and saw, near the centre of the front garden, the figure of a waving Ellery, wearing a cardigan over his pyjamas. He was standing in a spot just hidden from sight of the Decagon House by some trees.

The two quickly ran over to Ellery, but were rendered breathless when they saw what lay at his feet.

"He's dead," Ellery blurted out, shaking his head.

Leroux was lying on the ground. He was dressed in a yellow shirt, jeans and a denim jacket with the sleeves rolled up. Both arms were sticking out in front of him, as if he were pointing towards the Decagon House. His face, on its side, was half buried in the black mud. Near his stretched-out right hand lay his beloved round glasses.

"He was beaten to death. Probably hit on the head with one of the rocks or bricks lying around here," said Ellery, pointing at the red and black spot on the back of Leroux's head. An "Ugh" escaped from Van's lips, and he put his hand to his mouth. He was struggling to avoid throwing up again.

"Poe, would you mind examining the body? I know it's difficult, but please."

"Of course."

Poe kept a hand on his forehead, which was covered by locks of hair, as he bent forward next to the body. He lifted the mud- and blood-covered head slightly and looked into the corpse's face. Leroux's round eyes were wide open in surprise. His tongue was sticking out from the corner of his mouth. It might have been from fear or pain, but the expression on Leroux's face was incredibly distorted.

"*Livor mortis*," said Poe in a suppressed voice. "But the spots go away when I press on them. *Rigor mortis*… Hmm, quite advanced. The stiffening is also affected by the outside temperature, so I can't say exactly, but, yes, it's somewhere between five or six hours since he died. So…"

He glanced at his wristwatch.

"He was probably killed between five and six this morning."

"So at dawn," Ellery muttered.

"Let's carry Leroux back to the Decagon House first. We can't just leave him here like this," said Poe, and he reached out for the shoulders.

"Ellery, could you carry his legs?"

But Ellery didn't respond even after being called. He was looking silently at the ground, both hands in the pockets of his cardigan.

"Hey, Ellery."

Ellery looked up.

"Footprints…" he muttered, and pointed at the ground.

Leroux was lying roughly ten metres from the pine trees in the direction of the Decagon House, in the middle of the Blue

Mansion garden. The ground at this spot, as well as all of the burn site, was completely black because of the ash. But the rain last night had made the ash-filled ground very soft and footprints had been left here and there.

"Oh, forget it."

Ellery crouched and lifted the body's legs.

"Let's go. It's cold."

The two turned Leroux's body over and lifted him up. The sound of rolling waves provided a dirge mourning Leroux's death.

Van picked up Leroux's dirty glasses. Holding them to his heart, he followed Ellery and Poe on the way back.

4

Arriving at the Decagon House, they first carried Leroux's body to his room. They found his room key in his jacket pocket. Although his clothes were all covered in mud, they laid him down on the bed.

Van placed the glasses he had picked up on the bedside table.

"Could you fetch me a basin with some water? And a towel. We should at least clean his face," said Ellery to Van, as he covered the body with a blanket. Van nodded silently and left the room. He still walked shakily, but he seemed to have recovered from the shock. Ellery and Poe then went to retrieve Agatha's body from the bathroom. They carried her to her bed, joined her hands on her chest and straightened her dishevelled hair and clothes.

"So it was prussic acid…" Ellery muttered, as he looked at Agatha, who had entered an eternal sleep. "As they say, the smell of almonds."

"Probably about three hours since she died. So around eight this morning."

Van returned just as Poe gave his estimate.

"This was lying in front of the washstand. It's probably Agatha's," said Van, as he handed over a black pouch.

"A make-up pouch?"

Ellery took the pouch in his hands, seemed to think of something and started to search its contents.

"Van, this pouch: was it closed when you found it?"

"No, it was open. It was on the floor together with some of the contents."

"You put them back? Ah, too late now."

Foundation. Rouge. Hairbrush. Cream. Toner.

"Got it," said Ellery and he pulled out two tubes of lipstick. He pulled the caps off both sticks and compared the colour of each.

"This one."

"Don't put it too close to your nose, it's dangerous stuff," said Poe, correctly guessing what was going on in Ellery's head.

"I know."

One lipstick was red, the other pink. Ellery carefully took a sniff of the red lipstick, nodded and passed it to Poe.

"You're right, Ellery. Appears to be coated in poison."

"Funeral make-up. A white dress for her funeral clothes, and then she was poisoned. Like a princess in a fairy tale."

Ellery took another sad look at Agatha, then suggested they all leave the room. He closed the door silently as he left.

"Sleep well, Snow White."

The three went together to Leroux's room.

They cleaned his face with the water and towel Van had brought. They also cleaned his glasses and placed them on his chest.

"And he was so determined, our editor-in-chief."

With that, Ellery closed the door. The ominous plate with the red characters still proclaimed "The Third Victim".

And then there were only the three of them still alive in the Decagon House: Ellery, Poe and Van.

5

After going back to his room and getting dressed, Ellery sat down on the corner of his bed and took out his Salem cigarettes. After two of them had been turned into ash, he left the room.

The other two were already in the hall.

Poe was examining the bandage he'd put over the wound on the back of his right hand, while smoking another cigarette. Van had brought a kettle with hot water and poured some coffee.

"I'd like some too, Van," said Ellery.

Van shook his head and, covering his cup with both hands, sat down in a chair away from Poe.

"That's not very nice," said Ellery with a shrug and went into the kitchen.

He carefully washed a cup and a spoon. He also took a look at the drawer of the cupboard. The six plates that had announced the murders were still there.

"'The Last Victim', 'the Detective' and 'the Murderer'," muttered Ellery as he returned to the hall and poured his own coffee. Poe and Van stayed silent. He looked from one to the other.

"Assuming 'the Murderer' is among us, I guess he won't admit to it at this stage?"

Poe frowned and blew out a cloud of smoke. Van turned his head away and sipped his coffee. Ellery sat down on a chair away from both of them, his hands around his cup.

There was a disquieting silence. The three men sat apart from one another in the hall of the Decagon House and did not even try to conceal the distrust they had for each other.

"Can you believe it?" said Poe in an unnatural voice. "One of us here has killed four of our friends."

"It might've been Nakamura Seiji," replied Ellery.

An irritated Poe shook his head.

"I won't say it's absolutely impossible, but I do say you're wrong. I don't even agree with your idea of him being still alive. It's just too incredible."

Ellery snorted.

"So the murderer is one of us?"

"That's what I said."

Poe banged the table angrily. Ellery ignored the gesture and brushed his hair back.

"Let's examine everything from the beginning once again."

He leant back in his chair and looked up at the skylight. The sky was as dark as ever.

"It started with those plates, yes? Someone had to prepare them beforehand and bring them to the island. They don't take up that much space, so it would be easy to bring them along without anyone noticing. So any one of us could have done it. Are we agreed on that?

"But listen. On the morning of the third day, the murderer started to commit the deeds announced by the plates. 'The First Victim' was Orczy. The murderer entered her room through the window or door, and strangled her. Poe, you said the murder weapon, a cord, was still wrapped around her neck. The cord probably won't serve as a meaningful clue. But the first problem we need to look at is *how did the murderer enter Orczy's room*?

"When we found the body, the door and window weren't locked. It's possible that Orczy hadn't locked them in the first place, but I think it's unlikely. Especially the door. It was Orczy who first discovered those plates. She seemed very scared and anxious.

"So what does that leave us with? There are a number of possibilities, but I think we can basically bring it down to two. One: Orczy forgot to lock her window and the murderer came in from there. Two: the murderer woke Orczy up and got her to open the door."

"If the murderer came in through the window, why unlock the door?" asked Van.

"Either to find a plate, or to affix a plate he had already brought to the door. But if we limit ourselves to Poe's idea that the murderer is one of us, then I think we should focus on the hypothesis that Orczy herself opened the door to the murderer.

"Even in the early morning, even if Orczy were still asleep, sneaking into the room through the window would have made some noise. It would have been all over if the murderer had been seen then. If the murderer is one of us in the Mystery Club, he wouldn't have run that risk. It would've made more sense just to wake Orczy up with some excuse and have her let him in peacefully. Orczy was like that. She might have thought it strange, but she wouldn't have said no to one of us."

"But Orczy was still wearing her pyjamas," put in Poe. "Would she have let a man inside dressed like that?"

"She might have. If he'd said it was urgent, she couldn't very well turn him down, even if she'd wanted to. Except for Carr, after their falling out. But going on that assumption…"

Ellery shot a sidelong glance at Poe.

"You're the prime suspect, Poe. You were childhood friends, so she wouldn't be as much on her guard with you as with me or Van."

"Rubbish." Poe leant forward. "You're saying I killed Orczy? That's not funny."

"It wasn't meant to be funny. But, at least with regard to Orczy's murder, you're the most likely suspect. If it were you, her old friend, I would also find it easier to understand the psychology behind the murderer's peculiar act of neatly arranging Orczy's body."

"What about her hand? Why would I want to cut off her hand and take it with me?"

"Easy, Poe. I know this isn't the one and only answer. There are also other possibilities. It could have been Van, it could have been me. I just say that you are the most *likely* suspect.

"And as for the problem of the hand, it's obvious the murderer had in mind the incident that happened in the Blue Mansion last year, but I'll be honest and say I have no idea why the murderer is alluding to it. What about you, Van?"

"Maybe to confuse us?"

"Hmm. Poe?"

"I don't think the murderer would do something like that just to confuse us. Cutting off the hand without making too much noise must have been difficult."

"True. So there must have been a reason to cut off Orczy's hand. What could that reason be?"

Ellery cocked his head and took a deep breath.

"Let's just leave that problem for the time being and continue. The Carr murder. To start with the conclusion, I don't think we can come up with the one perfect answer for this case either. From the discussion we had after the murder, we can at least conclude that neither Poe nor Van had the chance to put poison directly in Carr's coffee. If the cup itself were poisoned beforehand, then anyone had a chance to do it, but there was no way to distinguish the poisoned cup from the others.

"Anyway, with Agatha now dead, the remaining person most capable of putting the poison in the coffee with a magician's sleight of hand would have to be, I regret to say, myself. However—"

"You're about to suggest I could have given Carr a slow-dissolving poison capsule, aren't you?" Poe interrupted. Ellery smiled.

"Precisely. Not that I think it would be a smart move. Suppose you had successfully given Carr the capsule, how could you have known he could get sick and die just as he was drinking coffee? If the poison had started working when he wasn't eating or drinking, then our doctor-in-training would be the first to be suspected. I don't think that you're that foolish."

"Sharp observation."

"But there's another possibility."

"Hmph, and that is?"

"Poe is a star of our medical faculty and his family owns one of the most prominent private hospitals in O— City. It could be that Carr hadn't been feeling well for a while and that he had been asking Poe for advice. Or he might have visited Poe's hospital. Anyway, let us suppose that Poe was familiar with the details of Carr's health problems.

"On that fateful night, Carr had some sort of attack. An epileptic seizure or something. Poe immediately ran to Carr's side and pretended to help him, but instead took advantage of the confusion to slip some arsenic or strychnine into Carr's mouth."

"You really seem to think I did it, but your story is just too far-fetched. Not even a sliver of reality."

"Don't take me too seriously. I'm just discussing possibilities. But if you claim this theory is too far-fetched, I could say the same of your sleight-of-hand theory.

"Perhaps I should take it as a compliment, but I think you are overestimating my magic skills. Hiding poison in my hand and putting it in another cup just as I reach out for my own cup is not as easy as it sounds. If I were the murderer, I would have avoided such a dangerous method. It would be much easier and safer to smear some poison on one of the cups and mark it in some manner."

"But the actual cup didn't have any marks or signs on it."

"Precisely. That's what's bothering me. *Was there really no mark on that cup?*"

Ellery cocked his head as he looked at the cup in his own hands.

"There's no chip. No crack. Just like the others, a moss-green decagon… No, wait."

"What's the matter?"

"We might have overlooked something. Something incredible."

Ellery got up from his chair.

"Poe, we set Carr's cup aside just as it was, I think?"

"Yes. It's in the corner of the kitchen counter."

"Let's take another look at it…"

Ellery was already on his way to the kitchen before he had even finished his sentence and he ordered the others to follow.

"You two come as well."

The cup stood on the table, covered by a white towel. Ellery pulled the towel away smoothly. There was still a little of the two-day-old coffee left in the cup.

"…I was right."

Ellery looked straight down at the cup and clicked his tongue angrily.

"We've been had. It's a mystery why we didn't notice it then."

"What do you mean?"

Van cocked his head. Poe too had a puzzled look on his face.

"It looks the same as the others to me."

"But it isn't," said Ellery solemnly. "A decagonal building with a decagonal hall, a decagonal table, a decagonal skylight, decagonal ashtrays and decagonal cups… *Distracted by this grand collection of decagons all around us, our eyes stopped working.*"

"What?"

"What do you mean?"

"There's something that sets this cup apart. There's something that makes it fundamentally different from the others. You still don't see?"

After a while, both Poe and Van yelled out simultaneously.

"You see?"

Ellery nodded contentedly.

"The decagon theme in this building was a major piece of misdirection. *This cup doesn't have ten sides, but eleven.*"

6

"So, back to the beginning."

Back at the table in the main hall, Ellery looked once more at the other two.

"Now we've discovered the cup was different, either of you or, of course, I myself, had an equal opportunity to poison Carr. One cup with eleven sides among the decagon cups. The murderer smeared poison on that cup, and if it had been passed to him, he would simply not have drunk his coffee."

"I wonder why that cup was there in the first place?" asked Van.

"Maybe one of Nakamura Seiji's jokes," said Ellery, a smile appearing on his delicate mouth. "Hiding a single eleven-sided object in a house of decagons. Fantastic joke, right?"

"Could it really be just that?"

"I believe so. It might also have another meaning, but that's not important. The murderer happened to discover that eleven-sided cup and decided to use it. I don't believe it was something he prepared beforehand. You can't get something like that unless you have it specially made. The murderer just happened to notice the cup after arriving on the island. And all three of us had an opportunity to do so."

Ellery put both elbows on the table, and joined his fingers at eye-level.

"The murderer waited until everyone had gone to sleep and sneaked into the room where Carr's body lay. He then went to all the trouble of cutting off the corpse's left hand, just as with Orczy, and throwing it in the bathtub. I've no idea why he did that, though."

"Agatha said she heard something. That was probably what it was."

"Yes, Poe. Everyone was a little bit on edge by then. The murderer committed himself to quite a risky job. So that means that there was an important reason to cut off the hands. But it remains a mystery to me."

Ellery frowned and continued:

"Anyway, as I said, all three of us had an equal opportunity to kill Carr. Let's go on to the next."

"Next is Agatha... No, Leroux first?" Van said. Ellery shook his head.

"No, first was the attempt on my life. Me, Ellery. In the underground room yesterday. The night before that—I think it was just before Carr collapsed—I mentioned the possibility of there being an underground room in the Blue Mansion. I suppose that having heard that, the murderer—probably after cutting off Carr's hand and sticking the plate to the door—sneaked outside and laid the trap. Everybody was there when I mentioned the possibility of an underground room, so anyone could have done it. Since I almost became one of the murder victims, I should be ruled out as a suspect, shouldn't I?"

Ellery watched the reactions of the other two. Van and Poe looked at each other and signalled their disapproval.

"But I admit there's nothing to prove it wasn't all a one-man show. I wasn't even badly hurt. And now to the murder of Leroux this morning."

Ellery gave it some thought.

"There were some strange features to that murder. It was committed outside and the victim was beaten to death. Unlike the two earlier murders, there was no cutting off of hands. This murder was different."

"I agree. But even so, any of the three of us could have been the murderer," said Poe.

Ellery rubbed his thin chin.

"That's true. Let's keep the examination of Leroux's murder for later, then. I need more time to think about it.

"Last is Agatha's murder. As we just found out, potassium cyanide or sodium cyanide, or something like that, had been applied to her lipstick. The only problem is *when and how was the poison put there*?

213

"Apart from when she was applying it, the lipstick had been in her room the whole time since she came to the island, inside her make-up pouch. Since the day before yesterday, following the murders of Orczy and Carr, Agatha had become extremely cautious and would always keep her door locked. The murderer wouldn't have been able to sneak into her room. On the other hand, Agatha did use lipstick every day. She died this morning, so that means her lipstick was poisoned between yesterday afternoon and last night."

"Ellery, just one thing."

"Yes, Van?"

"I think the colour of the lipstick Agatha used today is different from yesterday."

"What?"

"The colour she wore this morning was horribly bright. I couldn't even believe she was dead."

Van continued:

"Agatha was using a different shade of pink yesterday and the day before. Rose-pink, I think it's called."

"Aha."

Ellery tapped on the edge of the table with his fingers.

"Now that you mention it, she did have two tubes in her pouch, one of them pink. So I guess the poison was put on the red one earlier. It was put there on the first or second day, when Agatha wasn't yet on her guard and the murderer could easily sneak into her room. But she didn't use that lipstick until this morning."

"A time bomb," Poe said, stroking his beard. "And, again, any of the three of us had the opportunity to pull that off."

"That's what it boils down to. But Poe, if we believe the murderer to be one of us, it doesn't help to go on saying that any of us could have done it every time."

"So what do you propose?"

"A vote," Ellery said with a calm expression, before breaking into a smile. "I'm joking, of course, but let's hear what each of us has to say. Van, who do you think is the most suspicious?"

"Poe," answered Van surprisingly easily.

"What?" The colour drained from Poe's face, and he put out the cigarette he had just lit in the ashtray. "Damn it, it wasn't me. But I guess saying that's no good."

"We can't just take you blindly at your word, of course. I'm of the same opinion as Van: that of the three of us, you are the most suspicious," Ellery said squarely.

Poe was visibly disturbed and asked angrily: "Why? Why am I suspicious?"

"Motive."

"Motive? Motive, you say? Why would I want to kill four of my friends? Tell me that, Ellery."

"I heard your mother is being treated in a mental hospital," replied Ellery coolly. Poe choked back a reply and clenched his fists until the knuckles turned visibly white and started to tremble.

"It happened several years ago. Your mother was caught attempting to kill a patient in your hospital. Her mind had already become unbalanced, I heard."

"Is that true, Ellery?" Van's eyes were wide open in surprise. "I didn't know that."

"His father hushed it up. Because it would hurt the reputation of the hospital. The patient who was attacked was probably paid off. The lawyer who acted on their behalf is a friend of my father, that's how I learnt about it. The wife of a doctor must be under quite some mental stress. It might be too much for a woman with a weak mind. She might even imagine a patient was stealing her husband away..."

"Shut up!" Poe cried out angrily. "Don't you talk about my mother!"

Ellery whistled once and then kept quiet. Poe was still looking down, fists clenched, but finally a little laugh escaped his lips.

"So you're saying I might be insane? Rather a simplistic attempt at a motive."

Then his face grew dark and he glared grimly at both Ellery and Van.

"Let me tell you this first: both of you have motives too."

"Oh really?" said Ellery. "Please do tell us about them."

"First you, Van. Your parents were murdered by robbers when you were in middle school. Your little sister too. So you might have an issue with us, a group of students who happily write about people being killed."

Van turned white as Poe spoke, but nevertheless managed to reply.

"What happened to my family is in the past. And if I'd had a grudge against mystery writers, would I really have entered a mystery-fiction club in college?" Van spoke in a low voice. "What's more, I don't believe for a moment that mystery fiction praises murder. That's why I've been in the club all this time and even agreed to come here with you all."

"Well, you would say that, Van. Who knows why you joined the club, maybe to get your revenge on us?"

Poe changed targets.

"And next up is Ellery."

"Yes. What would my motive be?"

"You claimed it didn't bother you, but perhaps you'd had enough of being sniped at by Carr."

"That's it? I'd had enough of Carr?" Ellery looked surprised. "Oh, and I suppose the other three murders were camouflage.

That's just ridiculous. Too bad, but Carr wasn't even a nuisance as far as I was concerned. I don't really care what others think of me. You should know that. Do you really think I hated Carr enough to want to kill him?"

"You wouldn't have needed much of a motive. It would have been like swatting a fly."

"So you think I'm that cold-blooded a person?"

"'Cold-blooded' doesn't quite capture it, but you are indeed lacking something human. I think you're a man who could kill someone on a mere whim. Don't you agree, Van?"

"Maybe." Van nodded with emotionless eyes. A troubled expression appeared on Ellery's face for one fleeting moment, but it changed into a wry smile and he shrugged.

"Oh, well, I should probably mind my manners better."

And then the three fell silent.

The dark and sinister atmosphere of the hall seemed to freeze their minds, not allowing them to break free. The ten white walls around them appeared to be more warped than ever.

They remained like that for a long time.

They could hear the murmur of the wind in the trees. The noise was a harbinger of a light beating sound on the roof of the building.

"Oh, it's raining," Ellery murmured, gazing up at the water drops that had started to accumulate on the glass of the skylight.

The noise grew louder as the rain became heavier, more violent, as if to isolate further the three men who were already trapped on the island.

And then Ellery mumbled something and stood up, still looking up at the skylight.

"What's the matter?" Poe asked suspiciously.

"Ah, no, wait—"

Ellery hadn't finished his sentence before he suddenly pushed his chair back, turned around and sprinted to the entrance.

"The footprints!"

7

It was pouring. The sound of the rain mixed with the waves and reverberated throughout the island, like some unearthly melody.

Ellery ran through the rain, not caring about getting soaked.

He didn't take the roundabout way through the arc of pine trees, but headed straight for the ruins of the Blue Mansion. He would need to run right through the trees.

He stopped once to look behind him. Making sure Poe and Van were following him, he yelled:

"Hurry! The rain will destroy the footprints!" He put on another spurt.

His feet got caught in the undergrowth a couple of times, but he finally made his way through the trees. Arriving in the front garden of the Blue Mansion, he saw that the footprints around the place where Leroux had lain were still intact.

Poe and Van arrived soon after. Ellery pointed at the footprints as he caught his breath.

"Just memorize everything here as if your lives depended on it."

They stood there, following the lines of footprints left on the ground with their eyes, while the cold rain pelted them. They desperately tried to memorize the scene in front of them as puddles started to form and rivulets started to erode the prints.

After a while Ellery turned around, brushing wet locks of hair from his forehead.

"Let's go back. We'll catch cold."

† † †

After changing their soaked clothes, the three gathered once again around the table in the hall.

"Would you two mind coming a bit closer? This is important," said Ellery as he opened a notebook he had brought from his room and grabbed a pen. Poe and Van hesitated, but got up from their chairs and walked to Ellery's side.

"Let's draw the plan while it's still fresh in our minds, OK?"

Ellery drew a vertical rectangle that filled the page of the notebook.

"This represents the grounds of the Blue Mansion."

Ellery drew a smaller horizontal rectangle near the top of the page.

"These are the ruins of the building—the pile of bricks. And this is the staircase that goes down to the rocky area beneath the cliffs."

He marked a spot halfway down the left side of the large rectangle.

"The Decagon House is off to the bottom right. The bottom line here is the row of trees. And Leroux was lying in the front garden, around here."

Slightly to the right and below the centre, Ellery drew a human figure, representing the corpse. Ellery then looked up at the other two.

"And now the footsteps. Where were they?"

"First, there was a line of footprints which went from the entrance to the grounds—the arch of pine trees—to the staircase on the cliffs," answered Poe, restlessly scratching his beard.

"And then three disorderly lines of footprints which went from the entrance to Leroux's body and back."

"Precisely. Like this, I think. Van, this right?"

"Yes. I think that's how it was."

"OK, done."

Having finished drawing the diagram, Ellery placed the notebook where all three of them could see it clearly. (See Figure 3.)

"I discovered Leroux's as soon as I had come through the arch of pine trees and arrived on the Blue Mansion grounds. You two arrived soon after and we ran straight to the body. Poe and I picked up the body and, with Van behind us, we went back to the Decagon House the way we came. Therefore the three chaotic

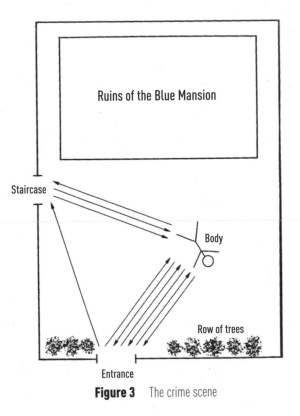

Figure 3 The crime scene

sets that went up to the body and back were made by the three of us, naturally. So if we remove those sets from our investigation…"

Ellery paused and swept his wet hair back.

"*Don't you see anything odd?*"

"Odd? About these footprints?" Poe asked, frowning.

"Yes. The only people who entered the crime scene were you, Poe, you, Van, and me, and of course the murderer. Taking Leroux into account, there should be five sets of footprints going to his body. And indeed, there are five sets. However—"

"Ellery, wait," said Poe, glaring at the diagram. "If we ignore the sets we made when we discovered Leroux's body, there remains one set going from the entrance to the staircase, two sets going from the staircase to the body and one set from the body to the staircase."

"So you see our problem?"

"Yes."

"I think we can safely assume the footsteps from the entrance to the staircase are those of Leroux. One of the sets going from the staircase to the body naturally belongs to Leroux himself. That means the remaining two lines were made by the murderer going to Leroux and back. *But where did the murderer come from?*"

"The staircase."

"Precisely. *But there is nothing but sea down there.* You remember? There were only sheer cliffs on both sides of the rocky area beneath the staircase. The only way to get onto this island is either from that staircase or from the steps from the inlet with the pier. So how did the murderer make his way to that rocky area? And where did he go from there? He'd have to go all the way around that projecting cliff if he wanted to get back to the inlet. The water is deep, too. He would need to swim in this weather. I wonder what the temperature of the water is."

Poe got out his cigarette case and groaned softly. Van's eyes were fixed on the notebook on the table.

"And?" Poe prompted.

"So the problem is *why did the murderer do that?* Well?"

Ellery was the only one enjoying these riddles under the tense circumstances.

Van remained silent, slipping both hands inside his down jacket.

"Hm." Poe cleared his throat and spoke. "The murderer is one of us three here in this house. So why would he go down to the rocky area to swim back here? Walking would have been easier. He could easily have just trampled on his own footprints to obscure their size and shape. It's not as though we have a forensics expert around here. So the fact he didn't do that means he had an important reason to return by sea."

"Exactly. And the reason is obvious, I think." Ellery nodded in satisfaction and stood up. "So let's get something to eat now. It's already three o'clock."

"Eat?"

Van looked suspicious. "How can we eat now, Ellery? Why did the murderer…?"

"Later, later. No need to get all worked up over the question now. We haven't eaten since morning."

Ellery turned round and went to the kitchen.

8

Having finished his lunch of emergency rations and a cup of coffee, Ellery began:

"Well now. Our stomachs are full, so let's finish this problem of ours. OK?"

"Of course. Stop making a show of it," replied Poe. Van nodded without saying a word.

Ellery's behaviour had been a source of confusion to the other two ever since he started talking about the footprints. They had kept an eye on Ellery during their meal, but he remained calm throughout and they even caught an occasional glimpse of his trademark smile.

"OK."

Ellery pushed his cup and plate away and opened the notebook again. The other two came round to his side of the table, each keeping his distance from the other.

"First, a review of the main points."

Ellery glanced at the figure of the footprints and began his analysis.

"We concluded that the only footsteps left by the murderer were the two lines between the body and the staircase. That means the murderer *came and left by sea*. Supposing that the murderer is one of us, let's try to trace the route he took.

"He would have left the Decagon House, gone down to the inlet, into the sea, swum to the rocky area and climbed the staircase there to arrive at the Blue Mansion. He would have taken the same route back after the murder. Poe just talked about an important reason for coming back to the house by sea, but could there really be such a thing? No matter how much I think about it, it seems like nonsense to me. There's no need to do it at all. There's not the slightest glimmer of reality about the whole idea."

"But that would mean that the murderer is someone besides us," said Poe. "Someone from the sea—someone from outside the island."

"And why shouldn't that be the case?"

Ellery closed the notebook.

"The most logical conclusion we can come to, given the circumstances, *is that the murderer is someone besides us*. We might not be able to leave the island, but there are plenty of ways for someone from outside to come to the island. That way, there's also no need to suggest silly ideas like someone swimming in the sea. *The murderer used a boat.*"

"A boat," muttered Poe.

"Why were both Orczy and Leroux killed in the early morning? Because the best time to get to the island unnoticed is in the middle of the night or in the early morning. What do you think?"

Ellery took out his pack of Salem cigarettes as he watched the expressions of the other two. Realizing the pack was empty, he threw it on the table.

"You want one?" said Poe, and slid his cigarette case towards Ellery.

"Poe seems to agree with me."

Ellery put a cigarette in his mouth and lit a match.

"And Van?"

"I think you're right, Ellery. Poe, could I have one too?"

"Sure."

Ellery passed Poe's cigarette case to Van.

"But Ellery, if you're right and the murderer isn't one of us, why did they make those plates?" asked Poe.

"You mean why was there a nameplate for 'the Murderer', as well as those for 'the Detective' and the victims? Because their real purpose was to act as a distraction."

Ellery, eyes half closed, blew a cloud of smoke.

"First of all, it had the effect of making us believe that 'the Murderer' was one of us seven. That way, we would be put off guard about the outside world."

"And secondly?"

"I'd say psychological pressure. As the group dwindled, the remaining survivors would become suspicious of each other, and might kill each other. The murderer was probably hoping for that. More bodies without having to dirty his own hands. Anyway, the murderer's final goal is very likely to kill all seven of us."

"That's evil," muttered Van as he lit his cigarette.

"One more thing I find curious," said Poe, pressing a thick thumb to his temple. "Why did the murderer go straight back towards the sea after killing Leroux?"

"What do you mean, why?" Van asked, as he returned Poe's cigarette case.

"The killer was trying to make it appear like the murders were committed by one of us. So wouldn't it have made more sense for him to leave more footprints, for example between the entrance and the staircase? It would have been simple to do."

"He might not have noticed he'd left any footprints."

"And he returned to the mainland right away? When did he stick that plate with 'the Third Victim' on the door then?"

"That's…"

Seeing that Van couldn't come up with an answer, Poe turned to Ellery.

"What's your view on that, Ellery?"

"I think it was like this," said Ellery and he placed his cigarette in the ashtray. "It could be, as Van said, that the murderer hadn't noticed the problem of the footprints. But supposing he had noticed it, he probably would have wanted to leave an extra set of footprints between the entrance and the staircase. The fact he didn't means the situation didn't allow him to do so. I think I can explain it by factoring in the particular circumstances of Leroux's murder.

"Leroux was beaten to death. Judging by the wild footprints that led from the steps to his body, I think we can deduce

225

that he was being chased by the murderer. My guess is that Leroux saw the murderer and the boat down in the rocky area, probably just as the murderer was preparing to leave the island.

"Leroux figured out what was going on and ran away. The murderer saw Leroux and ran after him. Leroux most likely yelled for help, so, after catching up with Leroux and beating him to death, the murderer panicked. Someone might have been woken up by Leroux's cries and could have arrived there at any moment. He could have hidden in the vicinity, but he couldn't afford to have his boat discovered.

"The murderer therefore left the footprints as they were, went back down to the rocky area and rowed the boat to the inlet, to see whether he could hear us come looking for Leroux. Fortunately no such thing seemed to be happening. He then came up to the Decagon House and, after looking through the kitchen window to check whether everybody seemed to be asleep, he sneaked inside and stuck the plate on Leroux's door. He gave up on the footprints and left the island. It would have been too dangerous, considering the time of the day as well, to go back to the Blue Mansion once again."

"Hmm. So the murderer was here on the island the whole night?" asked Poe.

"I think he's been here every night. He arrives on the island by night to watch our movements."

"Hiding beneath the kitchen window?"

"Probably something like that."

"And he leaves his boat in the inlet or at the rocky area?"

"He probably hides it. A small rubber dinghy can be folded up easily. He could carry it to the grove, or hide it underneath the water with a weight on it."

"A rubber dinghy?" Poe frowned. "Could you get to the mainland with that?"

"No need to go all the way to the mainland. There's a perfect hiding place just around the corner."

"Cat Island?"

"Precisely, Cat Island. I think the murderer is camping out there. You could easily row here from that island."

"True, it's not far."

"Let's reconsider what the murderer did once again."

Ellery closed the notebook and put it to one side. He produced his deck of blue bicycle cards out of nowhere, put it on the table and played with it as he continued his story.

"The murderer came here last night from Cat Island. He watched us, hoping for an opportunity to commit his next murder, but he drew a blank and so, this morning, he returned to the rocky area. It was still raining at the time, I think. That's why the murderer didn't leave any footprints going from the entrance of the ruins to the staircase.

"The rain stopped while he was preparing the boat in the rocky area. From then on, footprints would remain intact on the ground. At that point Leroux made his appearance, although I don't know what he was doing there.

"Leroux saw the boat and the murderer. In a panic, the murderer grabbed one of the rocks lying around, chased after Leroux and silenced him. Fearing someone might come running because of Leroux's cries, he moved his boat to the inlet. He waited a while to see if anyone was out of bed and then sneaked in here to hang the plate up. Something like that."

Poe's thumb had not once left his temple. With one elbow on the table, he asked angrily: "But Ellery, who is this murderer hiding out on Cat Island?"

"Nakamura Seiji of course," Ellery declared without any hesitation. "I've been saying that from the start. I wasn't serious when I said I thought you were a suspect just now."

"Suppose I accept the possibility Nakamura Seiji is still alive, for argument's sake. I don't know about anyone else, but I can't see what motive this Seiji could possibly have for wanting to kill all of us. I can't think of anything. Or are you simply saying he's mad?"

"A motive? Of course he has one. A strong one."

"What? What do you mean?" Poe and Van cried out simultaneously, leaning forward.

Ellery's hands skilfully gathered the cards he had fanned out on the table. "We talked about each other's motives just now, but Nakamura Seiji has a much more obvious one. I only realized it myself last night, after I'd gone back to my room."

"Really?"

"What is it, Ellery?"

"Nakamura Chiori. Remember her?"

Silence reigned in the gloomy hall, except for the distant sound of the waves. The rain had eased to a noiseless drizzle.

"Nakamura Chiori. You mean?…"

Van's voice had become weak.

"Yes, our junior member, who died because of our carelessness in January last year. That Nakamura Chiori."

"Nakamura—Nakamura Seiji, Nakamura Chiori."

Poe muttered the words as if he were chanting a spell.

"But it just can't be."

"It can be and it is. It's the only reason I can think of. Nakamura Chiori was the daughter of Nakamura Seiji."

"So that's it."

Poe frowned deeply, tapped a Lark cigarette out of his cigarette case and put it straight in his mouth. Van closed his eyes, his hands on the back of his head. Ellery gathered the cards, placed them on top of the case and continued:

"It was Nakamura Seiji who committed the murders that happened here on this island six months ago. He burned someone to serve as his body double, either the missing gardener or someone else of similar age and build and the same blood type. Nakamura Seiji is still alive and now he is acting out his revenge for his daughter—"

At that moment, he was interrupted.

"Uuurgh!"

An unnatural sound escaped Poe's throat.

"What's wrong?"

"Poe?"

His chair screeched across the floor, then Poe's large body tumbled forwards and fell.

"Poe!"

Ellery and Van rushed to him, trying to get him back up. Poe, doubled up with pain, pushed their hands away. Then, finally, it was over.

With one last violent convulsion, his four limbs thrust out stiffly in the air and he crashed back on the floor face up. That was the end of Poe.

The Lark cigarette Poe had thrown away after just a single puff was lying on the blue-tiled floor, smoke rising from it. Ellery and Van could only look in shock at the now motionless "Last Victim".

9

It was nearly dusk and the sky was still covered with grey clouds, but it didn't look as though it would rain. The wind stopped shaking the trees and the noise of the roiling waves had also softened into a melancholic melody.

Poe's body was carried to his room by the two survivors. On the floor lay the jigsaw puzzle, which had hardly been touched since Van last saw it. The cute upturned faces of the fox cubs looked terribly sad.

Ellery and Van made sure not to disturb the puzzle and placed Poe's large body on the bed. Van covered him with a blanket and Ellery closed Poe's eyes. From his painfully contorted mouth rose a hint of almonds.

After a moment of silent prayer, the two left the room without saying a word.

"Another time bomb. Damn."

Ellery's voice trembled with fury as he trampled on Poe's cigarette, which had turned to ashes on the floor.

"One of Poe's stock of cigarettes was poisoned with prussic acid. He probably sneaked into Poe's room and injected one of them with a syringe."

"Nakamura Seiji?"

"Who else?"

"It could have been one of us."

Van dropped into a chair. Ellery walked to the table and lit the lamp. In the flickering light, mysterious shadows started dancing on the white walls.

"Nakamura Seiji…" muttered Ellery as his eyes focused on the flame.

"Now I think about it, Van, Nakamura Seiji used to be the owner of this house. He'd naturally know all about the geography of the island and the layout of the buildings, and I'll bet he also has spare keys to all the rooms."

"Spare keys?"

"A master key perhaps. He took it with him after burning down the Blue Mansion and going into hiding. He can enter any room whenever he wants. It was the easiest thing in the world to poison Agatha's lipstick, or kill Orczy. The same for Poe's cigarettes. He made sure to stay out of sight and flitted around this building like a shadow. We're just the poor insects who flew into the trap called the Decagon House."

"I remember reading somewhere that he used to be an architect."

"I read that too. He might even be the one who designed this place. He was certainly the one who had it built… Perhaps—hold on a second!"

Ellery looked keenly around the hall.

"What's wrong, Ellery?"

"I was just thinking about the cup that was used to poison Carr."

"The eleven-sided one?"

"We now know it wasn't used to mark the poisoned coffee, but do you remember, Van? You asked the question. *Why was that cup there in the first place?*"

"Ah, yes, I did."

"I answered that it was just Seiji's joke. But I added that *it might also have another meaning. Hiding a single eleven-sided object in a house of decagons.* Doesn't that suggest something?"

"Something eleven-sided inside a decagon?" muttered Van, before his eyes suddenly widened in surprise. "It might mean *there are eleven rooms here.*"

"Precisely." Ellery nodded grimly. "I had the same idea. Apart from this central hall, the building consists of ten trapezoidal rooms of equal size. The toilet, bathroom and washstand are one room, the kitchen, the entrance hall and the seven guest rooms make nine more. If there's one more room hidden here some-where besides those ten…"

"You mean Seiji wasn't watching us from the kitchen window, but from that secret room?"

"Precisely."

"But where could it be?"

"Considering the layout of this building, I think it could only be underground. And I have a suspicion…" A smile appeared on Ellery's lips "…*that the eleven-sided cup is the key to the secret room.*"

They found it inside the storage space beneath the kitchen floor.

There was nothing strange about the storage space itself. A square part of the floor, about eighty centimetres on each side, could be easily lifted by pulling on a handle.

The hole was about fifty centimetres deep. White boards lined the bottom and the four sides. There was nothing inside.

"This is it, Van."

Ellery pointed.

"I figured that if the room really existed, it would be in the kitchen, together with the cup. And hey presto!"

They shone a torch on the bottom of the space. There was a small hole there, just a few centimetres wide, almost invisible unless you looked for it. A groove encircled the hole.

"Van, give me the cup."

"What about the coffee inside?"

"This is important, so just throw it away."

Ellery took the cup and crawled on the floor. He stretched his right arm into the storage space and slid the cup into the hole in the middle.

"Got it. A perfect fit."

232

The eleven-sided keyhole and key connected.

"I'll turn the key."

As he had expected, the hole turned following the circular groove. After a while, he felt something slide into place.

"OK, I'm going to open it."

Ellery carefully pulled the cup out of the hole. As he did so, the entire white bottom of the space started to tilt downwards noiselessly.

"Fantastic contraption," Ellery said. "There's a mechanism with cogwheels or something that prevents it from making any noise as the bottom angles downwards."

It didn't take long for a staircase leading to a secret underground room to be revealed.

"Let's go, Van."

"Should we?" Van had cold feet. "What if he's down there waiting for us?"

"Don't worry. The sun has just set. Seiji probably isn't here yet. Even if he is there, it's two against one. We can handle him."

"But…"

"If you're scared, stay here. I'll go alone."

"Ah, wait, Ellery."

A damp, acrid smell reached their noses.

Their way lit only by Ellery's torch, the two stepped down into the pitch-black hole.

It was a sturdy staircase despite its age. If they stepped carefully, it didn't even squeak. Ellery led the way and, making sure not to repeat the foolish mistake he had made the day before, advanced very cautiously.

After not even ten steps down the staircase, they arrived in the fairly large room they had already glimpsed. It started right under the kitchen and stretched out in the direction of the central hall.

The floor and walls were of bare concrete. There was no furniture. The ceiling was just a little higher than Ellery and perforated with small holes. Thin slivers of light shone down through them.

"The light from the lamp," Ellery whispered. "We're beneath the hall. Everything we said could be heard clearly from here."

"So Seiji really was here?"

"Yes. He must have been listening to our every movement. And I bet he also made a path from this room that leads outside the building."

Ellery shone the light on the surrounding walls. Dirty concrete with black spots. Here and there some cracks and signs of repair.

"There," said Ellery, and he stopped moving his light. To their right, in the rear, was an old wooden door.

The duo approached.

Ellery stretched out his hand out to touch the rusty doorknob. In a subdued voice, Van asked: "Where does this lead?"

"I wonder."

Ellery turned the knob. The door creaked loudly. Ellery held his breath and pulled harder. The door opened.

Suddenly, they both groaned and held their noses.

"What the!…"

"What a horrible smell."

An overpowering odour filled the darkness. It was so repellent that it made them want to vomit.

They guessed immediately what the source was, and shuddered in disgust.

It was the smell of decayed flesh.

Ellery's hand wouldn't stop shaking, but he clenched the torch tightly once more and pointed its beam towards the darkness beyond the door.

It was a deep darkness. As they had suspected, this appeared to be a path to somewhere outside.

He pointed the beam lower. As it swept over the dirty concrete floor, it fell on…

"Aah!"

"Urgh!"

They cried out at the same time.

They had found the source of the horrible smell.

A lump of flesh of a nauseating colour, its original shape unrecognizable. Yellow-white bones sticking out. Dark, empty eye sockets.

It was unquestionably the half-decomposed corpse of a human being.

10

It was past midnight.

There was nobody left in the decagonal hall. The lamp had been extinguished and only darkness remained.

The faraway booming of the waves played a melody from a different dimension. The stars peeked inside through the decagonal skylight, resembling an open mouth in the darkness.

And suddenly a sharp noise came from somewhere inside the building.

It was followed by a completely different sound, the noise of a living thing sighing. The sighing turned into whining, the whining into a roaring noise which enveloped everything.

The Decagon House was on fire.

The white building was wrapped in a crimson light. Smoke rose in thick clouds. A roar rumbled through the night sky. The gigantic blaze burned on furiously, as if trying to scorch the passing clouds.

The extraordinary light was even visible in S— Town across the sea.

TEN

The Sixth Day

1

He was awakened by the shrill ring of the telephone.

He finally managed to lift his heavy eyelids and glance at the clock next to his pillow. Eight in the morning.

Morisu Kyōichi raised his body sluggishly and stretched his hand out to the receiver.

"Hello, this is Morisu speaking. Yes… Eh? Could you repeat what… Yes. The Decagon House on Tsunojima gone up in flames? Are you sure?"

He threw off his blanket, clutched the receiver more firmly in his hand and demanded forcefully:

"But what happened to everyone?… Ah…"

Energy drained from Morisu's body as he nodded his head heavily.

"…Yes. And I am to… Oh, OK. Understood. I'll be there. Thanks."

He put the receiver down and reached out for his cigarettes. His sleepiness had been dispelled completely. He lit a cigarette, inhaled deeply and concentrated on keeping calm.

After smoking it completely, he put a second one in his mouth and picked up the receiver again.

"Kawaminami? It's me, Morisu."

"Ah, hey. What's up so early in the morning?" a drowsy Kawaminami Taka'aki answered from the other end of the line.

"I've got bad news." Morisu told him. "The Decagon House burned down."

"Wha-what?!"

"I was told everyone died."

"Impossible… How could… You're not joking? April Fool's Day isn't until tomorrow."

"I wish I was joking. I was just told over the phone."

"But—"

"I'm heading for S— Town now—you'll come too, I hope? Can you reach Mr Shimada?"

"Yes."

"I'll meet you over there then. All concerned parties are to assemble in the fishing union's meeting room near the harbour. Got it?"

"Got it. I'll find Mr Shimada and bring him along."

"OK. I'll meet you there."

Monday, 31st March. 11.30 a.m., Tsunojima.

A crowd was milling about in all directions.

The rubble of the Decagon House was still smouldering, resembling nothing so much as the burnt corpse of some grotesque monster.

The sky was clear. The blinding reflection of the surrounding sea was redolent of spring. The contrast between the peaceful background and the dark, tragic scene on the island itself was unbearably shocking.

"Inspector. We got a message that most of the families of the deceased are gathered now in S— Town," yelled a young police officer, holding a walkie-talkie in his hand.

The inspector, a portly man in his forties, yelled back with a handkerchief held to his nose: "OK. Bring them over. Tell me as soon as they arrive. Make sure they don't come up here."

He returned to his discussion with the medical examiner, who was inspecting a body burnt black beyond recognition.

"And this one?" he asked. It was unbearably hot and a penetrating stench filled the area.

"A male," answered the medical examiner from behind his large mask.

"A male of small build. Some deep lacerations on the back of his head. Could have been a blow from a blunt instrument."

"Hmm."

The inspector nodded wearily and turned his eyes away from the body.

"Hey, how are things over there?" he yelled as he walked towards another investigator looking at a different body, lying among some bricks further away.

"This was probably also a male. It also appears this was the source of the fire."

"Oh."

"Seems like kerosene was poured all round the room and then lit. Our corpse here seems to have poured kerosene over himself too."

"Oh, so it might be a suicide?"

"Well, we would need to compare it with the other facts, but I think there's a good possibility."

The inspector scowled and walked away rapidly. A police officer ran after him with a question.

"Shall we move the bodies?"

"Wait until the families're here," the inspector replied immediately. "If we're not careful, we might get all the corpses and the stuff around them mixed up. We won't be able to figure out who's who."

With speedy steps, he moved upwind.

"I won't be able to get lunch down my throat like this," he muttered to himself, as he removed the handkerchief from his nose and filled his lungs with the breeze from the sea.

The bright sea spread out on the other side of the grey, cold blinds. He was inside a large room, plain and bleak.

The meeting room of the fishing union in S— Town.

Chaotically arranged folding tables and chairs. Thinly scattered groups of people anxiously holding on to each other. Whispers being exchanged.

Sitting alone by the window was Morisu, who had lost count of the number of cigarettes he had put out in the cheap ashtray.

The Decagon House on Tsunojima, gone up in flames.

His heart beat furiously.

Everyone is dead.

It was almost one o'clock in the afternoon when Kawaminami and Shimada finally appeared. They recognized Morisu as they looked across the room and walked straight up to him.

"Any news about what happened on the island?" Kawaminami asked, without any preliminaries. Morisu shook his head silently.

"We've heard no details. Some members of the families have just gone to the island to identify the bodies."

"Is everybody really dead?"

"Yes. The Decagon House burned down completely. They found the bodies of everyone at the fire site."

Kawaminami's shoulders drooped and he stood still for a while.

"Was it arson? Or perhaps an accident?"

"No idea."

Shimada walked to the window and looked outside through the blinds. Kawaminami moved a nearby chair next to Morisu and sat down on it.

"Did you tell them about the letters?"

"No, not yet. But I plan to—I brought my letter with me."

"OK."

The two looked at each other with bewildered expressions.

"We were tricked," Shimada muttered, his eyes still staring outside through the blinds. Kawaminami and Morisu turned around in surprise and Shimada continued in a grave voice:

"This was no accident. It was murder. Revenge."

Several people in the meeting room stole a glance at the trio. Shimada quickly lowered his voice to a whisper.

"We can't talk here. Let's go outside."

Morisu and Kawaminami nodded silently and got up slowly from their chairs. The heavy steel door opened into a hallway and the three happened to overhear some men standing there.

"…I heard some of the bodies show signs of homicide."

2

The trio walked out onto the seashore.

They climbed down to the breakwater and sat next to each other on one of the concrete tetrapods poking out of the water.

Beneath the bright sun the calm sea offered a stark contrast to the state of their minds.

"So they all died."

Kawaminami's arms shivered as he sat down, hugging his knees.

"I've been an idiot."

"Conan," Shimada called out to him. Kawaminami shook his head several times.

"We went around, poking here and there, but what did we accomplish? Absolutely nothing. We even came to this very harbour just three days ago. We should have at least warned them on the island then."

"It's not your fault." Shimada stroked his chin and continued, as if to himself: "How many people would have taken those letters seriously and gone running around as we did? Even if we had gone to the police, they would just have told us not to take such things seriously and kicked us out."

"I wonder."

"I kept saying Nakamura Seiji was still alive and that everybody on the island was in danger, but that was all I did. I couldn't cross the sea and go to the island just because of a guess, not without some decisive evidence that showed that everybody on the island was indeed in danger of being murdered."

"Mr Shimada," Morisu interrupted. "If everybody on the island has been murdered, does that mean that Nakamura Seiji is indeed alive?"

"Well, I wonder," Shimada said evasively.

"But who else could the murderer be?"

"Who knows?"

"Mr Shimada, what's your opinion of those letters signed by Seiji? Were they related to what happened on the island?" Kawaminami asked.

Shimada grimaced:

"We can only assume they were, considering what has happened since."

"Is the same person behind the fire and the letters?"

"Yes, I believe so."

"Were the letters a warning?"

"I don't think they were a warning, exactly, and it was curious that they were delivered right after everyone had left for Tsunojima. I think the murderer had some other purpose in mind."

"Such as?"

"Conan, on the first day we met, you made an analysis of your letter and came up with three different meanings. Do you remember?"

"Yes. Accusation. Threat. An invitation to look into the Tsunojima accident of last year again."

"Yes."

Shimada gazed sombrely at the sea.

"Following that suggestion, we started a second inquiry into the incident that happened last year and managed to uncover the truth behind that. But I don't believe the culprit had foreseen that. The sender could not have guessed that we would actually be so meddlesome. So I think the culprit's real intention with the letters was to accuse you of murder and *to suggest the idea of Nakamura Seiji to us.*"

"Nakamura Seiji?"

"By signing as Nakamura Seiji, he planted the idea in our minds that the dead architect was actually still alive. The goal of that was, of course, to turn Seiji into a scapegoat."

"So Mr Shimada, the person you suspect is…"

"Nakamura Kōjirō?" Morisu asked carefully. "You mean that now we know that Nakamura Chiori is Kōjirō's daughter, the person with the motive for murder is not Seiji, but Kōjirō."

"Going by motive, I agree that Kōjirō is the prime suspect. But…" Kawaminami glanced at Shimada. "But he was in Beppu all the time."

"Conan, do you remember what that young man said?"

"Eh?"

"The son of the fisherman who took your Mystery Club friends to the island."

"Ah, yes."

"He told us that it wasn't difficult to go to and from the island in a motorboat. Can you be sure Kō didn't do just that?"

"Oh."

"Kō said he had been cooped up in his house the last few days to write a thesis, and shut out all visitors and phone calls. But was he telling the truth?"

Shimada nodded slightly, still staring at the sea.

"Yes. I find it hard to say this as his friend, but I have to suspect Kō. He lost his daughter, the only bridge between him and his unreachable love, and in such an awful way. And because of her death—remember what he told us?—his love was murdered by his own brother. He has more than enough of a motive.

"And Kō was also the previous owner of the Decagon House. It's not too far-fetched to imagine he somehow managed to hear that the people responsible for his daughter's death were going to the island. He wrote those letters to you to suggest Seiji was still alive, divert suspicion to Seiji and to vent his own pent-up rage. He sent one of those letters to himself, too. To make him appear to be one of the victims as well."

Now all three of them were looking silently at the sea.

"I agree," said Morisu finally, in a dull voice. "He's the only one I can think of with a motive to kill all of them, on that island of all places. Kōjirō is the most likely suspect. But Mr Shimada, this is nothing more than conjecture."

"I know, Morisu," Shimada answered ironically. "It's nothing more than conjecture. And, rest assured, I have no intention of looking for evidence. Neither do I plan to tell any of it to the police."

Noticing two boats appearing from beyond J— Cape, Shimada stood up.

"Police boats. They're coming back. Let's go back in."

3

"Who are those three?" the inspector asked a nearby police officer. He had just returned from inspecting the crime scene over on Tsunojima.

He had been told by a local estate agent, Tatsumi Masa'aki, the person currently in charge of the building on the island, that students from K— University had been staying in the burnt-down Decagon House. They were friends of his nephew and he had given them permission to stay there a week, starting last Wednesday.

Tatsumi had a list of names of the club members who had gone to the island and the police used that list to make enquiries at the university and to contact family. Some of the students had been living away from their parents' homes, in boarding houses, so not all the families had been tracked down. Still, they had managed to identify bodies to the point that they now had a good idea of which corpse belonged to which victim. The inspector had also started to question the families of the deceased, but had obtained little useful information from any of them.

"Eh? Which three?" the officer replied, and the portly inspector pointed towards the window.

"Those three over there."

"Oh, they're friends of the deceased from the same university club. They've been waiting all afternoon to ask about the case."

"I see."

The inspector cocked his large head. The two younger men were leaning against the window and talking. Next to them stood a lanky man in his thirties looking out of the window, his back to the police.

The inspector pulled his hands from his coat pockets and walked over to the three men.

"Excuse me. You're members of the same club as the deceased students?"

The two younger men looked up quickly.

"I'm from the police. I'm—"

"Ah, hard at work, I see." The lanky man, who had been looking outside, turned around. The inspector clicked his tongue.

"I had a feeling your back looked awfully familiar."

"What a coincidence. I was hoping it would be you, though."

"Mr Shimada, do you know this man?" one of the young men asked in surprise.

"I told you I knew people in the police, right, Conan? Let me introduce Police Inspector Shimada Osamu of the First Investigation Division of the Prefectural Police."

"Shimada? Ah, so you're?—"

"As you have correctly guessed, this man here is the second son of our temple family."

"Aha."

Inspector Shimada coughed loudly once and glared at the nonchalant face of his younger brother, whose physique was the complete opposite of his own.

"And what are you doing here?"

"I've been with these two here all this last week, for a certain reason. It's a long story, so I'll just keep it to myself."

Shimada Kiyoshi then turned to the two young men.

"This is Morisu, a member of the K— University Mystery Club, and this is Kawaminami, an ex-member."

"Hm."

Inspector Shimada turned to the two with a perplexed expression.

"I'm Inspector Shimada. These are really very tragic circumstances to meet under," said the policeman formally as he dropped

246

into a chair nearby. "Mystery... So detective fiction, I assume? A club for that, eh? Hm. I used to read mystery fiction a lot when I was young, too. What do you usually do at your club?"

"We have a reading circle for mostly mystery novels and some of us write," said Morisu, as a plain-clothes policeman arrived and gave the inspector a report several pages long. He flipped through it and nodded.

"It's the report from the medical examiner," he said to the two young men. "Just a preliminary one though. A thorough examination will be held later."

"If it's not against regulations, could you perhaps tell us more?" Kawaminami asked. "I want to know everything, no matter how insignificant it might seem."

The inspector glanced at his brother and pursed his lips.

"This guy will just come and pester me later anyway, so I suppose I might as well tell you myself."

"Thanks."

"Based on the bodies—all of them in bad shape—it appears that all of the deceased, except for one, were already dead before the fire. Very likely homicide. The remaining person actually died in the fire, burnt to death, but that one appears to be suicide. He had doused himself in kerosene and the fire probably also started in his room. We can't say for sure, but this man might have killed everybody and then committed suicide. Please keep this information to yourself. His name was..." The inspector stared at the report in his hands. "Ah yes, Matsu'ura. Matsu'ura Junya. You know him, of course?"

Morisu and Kawaminami gasped and nodded.

"Was it really suicide?" Shimada Kiyoshi asked in a rather surprised tone of voice. The inspector wrinkled his nose and scowled at his brother.

"I just told you we can't say for certain at the moment. I'm still waiting for the reports with more details on the causes of death of the other victims."

He turned back to the two young men.

"What kind of person was this Matsu'ura Junya? I'd like to hear what you think of him."

"What kind of person?"

It was Morisu who answered.

"He would have been in his fourth year at the faculty of law this April. Excellent grades, intelligent and eloquent, but he could be a bit peculiar."

"Thanks. And another question, Morisu."

"Yes?"

"Was this visit to Tsunojima some sort of Mystery Club trip?"

"I guess 'trip' might be the right word. But it wasn't an official activity of the Mystery Club."

"Then I assume they were a group of particularly close friends within your club?"

"Yes. Well, yeah. They got along quite well, I think."

The same officer returned and whispered something in Inspector Shimada's ear.

"OK. Got it."

The inspector stuck both hands in his coat pockets and slowly got up out of his chair.

"I have some other business to attend to now, but I think I might need to meet with the remaining members of your club in the near future. Kawaminami, if you could make it, I'd like you to come along, too, as an ex-member."

"I understand," replied Kawaminami obediently.

"Well then, goodbye."

The inspector gave his brother a glance and started to walk

away, but then turned back to Morisu and Kawaminami as if he had suddenly remembered something.

"Suppose this Matsu'ura Junya is indeed responsible for all this, do you have any ideas about a motive?"

"Hmm," answered Morisu, cocking his head. "I just can't believe it. To think that Ellery would do that."

"Who?"

"Oh, I'm talking about Matsu'ura. Ellery was something like his nickname."

"Ellery... Anything to do with that writer, Ellery Queen?"

"Yes. It's a bit of a club tradition. Members go by the names of famous foreign mystery writers."

"Oh, all members?"

"No. Just a select group."

"All of those who went to Tsunojima were members with nicknames like that," explained Kawaminami. An interested twinkle appeared in Inspector Shimada's eyes.

"Kawaminami, did you also have a strange name like that when you were in the club?"

"Well, yes."

"What was your nickname?"

"It is a bit embarrassing. I was Doyle. Conan Doyle."

The inspector laughed.

"Haha, one of the masters. Then I guess that Morisu here is Maurice Leblanc?" the inspector asked, amused.

Morisu frowned slightly and muttered a "no".

A self-deprecating smile appeared on his lips for a brief moment; then, with downcast eyes, in a low voice, he answered:

"I'm Van Dine."

ELEVEN

The Seventh Day

Tuesday, 1st April 1986. From the morning edition of the A— newspaper.

ANOTHER MASSACRE AT THE DECAGON HOUSE ON TSUNOJIMA

In the early morning of 31st March, the bodies of six university students were discovered in the ruins of the burnt-down Decagon House on Tsunojima, S— Town, Ōita Prefecture. The students were staying there.

All six deceased were students of K— University: Yamasaki Yoshifumi (age 22, 4th-yr Medical), Suzuki Tetsurō (22, 3rd-yr Law), Matsu'ura Junya (21, 3rd-yr Law), Iwasaki Yōko (21, 3rd-yr Pharmacy), Ōno Yumi (20, 2nd-yr Literature) and Higashi Hajime (20, 2nd-yr Literature). They had been scheduled to stay in the Decagon House for one week from Wednesday, 26th March.

Investigations have revealed the possibility that five of the six deceased were murdered before the fire broke out. The massacre and subsequent fire are considered to surpass even the quadruple murder that occurred last September in the Blue Mansion on the same island and [...]

From the evening edition of the A— newspaper (same day):

[…] Subsequent investigations have led to the discovery of a further body: that of a man who met with an unnatural death in a room beneath the Decagon House.

The remains are partly skeletal, with time of death estimated at four to six months ago. Age at death is estimated at mid-forties. Wounds suggest the man was beaten on the head.

The existence of the underground room was discovered after the fire. It has been suggested that the body is that of the missing gardener, Yoshikawa Sei'ichi (46), who disappeared after the incident on the island in September of last year. Efforts to identify […]

TWELVE

The Eighth Day

1

The large campus of K— University cuts through the side of a mountain and spreads out extensively in a peculiar shape. In one corner of the campus stands the Box, a two-floor reinforced concrete building housing the circles and clubs officially sanctioned by the university. It was the second day after the six bodies had been discovered on Tsunojima. On the afternoon of Wednesday, 2nd April, ten or so members assembled in the Mystery Club's room on the first floor.

Two conference tables had been crammed into the disorderly room. The students sat around them, packed close together. Among them was also ex-member Kawaminami. Shimada Kiyoshi, the younger brother of the inspector in charge of the investigation, was not present.

Maybe he is trying to be considerate. Or maybe he has something else to attend to?

Morisu Kyōichi felt slightly anxious, but quickly got over it.

It doesn't matter, he knows nothing. He hasn't noticed anything and won't, either.

Inspector Shimada arrived with two officers, slightly later than scheduled.

He frowned at the smell of cigarettes lingering in the room, recognized Morisu and Kawaminami and greeted them heartily. Then he turned to the whole group.

"I appreciate you all coming here today. My name is Shimada."

After a formal introduction, he sat down in the seat reserved for him.

After all the club members had introduced themselves, the inspector explained the outline of the incident. He then moved in a leisurely manner to the main issue, periodically looking up from the notebook in his hands to the faces of the students.

"I'll repeat the names of the six who died on Tsunojima once more. Yamasaki Yoshifumi, Suzuki Tetsurō, Matsu'ura Junya, Iwasaki Yōko, Ōno Yumi and Higashi Hajime. I am sure you all knew them well."

The faces of the six appeared in order in Morisu's mind as he listened to the inspector.

Poe, Carr, Ellery, Agatha, Orczy and Leroux.

"Of these six, five are thought to have already died by the time the fire broke out. Ōno and Higashi were strangled and beaten to death respectively. Yamasaki, Suzuki and Iwasaki were very likely poisoned. The last person, Matsu'ura, was still alive when the fire broke out. It appears he had doused the room and himself in kerosene and committed suicide."

"So Matsu'ura murdered the other five and then committed suicide?" asked one of the members.

"That's what appears to have happened. As for how he would have obtained the poison thought to have been used on the three victims: Matsu'ura's relatives own a big pharmacy in O— City and he often visited them. So that would explain it. We are working on that assumption for the moment."

"But we have been unable to find a motive. That is why I asked you to come here today. I hope you'll be able to help me."

"Could it have been someone else?"

"Very unlikely."

Morisu almost sighed with relief on hearing the inspector's answer.

"First of all, everything points to Matsu'ura Junya having committed suicide. Furthermore, the five others were murdered in different ways at different times. One of them had died more than three days earlier and each of them died under different circumstances. They say that even fishing boats rarely go out to the sea around Tsunojima, and I think it highly unlikely someone would have taken a boat to the island to commit a massacre lasting several days."

"But Inspector," interrupted Kawaminami. "Nakamura Seiji is thought to have been murdered and burnt to death under similar circumstances in the incident in the Blue Mansion last year."

"Well, there are all kinds of strange circumstances tied up with that case." The inspector shot him a sharp glance. "At the time, the disappearance of the gardener caused us to suspect that Nakamura Seiji had been murdered. One person who should have been on the island wasn't there, so suspicion naturally fell on that person. We assumed he was the murderer.

"But now we have found a secret underground room beneath the burnt-down Decagon House with the body of a murdered man inside. I think it was in yesterday's newspaper. Based on the time of death, age and physique, we suspect it's the body of the gardener."

"Aha, I understand."

"So we were forced to change our assumptions about the Tsunojima incident. We now suspect that Nakamura Seiji's death was a suicide by burning and that the whole tragedy was a murder–suicide carried out by him."

The inspector gave Morisu and Kawaminami a meaningful look.

"We got hold of some new facts that support this theory from a certain source."

Shimada Kiyoshi must have talked, thought Morisu.

But he had clearly stated he had no intention of passing any of the facts he knew, or the suspicions he had, on to the police. Morisu had believed him when he'd said that. Even if Shimada's own brother was a police officer. But that would mean that…

Was it Nakamura Kōjirō who had talked?

"But anyway." Inspector Shimada looked at everyone in the room. "How many of you knew those six were going to the island?"

Morisu and Kawaminami raised their hands.

"Hmm, just the two of you. Do you know who came up with the plan to go to the island in the first place?"

"They had been talking about it for a while," answered Morisu. "And then, thanks to some connections, they managed to make the necessary arrangements."

"Connections, you say?"

"Yes. My uncle—his name is Tatsumi—is an agent handling a large variety of properties. He bought the Decagon House from the previous owner. So I told them I could ask my uncle."

"Oh. Tatsumi Masa'aki, eh? So you're the nephew he was talking about. But you didn't want to go to the island yourself?"

"No. I didn't feel like going to a place where such a horrible tragedy had occurred just six months earlier. They all seemed happy about the trip, but I thought it distasteful. And then there was the problem of the number of rooms."

"Number of rooms? But there were seven guest rooms?"

"*Practically speaking, there were only six rooms.* You can ask my uncle, but one of the rooms was not in a usable state. Rainwater had ruined it completely."

There was nothing in that room except for some built-in shelves and some old pieces of furniture in need of repair. The room was covered in stains and the ceiling looked as if it might fall down at any moment. And one part of the floor had rotted away, leaving a hole.

"I see. And who of those six was the—how do you call it—organizer of the trip?"

"I told Leroux about the house—sorry, I mean Higashi. Because he was scheduled to become the new editor-in-chief—basically the leader of the club. But he also asked Matsu'ura for advice."

"So Higashi and Matsu'ura."

"Yes, that's correct."

"Besides their own luggage, I saw they had food, blankets and other stuff with them. How did they arrange that?"

"I helped with transporting the supplies my uncle had prepared for them. I had a fisherman's boat help me bring the stuff to the island the day before their arrival."

"Hmm, I shall need to check that out as a matter of routine, of course."

Rubbing his flabby cheek, the inspector turned his gaze upon the whole group once more.

"Does anyone here have an idea what Matsu'ura's motive could have been for committing these murders?"

Voices started to murmur. Morisu joined the discussion too, but he was thinking of something else.

A fair face.

A fragile body that would break if hugged too strongly.

Long black hair gliding down her neck.

Thin eyebrows, always with an expression of embarrassment. Almond eyes, turned away in sadness.

A small mouth with a little smile. A frail voice like that of a kitten.

256

Chiori.

Timidly avoiding the eyes of other people, the two of them had loved each other. Silently, but deeply.

Oh, Chiori, Chiori, Chiori...

He had not told anyone of this, not any member of the club, nor his friends, and neither had she. It was not because he was hiding it, nor was he embarrassed about it. It was simply because both of them were afraid. Afraid that the tiny cosmos they shared with each other would shatter if anyone knew about it.

But all of it was suddenly crushed that fateful day. That night in January last year. It was evident that those six had robbed her of her life.

If only I had been at Chiori's side to the end...

How often had he blamed himself, chastised himself. And how deeply he hated those six who had been there.

He had lost his father, his mother and his little sister in the past in the same way. Without any warning, the selfish, cruel hands of unknown persons had taken the warmth that was his family away to a place he could never reach. And just when he had finally found someone to love in Chiori, that night had come.

It was not an accident.

She was not a girl to drink irresponsibly. She knew her heart was weak. Intoxicated and helpless, she was forced to carry on drinking.

She was killed by them.

She was killed.

"Morisu," asked Kawaminami from the adjacent seat.

"Uh, yes?"

"What about the letters?"

"Hmm? What's that?" Inspector Shimada asked when he heard what the two were talking about.

"Actually, there's something we forgot to tell you last time," Kawaminami replied as he took the envelope with the letter out of his pocket. "This was delivered on the day the group went to the island. Morisu and I each got one."

"A letter from Nakamura Seiji?"

"Y-yes."

"Both of you got one?"

The inspector took the envelope from Kawaminami and checked the contents.

"The exact same letter was delivered to the homes of all of the victims—including Matsu'ura," he said.

"Could it be related to what happened on the island?" asked Kawaminami.

"I couldn't really say," replied the inspector. "But it might well have been just an unrelated prank. I mean, it was signed by a dead man."

Inspector Shimada gave a wry smile, showing his yellow teeth.

Morisu joined in with a chuckle, but he was silently reaching back into his memories.

2

He had known that Nakamura Seiji was Chiori's father even before she had told him. He had also heard that Seiji was living a somewhat peculiar life on a little island called Tsunojima off the coast of S— Town. More than six months had passed since losing Chiori, in which he spent his days as a half-invalid, filled with unrelenting sadness and anger. He was shocked when, one autumn day, he heard how Chiori's parents living on Tsunojima had met their tragic death. He could not have imagined at the time that this case would help him release his own frustrated anger in the future.

Confronting the six men and women who had driven Chiori to her death was constantly on his mind. But he would not be content with just accusing them, shouting in their faces that they had killed Chiori. He had been robbed of someone irreplaceable, someone he had needed in order to live. They had stolen her from him.

The only thing he wanted was revenge. But he had only been able to channel his feeling into a concrete plan—for murder—when he learnt that his uncle, Tatsumi Masa'aki, had purchased the island of Tsunojima.

The Blue Mansion on Tsunojima, where Chiori had been born. The tragedy with her parents. Six sinners who would go to the island just to satisfy their own curiosity. This mental image fuelled his urge to purge them, to paint a brand-new picture without the existence of those six.

He had first thought about killing all six of them on Tsunojima and then dying there as well. But that would have meant burying himself among those sinners, as though he were one of them.

He needed to pass judgement upon them. Revenge in the name of judgement.

After long contemplation, he settled on a plan.

A plan to kill all six of them on the island, but also a plan where he would stay safe and alive.

He fired the first shot in early March, certain his prey would walk into his trap.

"My uncle just bought Tsunojima. If you'd like to visit and stay in the Decagon House, I could ask him. How about it?"

Naturally, they swallowed the bait.

After it was all settled, he took responsibility for the preparations.

He selected the days of their stay based on their schedules and the long-term weather forecast.

For his plans to succeed, he absolutely needed days with clear weather and calm seas. Luckily, the forecast for late March didn't show any bad weather. It was risky to bet on forecasts, but he could always just cancel the trip on the day itself if the conditions weren't right.

And so a one-week trip was agreed upon, starting on 26th March.

He prepared bedding, food and other necessary supplies. He rented bedding *for six persons*. He was very careful to make *the six think he was going to the island with them, while leaving the impression with everyone else that only six people were going and he wasn't one of them.*

He wrote nine letters under the name Nakamura Seiji. The letters had two purposes.

The first was naturally "accusation". He wanted to let someone, anyone, know that those people had *murdered* a girl called Nakamura Chiori. As for their second purpose, the "letters from the dead" were the perfect bait to *get Kawaminami Taka'aki moving.*

Sending one of those letters with Nakamura Seiji's name to Nakamura Kōjirō had been a strategic move on his part, anticipating that Kawaminami would eventually pay him a visit. He knew Kawaminami very well. Receiving the letter, he would go sniffing around and finally turn to him, Morisu, for advice. Morisu was expecting him. Even if he had to contact Kawaminami himself, the strange letters going around would be the perfect excuse.

He used a word processor, which was available for student use in a laboratory at the university, to type the letters. He also made two sets of the murder-announcement plates with materials he bought at a supermarket.

On Tuesday, 25th March, the day before their departure, he posted the nine letters in O— City, went to S— Town and took the supplies over to the island in a fisherman's boat he had reserved in advance. He then returned to S— Town, lied to his uncle that he was going to Kunisaki and borrowed his uncle's car. In the boot, he had prepared a rubber dinghy with an outboard motor, a cylinder with compressed air, cans of petrol and other items.

His uncle used the boat for fishing. He had secretly taken it out of the storage in the back of the garage, but as his uncle only used it in season, between summer and autumn, there was no fear of him finding out.

Few people make their way to the other side of the J— Cape, even during the day. After hiding the boat and cylinder in some bushes near the shore, he returned the car after enough time had passed. He lied about his plans once more to his uncle, saying he was going back to O— City that night and would go to Kunisaki again tomorrow. In truth he only went to O— City to get his motorbike and return to J— Cape in the middle of the night.

It takes about ninety minutes for a car to travel from O— City to J— Cape in the afternoon. But you can make it in less than an hour if you go fast on a 250cc motorbike at night. And with an off-road bike, you can also cut across the empty fields and thickets next to the roads. He hid the bike in some woods near the shore, covering it with a brown sheet, so there was no need to fear someone would find it.

Next, he set up the boat he had hidden and changed into a wetsuit. And so it was that, by the light of the moon and the unmanned J— Cape lighthouse, a lone figure made its way across the sea towards Tsunojima.

The wind wasn't strong, but it was terribly cold. The visibility was bad at night, too. He had borrowed the boat several times in the past and was used to handling it, but because of his bad state of health, the trip proved to be much harder than he had expected.

As for why he was in a bad state of health, he had not drunk any water since the day before. His plan called for him to abstain from consuming water.

It took about thirty minutes from J— Cape to Tsunojima.

He landed on the rocky area. He needed to hide the boat here. He folded it up and used a rope to tie it into a bundle, together with the air cylinder and the outboard motor, which he had first wrapped in a waterproof cloth and then sealed inside a plastic bag. He then placed the package underwater between the rocks, where it would not be directly exposed to the waves, and weighed it down with a big stone. He also tied the package to a rock to stop it from floating away. Finally, he hid some reserve petrol cans among the rocks there, just as he had on the other side in the thickets of J— Cape.

With a large torch hanging from his shoulder, he made his way beneath the moonlight to the Decagon House. He took the room to the left of the entrance—the room with water damage and no furniture—as his own. He slept in a sleeping bag he had brought there in the afternoon.

And so the trap to catch the sinners was set.

3

The next day, 26th March, the six arrived.

They didn't suspect anything. They knew there would be no way to contact the mainland, no matter what happened on the island during the week. Even so, they showed no signs of anxiety and were all enjoying their adventure.

That night, he retreated to his room early, saying he wasn't feeling well because of a cold. This was the reason he had not been drinking any water.

He knew that the symptoms of mild dehydration resembled that of a cold. He couldn't have just faked an illness. That wouldn't have fooled Poe, who was studying to be a doctor. On the other hand, any suspicion about him would disappear if Poe examined him and declared him to be ill.

Leaving the cheerful chattering behind him, he changed into his wetsuit, put everything he needed in a knapsack and sneaked out of the window. He went down to the rocky area, set his boat up and went back over to J— Cape in the night. Then he raced his motorbike back to O— City, returning to his own room around eleven.

He was exhausted of course, but the crucial part of the plan was only just beginning.

He made a phone call to Kawaminami. He needed him *as a witness to the fact he was in O— City.*

There was no reply, but if Kawaminami was going around investigating as planned, then he was sure to call on Morisu eventually. He might even have called for him several times already. If so, Kawaminami would probably ask where Morisu had been, but he had prepared an excuse for such an eventuality. *The painting.*

He had prepared it *to prove what he was doing on the mainland, while the six were on the island.* The painting of the stone Buddhas. Or, to be precise, *paintings*, plural. He had made three paintings.

One was a charcoal sketch that he had only started to colour. In another, he had applied colour to the whole painting with a palette knife. And the third was a finished article. The three paintings were all of the same scene, of course.

It was a scene he had come across last autumn, when he had been wandering around with a broken heart and happened to arrive in the mountains of the Kunisaki Peninsula.

From memory he prepared three paintings in different stages, changing the colours of the light and vegetation to those of early spring.

He put the earliest stage of the painting on the easel as he looked at the letter he had sent to himself, waiting for Kawaminami's call. If he didn't manage to get in contact with Kawaminami, he would need to find a different "witness". He tried to quell the restless anxiety lurking in his feverish mind.

Near midnight, the phone finally rang.

Kawaminami had taken the bait according to plan. He said he had gone to the home of Nakamura Kōjirō in Kannawa that day. Morisu had felt slightly uneasy about the appearance of Shimada Kiyoshi, however, the man Kawaminami had met in Kannawa.

He decided that it would be better to have more witnesses. But he couldn't have someone sticking their nose in too much. When they asked Morisu to join their little detective game, that was just what he had been hoping for.

Fortunately the two were focusing on the past rather than the present, so at least he didn't have to worry about them following the six to the island. To suggest as strongly as possible to the pair that he was part of the investigation, he used the phrase "armchair detective", saying he would play that role in their group. After telling them that he would be going to Kunisaki the next day, he asked them to call again that night. His suggestion that they visit Yoshikawa Masako in Ajimu was designed *to distract them from the current events on Tsunojima.*

After the two had left, he slept for a while. Before dawn he rode his motorbike back to J— Cape again and hurried to Tsunojima in the boat he had left tied up at the coast.

Returning to the Decagon House, he made sure nobody was out in the main hall and arranged the plates on the table.

What were those plates for?

Did he wish for them to reflect on what it meant to become a "victim"? Was he bound to some sort of a weird sense of duty, thinking it would be unfair if he did not announce their "punishments" in advance? Or perhaps he simply relished the irony of these pretend detectives becoming real victims. The answer his twisted mind had come up with was a combination of those three reasons.

The second night, he managed to retreat to his room even earlier than the night before. There was a tricky moment when Carr accused him of being behind the plates, just as he was leaving the hall, but he managed to get out of that.

He was suffering badly from dehydration by now. Before he put on his wetsuit, he drank all of the water in the jug Agatha had given him to take with the medicine, leaving not a single drop. He was not planning to make any trips to the mainland after the third day, so he wouldn't need any more excuses for going to bed early. He needed to rehydrate and restore his health as quickly as possible.

The trip from Tsunojima to O— City was even harder than the night before. At many points he felt like giving up on his plan halfway through. Looking back, it was a mystery how all that energy could have been stored inside that dehydrated body.

After returning to his room on the mainland, his first thought had been to rehydrate further. Even after Kawaminami and

Shimada had arrived and started discussing the case, he still continued to drink several cups of tea.

He had no intention of returning to O— City from the next day on, so, after performing his role of armchair detective, he acted dismissively towards their plans. He declared that he was withdrawing from their investigation, thus making sure they would not try to reach him again.

The harsh words he had spewed against Shimada did, however, reflect his true feelings. He was truly angry when he discovered they were digging into the circumstances surrounding Chiori's birth.

Just as on the previous day, he returned to the island before dawn. He went back to his room in the Decagon House, where he calmed his anger in the darkness.

4

There were several reasons for choosing Orczy as his first victim.

First of all, it was something like an act of mercy. If she died early, she would be spared the subsequent fear and panic that would affect the other five.

Orczy had been good friends with Chiori. There was something about that girl, always looking away, that resembled his love. Orczy had also probably not actively contributed to the *murder* of Chiori. She had been a mere onlooker. But even so, that didn't mean he would exclude her from his revenge.

Another important reason was *the golden ring he had seen on the middle finger of Orczy's left hand.*

He had never before seen Orczy wear a ring on her finger. That is why he had noticed it. *It was the ring he had once given Chiori for her birthday.*

He remembered Orczy's tear-filled eyes at Chiori's funeral. She had probably been given the ring as a memento.

If she had been such close friends with Chiori, she might also know that Tsunojima was Chiori's home. She might even have known about his and Chiori's relationship.

His initials and Chiori's had been carved on the inside of the ring. "MK & NC". Even if Chiori hadn't told Orczy about it, she might have noticed the engraving in the ring after Chiori's death. Once the murders on the island had actually started, there was a good chance she would figure out the motive and the identity of the murderer.

That's why he killed Orczy first. He had no other choice.

He sneaked out into the hall and went straight to Orczy's room. He'd kept it a secret from the others, but his uncle had given him the master key to all the doors in the Decagon House. He used that to get inside her room. Being careful not to wake her, he quickly wrapped the cord around her neck and pulled it with all his strength.

Orczy's eyes opened wide and seemed about to pop out of her skull. Her mouth contorted. Her face lost colour before his eyes, her strength to fight back ebbed away. And finally she breathed her last. He arranged her body neatly simply because he felt sorry for her.

He tried to remove the ring from her finger. He wanted to keep it as a memento of Chiori, of course, but he was also afraid someone might notice the initials on the ring. But Orczy's fingers were swollen, perhaps because of the island's new environment she wasn't used to, and he could not get the ring off.

As long as the ring stayed on Orczy's finger, the initials weren't visible. But he couldn't just leave behind this precious memory he shared with Chiori.

He decided to use brute force *and take the whole hand.*

If he only cut off the middle finger, he'd be calling attention to the ring that had been there. Also, the act of cutting off the left hand would serve as an allusion to what happened in the Blue Mansion the year before. He thought that this connection might lead to interesting reactions. In the words of Shimada Kiyoshi, it would suggest the idea of Nakamura Seiji to the gang on the island.

Using the knife he'd prepared as one of his murder weapons, he managed, after a struggle, to cut off the hand from the body. He buried it behind the building for the moment. He would dig it up and take off the ring after everything was over.

To suggest the possibility that an outsider had done it, he unlocked both Orczy's window and her door. And then, the final touch. He took out the plate with 'The First Victim' from the cupboard drawer in the kitchen and glued it to the door.

He'd smeared prussic acid on Agatha's lipstick the day before, in the afternoon of the second day, the 27th. The plates had already made their appearance on the stage, but nobody was acting very cautiously yet and he found a chance to sneak into her room.

He'd imagined his trap would yield results around the same time that Orczy's body was discovered. But he was in a hurry and he could only smear the poison on the one lipstick he found. His "time bomb" took much longer to go off than he'd expected.

The eleven-sided cup was next in line.

He'd discovered the existence of the strange cup the night everyone arrived on the island. He was handed it by chance, and realized he could use it.

On the morning of the second day, after arranging the plastic plates, he had taken the cup with him to his room. There were extra cups in the cupboard, so he took one out to replace the one with eleven sides.

The poison he had brought with him had been stolen from a laboratory at the science faculty. Prussic acid, potassium cyanide and arsenous acid. The poison he smeared on the cup was the odourless arsenous acid. At some time before dinner on the third day, he managed to switch the poisoned cup with one of the six cups set on the kitchen counter, unseen by the others, who were all still in shock.

There was a one-in-six probability he would end up with the eleven-sided cup, but he would simply not drink from it if that happened. It turned out there was no need for that and Carr became "the Second Victim".

Carr died of poisoning in front of his very eyes. That was more visceral, more horrible than Orczy's death. *He was committing a terrible crime.* This realization made his heart ache. But there was no turning back now. He would need to set body and soul to it and cold-bloodedly and daringly complete his revenge.

The group finally split up before dawn. He waited until everyone had fallen asleep to sneak into Carr's room, cut off the left hand of the corpse and throw it in the bathtub. This was to stay consistent with his "allusion" and to camouflage the real reason for cutting off Orczy's hand. He then picked the plastic plate with "The Second Victim" from his own spare set and glued it to the door.

Then he went to the ruins of the Blue Mansion.

He could still hear the words Ellery had spoken just before Carr collapsed: *There might be an underground room there.*

His uncle had told him about the underground room. The plastic tanks full of kerosene that he had transported to the island along with the other supplies on the fisherman's boat had been hidden there among the rubbish.

Ellery seemed to suspect someone was hiding down there. It was obvious he would go to look around.

Morisu wiped the floor with pine needles and left traces to suggest that someone had been living there. Next, he took some line from Poe's fishing gear and strung it across the staircase. As he had expected, Ellery got caught in his trap the following day.

Oh, foolish Ellery.

Ellery did indeed have an extremely sharp mind. But he was also unbelievably careless and stupid. Nobody who would cheerfully dive into a suspicious underground room without taking any precautions deserved the glorious title of "detective". Ellery got away without any serious injury, just a sprained ankle. But even if Morisu had silently hoped for a deadlier outcome, he had not seriously been expecting that adding to the body count would be such child's play.

One thing he had not anticipated was the situation with Agatha's lipstick. Watching her closely, he'd realized that the lipstick she was using was of a different colour from the one he had smeared poison on. If she was still unharmed by the following day, he would need to think about taking other measures.

He became slightly anxious when Poe suggested they search all the rooms.

He had, of course, reckoned on such a possibility. The plates, glue and knife were hidden among the trees outside and he had buried the clothes that had been covered in blood when he cut off the hands. The tanks of kerosene were in the underground room and he was carrying the poison on his body. It was unlikely they would do a body search. The only thing left in his room was his wetsuit, but even if they saw that, he could just make up an excuse for it.

But he definitely did not want the others to know about the state of his room. He could just have said that he took the worst room because it was his responsibility as the one who arranged everything, but it would be better if they didn't find out. That's why he objected to Poe's suggestion at the time.

And that night, due to Agatha's hysterics, everyone went back to their rooms unexpectedly early. He had not planned to leave the island that night, but there was no reason for him to spend one whole night doing nothing. If he could go back to O— City and meet up with Kawaminami, he could make sure his alibi was airtight.

He was feeling really ill. The cloudy sky worried him, but the weather forecast on the radio said there was little chance it would rain and that the waves were peaceful. He made up his mind to make his way to O— City as he had done the previous two nights. First he went back to his own room. Then he set his canvas holder on his motorbike to make it appear he was on his way back from Kunisaki and only then headed over to Kawaminami's place.

5

A light rain fell during the night, but it did not interfere with his plans and on the morning of the fifth day, 30th March, he managed to return to the island safely around the time the sky started to lighten.

He stopped the motor as he approached the rocky area and paddled to the coast. He had just tied the boat to a rock and was pulling it on to the shore when it happened. An unforeseen incident.

He heard a short cry and felt someone's eyes on his back. He looked up. Standing in the middle of the staircase, looking down at him with an alarmed expression, was Leroux.

I have been seen! I must kill him, Morisu thought instantly.

There was no time to think calmly about what the timid Leroux was doing there alone at that time of day. He might have seen the rope tied around the rock at some point, and now, thinking it suspicious, have come back to investigate. Anyway, Leroux had seen him. He probably hadn't figured it all out, but now he knew more than enough to work out what was going on.

Morisu picked up a stone from the ground and ran after Leroux as fast as he could.

He was in a panic, but Leroux was panicking even more. He stumbled over his own feet as he tried to run away and the distance between the two quickly shortened. Leroux cried out loudly for help from the Decagon House. Morisu had almost caught up with him by then and threw the rock at the back of Leroux's head. It hit its target with a dull sound and Leroux fell forward. Morisu picked the rock up once more and aimed for the crack in Leroux's head again and again…

After making sure Leroux was dead, he hurried back to the rocky area. He had noticed the footprints, but he was in too much of a panic to handle that problem coolly. Someone might have heard Leroux's cries and be on their way over already, he feared.

He swiftly checked whether the footprints had any distinguishing characteristics. He saw nothing that could connect the footprints to any particular individual. They would only be inspected by amateurs, not the police, so leaving footprints like these should be fine. With that conclusion, he forgot about the problem of the footprints.

What he feared the most was that someone would come running down from the house. If his boat were seen, all would be over.

He first moved the boat away from the rocky area towards the inlet. There was plenty of room under the pier and the water surface, so he manoeuvred the boat there for the moment, then waited out of sight, listening. Nobody was up. He had been lucky.

He climbed onto the pier, folded the boat up and hid it in the boathouse. It was risky, but it would be even more risky to return to the rocky area.

He sneaked into the Decagon House and glued the plate with "The Third Victim" on the door of Leroux's room. After that he finally managed to slip inside his sleeping bag.

His excited nerves only allowed him a light sleep. His whole body felt numb and tired. He felt sick to his stomach. Awoken by the alarm of his wristwatch, he left his room to drink some water and discovered Agatha's body. She had changed lipstick colours that morning.

He'd had enough of murders. He'd had enough of seeing corpses. He cried out in his heart. He lost control over himself and couldn't suppress the sudden urge to throw up. He knew that both his body and mind were at their limit.

But he couldn't just give up now. He couldn't run away.

In his mind, distorted by pain, flashed the face of his love who would never return.

He was sitting at the decagonal table together with the remaining two, Ellery and Poe. They were nearing the last act.

For Poe, the situation seemed to have taken a turn for the worse. Ellery denied he had been serious about it afterwards, but Poe was close to being fingered as the murderer.

Earlier, Morisu had thought his heart would stop beating when Ellery was so interested in the footprints at the scene of Leroux's murder. *Don't panic. It should be OK. Don't panic, don't panic…*

he kept telling himself, as he fought the urge to throw up again. Then Ellery turned away and Morisu sighed with relief.

But now, as they sat round the table and the rain began to fall outside, it was clear Ellery hadn't forgotten the footprints at all.

Morisu began to worry that he might have made an oversight. Perhaps a fatal one. He ran after Ellery to the Blue Mansion and was told to memorize the footprints as they were. It was then that he realized his mistake. He cursed his own stupidity. It was all over, he thought.

As the number of victims grew, Morisu knew the number of suspects would narrow and he had anticipated it would become more difficult for him to manoeuvre. He had some things prepared in case the situation called for him to take drastic measures. In the worst-case scenario, he might need to fight with multiple people. He always carried a small knife in the pocket of his coat just in case.

As Ellery proceeded with his examination of the footprints, he thought several times of attacking Ellery and Poe there and then with the knife. But if he acted rashly and was taken down by them, then the game would be up. At this point, he still couldn't be sure whether he would be accused or not.

Morisu felt the pressure rise as he listened to Ellery's clear voice outlining his theory, all the while thinking about how he could deal with his two opponents.

Thankfully Ellery's thoughts had gone off in another direction and reached the wrong conclusion. He thought the murderer was an outsider, not one of the three surviving Mystery Club members.

Ellery was thinking of Nakamura Seiji. He really believed that Seiji was still alive. Morisu had never thought that his *suggestion of Nakamura Seiji* would come back to protect him at such a crucial time.

His head cleared.

Ellery ran out of cigarettes and Poe passed his cigarette case to Ellery. Morisu decided that this was the perfect opportunity.

He quickly took a certain object out of his coat pocket. It was a small, thin box. Inside it was a single Lark cigarette that he had laced with potassium cyanide. He had been carrying this weapon around from the start, planning to use it on Poe if the chance arose.

He also said he wanted a cigarette and was passed the cigarette case. He made the switch underneath the table. He took out two cigarettes, put one of them in his mouth and the other in his pocket. Then he placed the poisoned cigarette in the cigarette case.

Poe was a heavy smoker, so he would probably smoke another one the moment he got the cigarette case back. There was a chance he wouldn't smoke and the cigarette case would be passed on again to Ellery, but it did not matter as long as one of them died. He could work out some way to deal with the last remaining person.

It was Poe who smoked the poisoned cigarette.

6

And then only two of them were left in the hall.

Even now that Poe had died, Ellery was still convinced that Seiji was the murderer. He showed no sign of suspicion towards Morisu at all.

It did not seem as though Morisu would need to finish the job quickly. He decided to await his opportunity calmly. For, if possible, he wanted the last person to commit "suicide" for him.

Foolish Ellery...

Ellery helped him all the way until the end.

Ellery thought himself the great detective, but he was nothing more than a helpless clown. By chance, Morisu had actually predicted this outcome. "The Detective" and "the Murderer" were the final two survivors.

But Morisu had to admit he was impressed by Ellery's masterful reasoning, starting from the eleven-sided cup, which led them to the eleventh room inside the Decagon House. He himself had been puzzled by the existence of that cup. He could never have dreamt that it was the key to a secret room, even though he had been told about Nakamura Seiji's love of gimmicks by Kawaminami on the mainland.

Even so, this development did not endanger Morisu's position. The discovery of the hidden room actually helped solidify Ellery's theory that Seiji was the murderer.

The two of them entered the underground room. Ellery started searching for a path leading outside. Then they discovered that horrifying corpse.

It came to him the moment he saw the body. It was the body of the gardener who disappeared, Yoshikawa Sei'ichi.

Yoshikawa had been murdered six months ago. Attacked by the insane Seiji, he had fled from the Blue Mansion to this place, where he had died. Or perhaps Seiji himself had dragged the gardener here to kill him.

He said this to Ellery, who stood quietly in front of the body. Ellery nodded several times, his hand still covering his nose, saying:

"Indeed. So that means that Seiji got his body double from somewhere else, in the incident last year."

He continued.

"Let's go, Van. We need to see where this passage leads."

They walked around the body and stepped deeper inside the passage. *I'll just accompany you until the end, then*, Morisu thought.

He also started to wonder whether Ellery might actually be suspicious of him now.

It was, for example, obvious from the dust lying on the floor that neither Nakamura Seiji nor anyone else had entered this place for a long time. So perhaps Ellery was merely pretending to suspect nothing and waiting for a chance to take him down.

Morisu followed Ellery into the darkness, his right hand holding the knife in his pocket.

The passage ended at a door. They could hear the sound of waves nearby.

Ellery opened the door. The sound of waves grew louder.

They were standing halfway down the cliff facing the inlet. Outside the door was a little ledge like a small terrace. Beneath it was only deep darkness. It was quite a distance to the water surface.

Ellery carefully watched his feet as he took a step outside and let the light of his torch check their surroundings. He turned round with a satisfied expression and said:

"This door is at an angle that makes it hard to spot from either above on the cliff or below from the sea. And with a little effort, it would be possible to make one's way to the stone steps running along the rock face. Seiji must have used this way to get into the Decagon House."

"I'm sure Seiji will come again tonight," said Ellery as they returned to the hall. "And we found the secret passage. Whether he comes through that passage or the front door, we have nothing to fear as it's two against one. Let's try to capture him."

Morisu nodded as he made coffee for two. He had secretly taken a number of sleeping tablets from the bottle the day Poe handed them out and he slipped several of them into one of the cups, making sure Ellery didn't notice.

With an innocent air, he placed the cup in front of Ellery. Without a hint of suspicion, Ellery drank all of it.

"I'm a bit sleepy. Yes, with much of the tension gone now... Van, would you mind? I need to take a little nap. Just wake me if something happens."

That was the last line spoken by the great detective before he left the stage.

Soon Ellery was lying with his face on the table, sleeping innocently. Morisu made sure Ellery was fast asleep, carried him to his room and laid him on the bed.

He had decided that Ellery would need to commit "suicide by burning" for him. The sleeping pills could be discovered from an autopsy of Ellery's corpse eventually, but he reckoned that the police would discover the corpse of Yoshikawa Sei'ichi, come to the conclusion that Nakamura Seiji's death last year was suicide and see this as a copycat case. The circumstances of that case were similar to this one, so that would no doubt also influence the police's opinion.

The rain finally stopped. It didn't seem as though it would start again soon.

He went down to the inlet and prepared his boat, then returned to the ruins of the Blue Mansion to retrieve the kerosene from the underground storage. He dug up Orczy's buried left hand, removed the ring and returned the hand to her room.

The remaining plates, clothes with bloodstains, the poison, the knife: everything he needed to destroy, he moved to Ellery's room. He opened the window and doused the room in kerosene. After pouring it around the other rooms too, he carried the propane-gas tank to the hall and opened the valve. He went outside, moved to the open window, soaked Ellery with the remaining kerosene and threw the empty tank inside.

That seemed to rouse Ellery. But by that time Morisu had already thrown an oil lighter at the kerosene-soaked bed.

He jumped several steps back and closed his eyes.

The after-image of the fire on the back of his eyelids danced and swirled violently.

The next morning, after a long, almost eternal, sleep he was awakened by a phone call from his uncle telling him about the incident. He called Kawaminami and arranged to meet him in S— Town.

But first he went to his uncle's house and borrowed his car, saying he was going to J— Cape to see what was happening on the island. He hurried there, as he said, and put the boat and gas capsule he had hidden there in the boot. At that time, everyone had their eyes on Tsunojima, not on J— Cape.

After returning the car to his uncle, he put the boat back in storage in the garage. Having finished everything, he went to the harbour to meet with Kawaminami and Shimada.

7

After the meeting in the box room of the K— University Mystery Club had ended, Morisu Kyōichi quickly hurried home alone.

Ellery, or Matsu'ura Junya, had killed his five friends and committed suicide by burning, because of some unknown motive or possibly insanity. It appeared that the police had settled on that. A definite motive had not come up in that day's meeting, but several suggestive tales about the kind of person Ellery was seemed to have caught the interest of Inspector Shimada.

Everything had gone even better than he had hoped.

He had already got rid of two of the paintings he had made to prove his alibi on the mainland. He had done everything that needed to be done. He had nothing to fear any more.

Everything was over now, Morisu thought.

It was finally over. His revenge was complete.

EPILOGUE

The sea at dusk. A time of peace.

The waves, shining red in the setting sun, came from far away to wash against the shore and retreat back whence they came.

Just as he had once before, he was sitting alone on the break-water, staring at the sea at sunset.

Chiori...

He had been repeating her name in his mind for a while.

Chiori, Chiori...

He closed his eyes and the fire of that night came back to vivid life. A giant fire of remembrance, which enveloped the decagonal trap that caught his prey and burned through the night.

Her image joined that sight in his mind. He tried calling out to her. But she was looking away and did not answer him.

What's wrong, Chiori?

The flames danced more furiously and burned brighter. The image of his love was caught in the fire, until its contour was swallowed completely and she disappeared.

Silently he stood up.

Several children were playing in the water. He stood there, staring at the view through narrowed eyes.

"Chiori."

He muttered her name once again, this time out loud. But she did not appear any more, whether he closed his eyes or looked up at the sky. A fathomless sense of emptiness tortured him, as if something had been ripped away from his heart.

The sea was about to blend in with the night. The waves carrying the last light of the setting sun lapped silently.

Suddenly, he felt a tap on his shoulder. He turned around in surprise.

"Hey, it's been a while."

A tall, lean man with a friendly smile was standing there.

"I asked the caretaker of your apartment building and he told me you often come down here to the shore."

"Oh."

"You look down. I've been watching you for a while, but I didn't want to disturb you. You looked as though you were thinking about something."

"Not really. But why did you come looking for me?"

"Oh, nothing important." The man sat down next to where he was standing. He put a cigarette in his mouth as he muttered: "One a day."

"It's been a while since everything that happened," the man went on. The police seem to be all done with their investigation. What do you think?"

"What do I think? Ellery did it."

"No, no, I am asking you whether you think there might be a different truth behind it all."

What is this man trying to tell me?

He looked out to the sea in silence. The man looked up at him as he lit his "one a day".

"I told you once I thought that Kō might be the murderer, but as I have an abundance of spare time, I tried casting the nets of my imagination wider and I caught an interesting idea. And I'd like you to listen to it."

Could he have seen through everything?

He didn't answer and turned away from the man's eyes.

This man... Impossible.

"Don't be so cold and please listen to me for a while. It's a rather incredible idea and you might even laugh at it. You might even scold me again, but just consider it simply a product of my imagination."

"Please keep your ideas to yourself," he said in a flat voice. "Mr Shimada, it's a thing of the past now."

He turned around, ignoring the man's calls, and went down to where the children were playing.

He thought it pitiful how disconcerted he felt.

Impossible.

He shook his head heavily and tried to calm himself.

Impossible. He could not have noticed it. Even if that man's fertile imagination had by chance brought him to the truth, so what? There was no evidence. There was nothing he could do now.

Right, Chiori?

He asked his girlfriend. But she didn't answer. She didn't even show herself.

Why?

His anxiety turned in an instant into a tsunami. The heavy, wet sand clung to his feet. And then, there at his feet, he saw something glistening.

This is...

He crouched down with a stunned expression on his face. His mouth twitched and he let out a deep sigh.

It was a small green glass bottle. It had been half buried in the sand at the water's edge. There were several pieces of folded paper inside.

Oh.

He picked the bottle up with a faint, bitter smile. He turned round to the man who was still sitting on the breakwater, looking at him.

So this is to be my judgement?

The children were about to go home. He slowly walked to them with the bottle in his hand.

"Hey, kid."

He stopped one of the boys.

"Could you do me a favour?"

The boy looked up at him with puzzled eyes. Smiling as calmly as the sea in the evening, he gave the bottle to the boy.

"Could you give this to that man over there?"

Seishi Yokomizo

PUSHKIN VERTIGO

THE
HONJIN
MURDERS

The award–winning
murder mystery classic

'Readers will delight in the blind turns, red herrings and
dubious alibis... Ingenious and compelling' ***Economist***

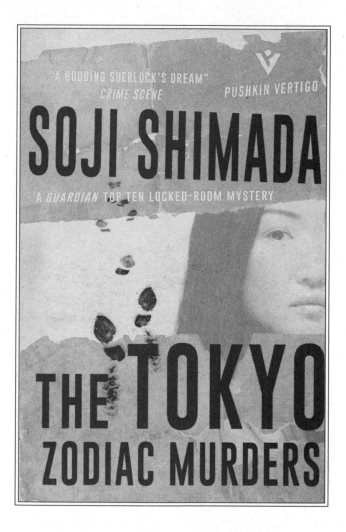

'The solution is one of the most original that I've ever read'
Anthony Horowitz, author of *Magpie Murders*